CRYPTIC KINGDOM

N. B. AUSTIN

CRYPTIC KINGDOM

THE CIVILANDS SERIES: BOOK 4

MOORE BELL

～

To the one who taught me the reasons why:
This book is the best illustration I could possibly draw of
what I learned.
So it could only be for you.
And by the time you finish reading it, I hope you'll
understand the reasons why.
I love you, mom.

～

CHAPTER 1

THE PRESTIGE

The short, anxious walk through the streets of Harran was brutal—it could be his last one, after all. No amount of accepting it could kill Dominic Turner's fear. Having gathered all the things he needed, he kept his head down and marched toward the hotel, cracking his knuckles the entire way.

Inside, the elderly owner, Donald Schneider, sat at his desk. Though their eyes met, neither said a word or acknowledged Dominic's entry. He headed toward a corner of the lobby—a study of sorts—and lifted up one of many books lying around before taking a seat in a large chair, which was carefully positioned so he wouldn't be easily seen.

Unsure if it was because he wanted to be distracted or because of how long the signal was taking, he soon found himself five pages into the book, *The Great Danton*. It was an interesting enough story, though he was only at the start. Part of him wondered how it would end—and if he would ever get to find out.

Heavy steps storming down the stairs interrupted his thoughts. By the sound of it, two men had entered the lobby.

"Hey, Donald, you awake? Hell of a day," Frankie Covington said.

A strange cough emanated from the hotel owner. "Well, heck,

1

what time is it? Course I'm awake. An' every day seems ta be a hell-ov-a-day. What are ya thinkin' makes this one any different?"

"Something in the air."

There's the cue.

They'd set it up the day before, after Frankie had accidentally ruined the plan to frame Charles Langston. This was his way of making up for it.

For, unbeknownst to Donald and the other townsfolk, Dominic had only shared part of his plan with them. He'd told them that he planned to plant dynamite in Clovis's hotel room but not that he intended to get caught, nor that he'd made Frankie swear to tell Clovis that he, Dominic, was the lone perpetrator of all Harran's mischief against the Keagan gang. He wasn't, of course, but for the sake of his plan, he needed Clovis to believe he was.

And now, with those words, Frankie was conveying that the smoke bomb Dominic had set to fog the area and slow the V'ahani down had been triggered. The natives were on their way for vengeance, which meant that Dominic had his opening. He lowered the book to his lap as he readied for his coming execution, an execution that would make clear to V'ahani Grand Chieftain Varek which Easterners were the *true* enemy.

"Whatever you feel in the air's only passing by y'all," Daniel Keagan said. He must've been the other pair of steps Dominic had heard. A moment later, the lobby door echoed shut.

It was time. Rubbing his sweaty hands on his pants, he took a moment to breathe.

"Ya ready ta make yer move, then, Dominic?" Donald interrupted his attempt to calm himself.

Dominic rose from the chair and turned toward the old hotel owner. "You want me to be honest or to tell you I'm all-good and ready?"

Donald remained silent.

Dominic blew out a breath. "It doesn't matter anyway. The time's come. If I don't get to talk to you again—it's been a ride, Donald."

"That it has, friend. Now off with ya. Go an' blow this place ta the ground. I've seen all I was needin' ta see. Make sure those Morrell youngsters an' everyone else in town knows I loved 'em. An' same goes fer you, boyo. Be seein' ya on the other side."

With a frown and an uneasy nod, Dominic rushed for the stairs. Though Donald was okay with the prospect of death by the explosion, Dominic could not accept the responsibility of flipping the switch on Donald's life or the lives of any of the other people who resided at the hotel. It had been difficult enough to murder in self-defense, and his line had been drawn. Underneath his coat, he was strapped with the fake sticks of dynamite he'd use to implicate himself. From his jacket pocket he removed six bullets that he loaded into his revolver. They felt light in his shaky hands.

When he reached Clovis's room, the first thing he noted was how much of a mess it was: clothes were strewn along the floor, the bedsheets hung half off the mattress, and open liquor bottles were everywhere, creating a rotten stench. Despite his disgust, Dominic knew this would be perfect; it would be easy to "hide" the fake explosives. Right beside the opening to the door was a large dresser. On the corner nearest to the door, he placed his pistol. He walked to Clovis's bed next, placing the fake dynamite underneath, and for a while he fiddled with the sticks, ensuring they looked

3

real. Beads of sweat trickled down his face as he doubted the result of his work.

A ring of deep voices picked up outside as the Keagans returned. Downstairs, Donald reacted to them—surely trying to stall them since he believed Dominic's dynamite play to be his true intent.

The distraction was short-lived; the pounding of boots on the wooden stairs signaled they were closing in. Dominic covered the stack under the bed, just poorly enough to keep its presence evident. If he survived, if the plan worked, this would be the greatest trick he ever carried out. Remaining on his knees, he readied himself for a desperate acting performance. The plan replayed in his mind: look surprised, dart for Clovis, empty Clovis's pistol—

Crack!

The door burst open off its hinges, and he turned as Clovis stormed in. Dominic's eyes widened before shooting up toward his revolver on the dresser. With Clovis's attention brought to it as well, the weapon was swiped before Dominic could come close to reaching it.

Hook. Dominic charged into Clovis's waist and grabbed for the gun holstered upon it. A sharp pain rang through his back when Clovis slammed the butt of Dominic's own pistol down on him. He yelped but fought through it, taking hold of Clovis's revolver and emptying the bullets from the cylinder.

Line.

As soon as his pistol hit the floor, Clovis went into a fit of inhuman rage. Dominic stood no chance; Clovis threw him into the dresser, its metal handle ramming into his back. The sharp, blistering pain became an afterthought, though, as Clovis's fists slammed into his gut. One after another, they contorted his ribs and knocked the wind right out of him.

"Clovis, please!" he heard Daniel say. It was enough to stop the barrage for a moment, and Dominic collapsed to his hands and knees, wheezing for air.

Out of the corner of his eye, he saw Clovis lift the closest revolver off the floor—Dominic's own—and check the cylinder. The psychopath wouldn't know the six bullets were blanks.

His vision continued to blur as he whispered to himself, "Sinker."

*

Though Clovis had just bloodied him, accused him of several "unjust" murders, and made an example of him in front of all his friends in Harran, Dominic Turner was happy. A town full of people stood before him, all of whom had the strength and bravery to resist the monster. They stood united against Clovis's gun-toting Keagan gang, attempting to take credit for crimes to which Dominic had already confessed. If he contributed to their unity in the slightest way, this would all be worth it.

"And I knew about all of it, Clovis," Daniel Keagan said to Dominic's left. "So now you know. We're all guilty. Every single one of us."

Dominic considered the sentiment, and his spirits lifted even further.

How right Daniel is.

He too was guilty—of course he was. Yet despite all he had done, despite how it had eaten at him in the past, he realized he'd always acted how he believed was right at the time. So he knelt,

5

head held high, conscience clear, and accepted his past as much as he accepted the risk he was about to take.

Clovis moved toward his restrained, now-enemy brother, a revolver jostling in his loose grip. "All guilty, you say?"

Every single one of us.

"Yes, brother. And you're no exception."

After a moment of pause, Clovis perked up. "Seems you've lost sight of one thing, Daniel: I just don't give a fuck. Goodbye, brother."

This is it.

"No! Don't! Clovis, no!"

As all of Harran whipped into a fury, Dominic smiled at the crowd with a tear dripping down his cheek. The floorboard creaked, and he rotated to see Clovis's gun raised toward his upper body. Dominic was ready and would make sure his killer knew it.

"Welcome to Harran," he said as coldly as he could to Clovis.

When his weapon blasted, Dominic grabbed at his chest and squeezed. The fake blood bag hidden beneath his shirt opened and began to leak. As the thick liquid seeped out, he collapsed to the floor and shut his eyes slowly.

He continued to give the best acting performance he could, remaining frozen and limp as the people of Harran shrieked in horror at the sight of their fallen friend. It broke his heart in particular to hear Jeannie Morrell shouting his name and crying at the top of her lungs. Dominic heard her brother, Harrison, trying to console her, and he wished more than anything in that moment that he could reassure her himself. But he couldn't. For his plan to work, he needed everyone to believe him dead. No matter how long it would take, he'd wait until the perfect opportunity to make his move on Clovis.

A deep, blaring roar overpowered the crowd's crying. It took all the willpower inside him to keep from flinching at its terrifying suddenness and ferocity. In the position he had fallen in, he was facing the northern direction of town, from where the sound originated. Even before he peered through the tiniest slit of his eyelids, however, he knew it was the V'ahani grizzlies. Though he still worried for the townsfolk standing out in the open on the streets, it became clear that his plan had worked to perfection—the natives waited for and witnessed the execution. With their alliance to the Morrells of Harran and the honor they were guided by, the V'ahani warriors would not prey upon the Easterners with whom they sympathized but instead upon those bearing the Lion's Paw pin of the Keagan gang. And having experienced Varek's harsh stance against Easterners as a whole firsthand, Dominic knew this was the only way to inspire an immediate sense of camaraderie in the grand chieftain. Clovis's reign of terror was at its end.

Through the slit in his eyelids, Dominic could see that one tremendous grizzly led a mass of men and other bears, all barreling toward Harran. When they reached their target, the carnage began. The other five shots of Dominic's revolver tore overhead as Clovis emptied the weapon at the attackers. Dominic was comforted to know none of Clovis's shots would connect, even as other gang members fired rifles. Though V'ahani warriors fell and their beasts slowed, the numbers favored them by a wide margin. For the most part, it seemed they were focusing their malice on the Keagans, so Dominic held on hope for minimal collateral damage.

A loud splintering sound came from right beside his head. Opening his eyes again, Dominic saw that a thrown spear had just missed cracking his skull in two. While his position on the platform was somewhat apart from the fight, he wasn't safe there. The charade could end now. He needed to find cover, so he rolled off the platform and into some debris remaining on the backside of the burned-down jail over which he had been lying.

From his hiding place, he could hear the pattering of horses. He craned his neck to see that Clovis and Devin Turpin had climbed atop two black mares, Clovis's with a white strip between its eyes and down to its nose.

They can't be allowed to escape.

Weaponless but desperate, Dominic tried to come up with a plan as he watched Clovis ride up to Daniel. "Take my hand! Brother, we need to get out of here!"

Daniel refused, and a brief look of betrayal and fury showed through Clovis's usually sardonic mask. It was quickly replaced by fear, however, when a grizzly started racing for them just before Dominic had been about to do the same.

Dominic watched the grizzly lunge forward but land short and in awkward fashion when a shot from behind halted its attack. His heart sank both at the wailing of the defeated beast and at the sight of Clovis riding off to freedom. Refocusing his attention on the bear, Dominic saw Daniel stop the man who had weakened the beast before he could finish the job—making the full turn against his own gang clear, if it had not already been so before.

The bloodshed continued until only three injured members of the Keagan gang remained from the enemy side. Dominic winced when he saw Varek order the execution of the three gang members after things settled down.

At least the brute is showing a bit of restraint for the righteous Easterners of Harran.

Varek ordered Daniel forward for execution next, but Hanzah and Harrison Morrell, who was reemerging from hiding with Jeannie, protested and paused the action.

"If we are to find Clovis, there is no one better to help us in doing it," Harrison said. "You'd be killing one of our greatest assets."

"Would you agree?" Varek asked Hanzah, with salt in his tone. "Do you think he could help us?"

"I do," Hanzah said.

Varek, frustrated but apparently accepting the value of keeping Daniel Keagan alive, took Daniel aside with Chieftain Orrin. Varek's face, including his scarred, misty eye, was stern and permanently fixed.

With Harran won, Dominic was ready to emerge. Climbing up from the rubble of the jail, he marched toward the crowd. "For what it's worth, I think saving Daniel is a good idea too."

Mouths gaped, none more than Jeannie's; she seemed frozen in place.

Hanzah took a step forward and stopped. "My eyes deceive me."

As with any performance, Dominic couldn't help but be filled with joy at the wonder on all their faces. Though it'd been necessary, though it'd been life and death, it had also been his greatest performance. So he replied with a line from his shows. "Our reality is what we make it, my friend."

Giving Hanzah a hug, he looked at Jeannie, who remained

still. With Harrison right behind her, her small frame trembled. Dominic crept toward her, understanding why she'd be shaken.

"Go away," she said, to his despair.

Dominic halted. "I'm sorry, Jeannie."

"You should've told us."

"I couldn't have." He crept toward her again. "But you're safe now. *We're* safe now, and—"

"Jeannie! Harrison!" He recognized Debra Kennedale's shout from the direction of the hotel and saloon.

As Jeannie trotted that way, Dominic followed close behind with Harrison.

The dirt road was stained with thick spatters of dark red blood from the scattered fallen corpses. Neither the grizzlies nor their V'ahani masters had shown mercy to these Keagan men. While he couldn't stomach the sight of their mangled limbs, Dominic also couldn't turn away. He cracked his knuckles on each hand—a long-standing habit—and scanned the bodies. Along with searching for any townsfolk among them—there were a few, the sight of which chipped away a piece of his heart—he for the first time acknowledged the youth of some of his deceased enemies. In them he saw both a victory and a loss, which brought him to his newest worry.

While Clovis's ego would be damaged by defeat, and while his numbers had been shrunken, Dominic knew allowing him to escape would come at a great cost. He resented his failure in that respect.

"Dominic?" He looked up to see Cassie Kennedale running to embrace him.

Over her shoulder, he noticed Debra was crouching on the

ground beside Jeannie, trying to console her from within a crowd of a few other townsfolk.

Debra passed Jeannie off to Harrison before rising to follow her sister. "You son of a bitch."

"I'm sorry, but—" The words wouldn't come out when he saw who Jeannie and Harrison were hunched over. "Donald?"

Walking beside him, Cassie placed a gentle hand on his shoulder. "Donnie got hit, hun. We had the doc take a look, but I'm afraid he ain't got much time. We tried our best to make him comfortable for now."

Once he'd shifted through the onlookers, he could see the gunshot wound in Donald's hip. The old hotel owner's mouth was gaping, and his skin was pale, but his eyes were open. As Dominic came down to a knee by his side, Donald wheezed.

"Hey, Donald. How you holding up?" he asked.

Another labored cough was directed in his face as Donald squinted up at him. "Dom? Dom, is that you?"

"Yes, sir," he replied, nodding his head and sliding his hand into Donald's grasp, which was as frail as his strained voice. "I'm here. We're all here with you."

Beside him, Jeannie rested her head on his shoulder.

"Did we—?" As he tried to speak, Donald winced in pain. "Did we get him, boyo?"

A sniffle and whimper from Jeannie.

"Yeah—yeah, we got him. The people of Harran are safe now," he replied. Harrison leaned over Jeannie to give him a curious look, but Dominic nodded and pursed his lips to affirm his lie about Clovis's capture.

Donald released a deep, exhaustive breath, then slightly tightened his grip on Dominic's hand. When he exhaled, his free hand came up to his cylindrical hotel hat, which rested on his chest. He smiled, yet his eyes also appeared to water. "I just wanted ta … I just …"

"We know, Don," Harrison said with a crack in his voice.

Donald's head rolled slightly toward the eldest Morrell. "Harrison, I—" The old man broke down, and like a switch, Dominic couldn't fight back his emotion any longer. He rubbed at the tears in his eyes with his arm sleeves. "Harrison, yer father … there's just so much strife an' turmoil in this world an'—" Donald's misty eyes widened, and he paused as if coming to a realization. "An' yet, he still gave a little ole coot like me a chance." As all who stood around them joined the hotel owner in a sorrowful sigh, Dominic nodded and placed his free hand around Jeannie and on Harrison's shoulder. "An' you all jus' have ta promise me that … that none-a-ya will ever let the hooligans out there keep ya from doin' the same. From losin' every inch-a yer trust and faith in folks."

"We promise, sir," Harrison said, his head upright. "And I swear to you we'll keep that promise, just as you have with us."

The slightest bit of Donald's lip twisted at the pain, and his head began to slump. Though he continued to breathe and seemed aware, he was fading. When Dominic realized this, he asked the Kennedales to lead the others in tending to the rest of the wounded. The request was followed after each sister gave Donald a kiss on the forehead. One by one, the remainder of Harran's inhabitants gave the old hotel owner their thanks as well—Daniel Keagan and a distraught Johanna Fontaine included—until there was no one left but Dominic and the Morrells.

After a few moments of silence broken only by Donald's weak inhales, Jeannie wiped her nose. "When you sound the call with spirit true," she sang in the quiet of their group. Dominic recognized it right away as the song she'd sung when he had first rescued her from the V'ahani. "I swear I'll hear that sound in you. And even when the black night hums, still don't look back, the sun will come. No, don't look back, the sun will come."

With Donald's hand still fixed in his, they stayed there together until the moment their friend and companion drew his final breath.

*

After a few hours of aiding in the post battle cleanup, Dominic was in need of a break—especially as Donald's funeral was still ahead of them. As he sat atop the same platform on which his false execution had taken place, his mind was clear in a way that it hadn't been for a while. Within this window, he registered only the basic parts of his surroundings: blades of grass blowing in the breeze, flies buzzing about overhead, clouds flowing by at a pace brisker than usual, he noticed. Perhaps, he thought, everything that had happened was so overwhelming, he no longer had the capacity to process any of the more depressing things. Or maybe simplicity wasn't a symptom but rather a remedy. The latter seemed more proactive, so he decided to buy into it instead, since he longed for the days where his performances were his main focus.

In his distraction, he didn't much notice Jeannie until she took a seat beside him, a basket of apples in her hand. Without a word, she handed a green one to him. As she looked down to take a loud bite out of her own apple, he lowered his between his thighs to hide it while he cut out a bite-sized slice. It occurred to him how instinctive the calculated move was, and he tried to restrain a grin. After taking a moment to make sure Jeannie hadn't observed his moves, he gave her a poke. She looked up with her mouth full as she chomped away. Presenting the hole in the apple, he raised a questioning brow, to which she nodded her understanding. A magic trick was about to commence.

Bringing up his left hand, which had been hiding the other piece, he used his right to play theatrics and cover the hole while the left suctioned the chunk back into place out of her sight. In an excited display, he revealed the recovered apple with a rotation, and her eyes bulged, a smile showing through her full mouth. He gave the fruit a careful toss in the air before taking an actual sour bite.

A hawk blared overhead, prompting Dominic, Jeannie, and each of the V'ahani nearby to avert their attention upward. He couldn't help but feel frustrated by the disruption to the peaceful moment, but he still noted the look exchanged between Hanzah, Orrin, and Varek. Hanzah nodded and ran off underneath the bird, coming to his knees just a bit further off the main road of the town. The bird circled and chattered, and Hanzah spoke back in an incomprehensible language.

At the same time, Daniel was having a word with Varek. To this point, Daniel had been helping the V'ahani by tending to their fallen and injured comrades. With a nod from the V'ahani chieftain, he approached Dominic and Jeannie.

"Hey, y'all," he said as he slicked back his hair. "I had a talk with the grand chieftain, and he agreed to let me have a go at finishing this."

"To track down Clovis?" Jeannie asked.

Daniel lifted a revolver and spun open the cylinder. "Yes, ma'am. It's well past time."

"I'd have to agree," Dominic said, knowing full well it was Daniel's responsibility more than anyone else's.

"Yeah, well, you know … the reason I came to tell y'all was just because I was kind of hoping …" Daniel said, whipping the cylinder back into place and holstering the weapon. "I could really use someone as resourceful and apparently immortal as yourself along the way, Dominic."

With a sigh, Dominic looked at Jeannie and back down at his apple. Inside him had grown the tiniest sliver of hope that his passions and his community would once again consume his life. With Clovis gone from the Riverlands, he'd hoped to reclaim those things. He resented the thought of being taken away from it now, after having already given so much, just because the Keagans had made a mess of things and didn't know right and wrong when it came to their own brother.

Varek and his Masters approached with Orrin behind, looking first at Jeannie and then at Dominic. "The V'ahani of the Riverlands have been imprisoned at the Tokali Hold for far too long. Daniel will march us south and order that they be freed, or we will free them ourselves. We will leave as soon as—"

"Wait," Hanzah said, charging up to the group, his cheeks rosy. "We cannot go south. Not yet."

"What did you hear, my boy?" Chieftain Orrin, Hanzah's uncle, asked.

"Latera, she has …" Hanzah smiled at Daniel. "She has captured your brother William."

"Captured?" Daniel asked.

"Yes, at his mansion in Fayette," Hanzah said, this time to his V'ahani elders. "The group she has been traveling with came upon his mansion and took him hostage with the help of someone you all may know from Harran. A mayor named Charles Langston. Now Latera is marching William south to the Hold to demand the release of our people!"

Daniel lowered into a squat and rubbed his fingers along his forehead, muttering and moaning to himself. "Charles Langston … well, fuck."

"Charles is in Fayette with them?" Dominic asked, shocked that the dimwit had made it so far. "You gotta tell her to abandon him. He's no mayor—he's only a danger to her."

"She orchestrated the attack?" Varek asked, not without skepticism.

"That sister of yours," Orrin said to Hanzah, stroking his beard, the corners of his moustache raised straight up.

"She said when she has our people secured, she will march them back to the Riverlands. As for Charles, he is no longer her concern. In exchange for their freedom from the Keagan held Hold and safe passage north, she left Charles for William to deal with at the mansion upon his return. I was told we must not descend on Fayette. These were the demands William gave."

Daniel stood and spoke up as he shook his head. "Billy's still dealing with the loss of his wife. He's too fragile to be their hostage—especially with his wife's killer at the mansion behind him. No … this is not a good idea. Please. I'll go south and take his place, and Latera can use me to order your people's release."

"Do you ask me for empathy after I have just allowed you to live, Daniel Keagan?" Varek asked.

"I … yes, I—"

"It is not granted." Dominic shuddered at the iciness in the grand chieftain's tone, flashing back to the V'ahani prison he was once held in. As much as he understood distaste for a Keagan, he was not a fan of Varek. "You will not have any involvement whatsoever in the predicament your brother finds himself in," Varek went on. "Your life has a single purpose now: finding Clovis. And you will only answer to me in fulfilling this mission."

"I'll find him. But please," Daniel faced Hanzah and Orrin, "just ask her not to rattle him any more than she needs to, y'all."

Varek stepped before Orrin and Hanzah. "It is time to lay our fallen to rest. As soon as you have had the opportunity to pay your own respects, you will go." Then he stalked away, Orrin and Hanzah pivoting to follow.

In the silence, Dominic tried his best to fight off the realization that Daniel would not be able to handle the journey alone. Without V'ahani support, Daniel would be going after his brother, a monster, who still had plenty of reserves at the Hold. He'd never survive, let alone succeed.

"Right. Well, I just wanted to thank y'all for everything," Daniel said in a sulk. "Y'all got something real special here. I'm sorry for all the trouble, and—"

"Varek's right," Dominic said. "Let's lay Donald and the others to rest. We'll talk about what comes next after."

A knowing nod from Daniel wasn't returned with any pleasure. It was time to thank the fallen for their sacrifice in securing their beloved home of Harran. And, along with that thanks, they had to promise them their loss would not be in vain.

∗

Behind Donald's hotel, Dominic stood with Jeannie, Harrison, the Kennedale sisters, and Frankie. He'd been relieved to discover that Frankie had survived by remaining hidden after helping the Morrells to shelter before the fighting had broken out. The young man had turned up during the cleanup and had missed saying his own farewell to Donald. Dominic supposed he'd have a chance to say goodbye now—they all would.

This group was the only family old Donald Schneider had left in the world, and they agreed there was no more appropriate place to bury him. Several hours had gone by since the fight, and the time of mourning came with the setting sun.

From behind the gravestone they had fashioned, Dominic faced the others. Jeannie's hands were extended up, each clasped by a Kennedale sister. Her short hair had been growing of late and was held back by a black bowed headband. As mellow as her ensemble was for the occasion, Dominic noticed how it matched the Kennedales'. Harrison stood beside them with his hands held before him, wearing a suit Dominic had helped him pick out earlier. It was a touch oversized for the young man, but he wore it well, looking every bit the son of Adonis Morrell. With Harrison's nineteenth birthday in the coming month, he was approaching the time to take up the Morrell mantle if he wanted to restore his family's influence in the Riverlands.

"There are people among us who are just so attentive and focused and polite," Dominic started. "Donald Schneider wasn't one of those people."

The others let out a snorting chuckle.

Jeannie smiled, her runny nose dripping over her upper lip. "He was focused on his hotel."

Debra released Jeannie's hand and placed her own on the young one's head. "And his coming 75th birthday."

"He made sure we were all focused on that," Cassie said.

Dominic nodded and pointed her way. "He was a man of interesting thoughts and speech, for sure."

"Hey, there," Harrison said, mimicking Donald's accent. "Ya outta be respectin' yer elders there, boyo."

Dominic huffed and winked at Harrison. "I'll be doin' my best there, Harry."

"Oh, God, I won't miss being called that."

"But you know what, Harrison—in time you will."

As Harrison's grin faded away, Dominic realized this was the first time since the fire that the Morrells would be able to mourn. This wouldn't just be about Donald but about all they'd lost—their family included. With that thought in the forefront of his mind, he continued with the service that the Kennedales had asked him to lead.

"We'll miss him for the things we couldn't stand as much as for the things we loved about him. Perhaps, in a way, we'll miss the bad even more because we don't give our appreciation for the bad. But our quirks are what separate us. They give each of us our own distinct flavor. And when we walk through the lobby of that hotel and see that silly little hat, we'll think of all the things that made Donald who he was." Dominic pulled out of his pocket the lobby-boy hat Donald always wore and presented it to the others before placing it on the gravestone. "When his birthday comes, we'll be filled with the same giddy joy he felt for each passing year. Just like we thought of Donovan and your parents when we saw our people standing together against Clovis," he said, nodding to Jeannie and Harrison.

The sounds of love and sorrow began to choke out of the others. He'd let the overdue emotions bleed. Harrison stepped forward with a smile. "They have been and always will be with us. Through the love they gave, the jokes they told, the wisdom they shared: they shaped us. So when we leave our mark, we leave theirs too. In the end, that's all Donald ever wanted: to leave this world a little better than it was when he came into it."

When Dominic looked up, he saw the cloud cover from earlier in the day had all but vanished. He took a deep breath and rubbed his eyes before continuing. "And he did that, you know? But it's on us now. It's our responsibility to make sure we continue that legacy for him. For the sake of our town."

"And we will," Harrison said in affirmation.

"We will," Jeannie echoed.

"For Donald," Cassie and Debra said in unison.

"For Donald," they all repeated before falling silent.

The back door of the hotel creaked open behind him. The others kept their heads bowed, but Dominic turned and saw Daniel, who mouthed his apologies.

Dominic nodded for Daniel to come over.

Though his execution survival stunt was mostly a success in its intent to remove Clovis from a now-liberated Harran, he accepted that those responsible for its undoing had not truly answered for their crimes. And someone would have to make them.

"You're leaving us again, aren't you?" Jeannie asked. Dominic met her gaze and realized she'd watched the exchange.

"The V'ahani are here in Harran to stay—at least for now," he said, scratching the back of his sweat-misted neck. It had been hard enough for him to accept that he needed to accompany Daniel—telling his friends would be just as difficult. He began with a truth none of them could deny. "But our town and the Riverlands need rebuilding. They need the Morrells."

"But Dominic, you can't—" Jeannie began, falling silent when Dominic approached her and Harrison. Standing before them, he placed a hand on each of their shoulders.

"I—" he paused, looking back at Daniel, "*we* have to give you that opportunity. If Clovis returns, if we don't stop him for good … he'll burn everything to the ground again."

Daniel, who appeared to be a combination of relieved and grateful, stepped forward to his side and looked at the Morrells. "Now's y'all's chance to reclaim what's yours."

"Promise you'll return," Jeannie ordered, keeping her eyes trained on Dominic.

Harrison shook his head. "He can't, Jeannie. But he'll be with us as we'll be with him. And the mark we leave on this territory will belong to us all."

There was a brief moment of stillness before Jeannie nodded.

"Are we leaving today?" Frankie asked. Knowing it wasn't to be, Dominic shook his head at Daniel. "What?"

Harrison lifted up Donald's hat from the gravestone and brought it over to Frankie. "We're gonna need someone to run the hotel. But there's a big hat to fill."

Though Frankie took it in his hand, he seemed hesitant. "Me? The hotel?" he asked as he looked to it. "I don't know, Harrison. I couldn't ask that of y'all."

"You didn't ask," Harrison said. "We offered."

Jeannie came to Harrison's side. "Try it on, Frankie."

With a toothy grin, Frankie placed the hat on his head.

"So?" Harrison asked. "Think you'll be up to it?"

"Well, it'd just about be the greatest honor I could 'magine, friendo," Frankie said before shaking each of their hands.

Well done, Harrison, Dominic thought, as Donald's words rang in his head. *"An' yet, he still gave a little ole coot like me a chance. An' you all jus' have ta promise me that … that none-a-ya will ever let the hooligans out there keep ya from doin' the same. From losin' every inch-a yer trust and faith in folks."*

With pride for his home in his heart, Dominic went on to say a difficult goodbye to the Morrells and the Kennedales, while Daniel went and did the same to his lover, Johanna Fontaine.

As he hugged Jeannie and exchanged parting words with the others, he focused on the task ahead. Clovis and his gang were monsters. Theirs was the shadow lurking over every crevasse of the

Murrieta Territory. No one would be safe, and there would be no true magic until its shroud was lifted.

For, however unlikely allies he and Daniel were, the time for justice was now.

Now it was time to hunt.

CHAPTER 2

WHISPERS

As the natives in the front hall of William's mansion celebrated his capture with their apparent leader, Latera, William fixed his gaze on her. There was beauty in her frosty eyes, tied-up hair, and general youthful appearance. He frowned with the guilt of noticing it but didn't look away, even when Latera caught him staring.

Not on your level, of course, Judith. It was a simple observation. There is no one as beautiful as you.

With a toothy smile, he thought of Father Kubler's promise to bring her back.

We'll be together again soon, my love. And the Murrieta Territory will be ours—just like I told you. I'll do whatever it takes.

Blinking himself back to awareness, he noticed Latera staring back at him in confusion. He had been smiling and gaping at her, even if he'd been unseeing at the time. He forced his face back into a blank mask. Latera squinted back with a furrowed brow.

Yes, I see you, girl. You, who thinks you've bested me with your self-endowed righteousness.

An unconscious Charles Langston was being hauled off by Gregory Calloway and the Tokali Elan, who he noted was also focused on Latera, despite the task at hand. A thump on a doorframe and an apology from Elan signaled the level of the young man's distraction.

Once they disappeared into the cellar, William marched toward a table in the hallway along the dining-room wall. Keeping his eyes trained on Latera, he shot his hands into the air, prompting a jump from her. She began rubbing the fingers of her right hand together—a nervous tick, perhaps. He smiled again and started to undo the cuff links on his shirt.

You know nothing of the higher powers in this land, girl. Not even those of your own belief system. Unlike you, I've met Nova, your Walking Widow—your so-called vessel of your goddess among us. I'm getting to know the Enigma too. It's only He who has provided promises of being reunited with the one I love. Who is "the Mother" to claim dominion when such a generous god as the Enigma exists? No one. She's nothing but a liar. Nova must be a liar. And to think I felt any bit of guilt for not upholding the agreement I made with her in Prayer's Passage.

Placing the cuff links on the table, he rolled up his sleeves before squaring up to Latera from across the room. He lifted his hands again to show there was nothing he was hiding, then made a slow descent to his knee. Keeping his eyes on her, he lifted his pant leg, revealing a holstered blade. She started to turn to her companions, each distracted with their own tasks, but stopped herself and folded her arms.

Brave girl. But just a girl.

"You think y'all won here, huh?" he said.

"What are you talking about?" Latera asked, unfolding her arms and shaking her head.

You haven't. And I will show you the truth. Because it starts now with you and yours, girl: my earning of His graciousness and my true journey into ascension. Now it begins.

William was steady in removing the knife, holding it pointed toward the ground between his pointer finger and thumb. Rising back to his feet, he stood with both hands above his head before gripping the knife in a tight fist and stabbing it into the table.

Latera rolled her eyes.

"I ain't what y'all think I am. But in time," he nodded with a grin, "in time y'all will see: William Keagan's a uniter."

She scoffed, which irked him more than he should have shown. "Have one of yours fetch us horses, a meal, and some rope to bind your hands. We leave as soon as that is done."

"Well, sure, but I need to talk to my priest before we go—"

"Why?"

"Why?" he asked, trying to buy time. He hadn't been church-going enough to spit out an excuse off the cuff.

"Yes, why? I was under the impression you people did not believe in anything."

"Well, you're wrong."

"Am I?"

"I want to go to … you know, to pray for a safe return and all."

"Uh-huh," she said with a grin as she spun away. "Look, just do as I asked. Or would you like us to take Charles with us—?"

"Would *you* like to ever see your family and friends from the Riverlands again?" William asked with a snap.

Latera whirled back around to face him, and he recognized the need for calm as soon as her fists balled.

You called yourself a uniter, William. Be a uniter. It's the only way to get Judith back.

"Look, I'm gonna do what you asked," he said, attempting to channel the calm of Father Kubler.

"Oh, I know you will."

William bit his tongue. "Right. You're gonna see your people again soon. But ... but in the meantime, I hope to be treated with respect. We've all been through a lot here, so let's just be on the same side for a while. What do you say?"

"The hands on your large fancy clock point down. I take it this means it is the bottom of the hour?" she asked.

"Correct."

"Good. See to my horses. We leave at the top of it." Latera stormed off to catch up with a couple of her comrades who had exited out the front door of the mansion.

Left behind to meet all the girl's demands, William found Gregory, who was ascending from the cellar where he had helped tie up Charles. Maria Abigale, the mother of William's late wife, was by Gregory's side as well, though she didn't look pleased.

What's going on between those two now?

He decided to ask Gregory when they had some privacy. After greeting Maria, he summoned his butlers. With food and horses on the way, he explained to Gregory his need to go see the priest, and they hurried toward the Church of the Humble Followers under the escort of two young Tokali men. One was armed with a rifle and the other a blade. Though he had no plans of resisting anyway, he couldn't deny a feeling of intimidation. Though he was taller and had about ten years on them, the physical imposition of the one with the dagger had him bested. As for the other, the certainty in his step with the gun in his hands was enough.

"Trouble in paradise?" William asked Gregory as they walked.

"Paradise? You call *this* paradise?" Gregory snapped with an uncharacteristic bitterness before shaking his head. "Not in my book."

"Now hold up a second. What's going on?"

"It's nothing."

He spat. "Shit."

"No, really, it's nothing. Maria just kind of worries over things sometimes."

"What things?"

"Like her family—what's left of it, anyway—and you and the, uh … the priest and stuff."

It disgusted him to hear she'd speak ill of the man who'd help bring back her daughter. "What about *the priest and stuff*?"

"I mean, he can be a little pushy sometimes, you know? And you've been through a lot, so she just doesn't want to see your vision for a peaceful Murrieta get clouded."

"*She* doesn't want that?" William gave his friend a plate of side-eye.

"That's right."

"Well, you tell her I'm seeing fine and clear. We're doing what needs to be done. Now, is that gonna be a problem?" After a moment, Gregory shook his head. "Good. Then let's dig that gripe a six-foot hole and throw it in."

They walked in silence until the church came into sight. Father Kubler emerged from the doors before they reached the front lawn.

The young priest remained just in front of the entryway, with his arms folded together in his white robe. He wore a mask of harsh reprimand, eyeing the natives flanking William and Gregory. William remembered the tale of Kubler's friend who had perished at the hands of the V'ahani. Though these young men were a different clan, he assumed their presence had an effect all the same.

Reaching into his shirt at the neck, William pulled out the Cereb crescent pendant, which fell beside the Lion's Paw pin on his chest. Kubler's characteristic smile returned, his gentle hands raising into the air to welcome them. "William. Gregory. Sons of the gracious Enigma. To what do I owe the pleasure?"

William addressed the Tokali. "We'll need a word of prayer with our priest before our trek south. If y'all don't mind—"

"Ten minutes," the one with the rifle said before the two strolled out of earshot while maintaining a line of sight.

Once they were far enough away, William began. "Since I ain't got much time, I'll be brief. The natives will be marching me south to the Hold to free their people from our forces there. So, Father, before I go, I need to know what the Enigma asks of me in order to fulfill your promise."

Kubler's brows raised before he looked down to straighten his robes. He said nothing.

"Well? What do I need to do to bring her back?"

Again, the priest grinned and patted his mushroom hair, his attention averted.

"So help me, if you were lying to me, I—"

"Ah-ah-ah," Kubler said as his finger raised. "There is only one way Judith will be returned to you, William, and this is not it."

Gregory frowned, but William ignored it and carried on. "Well, that's why I'm asking you what I need to do. Please, Father."

"What you need to do is *believe*," Kubler said, his hands balling into passionate fists and his overall composure increasing in excitement as he drew out the last word in emphasis. "The great Enigma asks for your faith and devotion. Reverting to threats as you were about to tells me he has not been granted either."

"I do believe, okay? I do. It's just that … it's gonna take time."

A gentle hand came to his shoulder as Kubler took an elongated breath. "I know it will, and so does He," the priest said, nodding with his eyes closed. "When they take you, focus on strengthening your faith by praying once every morning, afternoon, and evening. And be sure to always do so in the face of the natives. If your intent is pure, it should serve as a light for them. Your goal should be to help bring them to that light." Having gestured as if pulling something in toward his heart, Kubler looked up at William. "Convert them. As many as you can. Provide Him believers, and He will provide you with your love."

"Billy, I—"

"The Tokali hearts should be the easiest to win over," William said, interrupting Gregory. "Maybe I can start with them."

"Perhaps. But easy choices are not always the ones we are best served in making."

Pondering this, William turned his thoughts to Latera. Maybe it needed to be her. If he could turn her, he could turn them all—if he could turn her, the Enigma would answer his prayers. He nodded. "Thank you, Father. I'll make Him proud."

"Five minutes!" shouted the Tokali with the blade.

"Okay, Gregory, I need two things done while I'm gone," William said, the pace of his speech quickening.

"But I don't—"

"None of that, you hear me? I won't have it. Not now." With a reluctant pursing of his lips, Gregory nodded. "All right. First, gather whatever men we have left here, and send two or three of them to New Berkeley. Have them figure out if Henry's made any progress on dealing with Forrest Hayes. If not, I want the fucker dead. Tell the men they'll have a place in the mansion when they return with news of his assassination."

"We can send the Hawley brothers. But two or three might be all we have left here in Fayette without them," Gregory said, scratching furiously at his peach-fuzz head of hair. "With Clovis's smaller group to the north and the rest of our forces at the Hold, we have no more defense here."

"Which is why I'll need you, both of you, to recruit more men for me." William leaned in and gave a gentle elbow nudge to the priest. "Converts."

Father Kubler grabbed and rubbed his Cereb crescent pendant with his thumb. "Hmm, yes." His pleasure at the word sounded almost sexual. "You make the Enigma proud, child. Of course, I will help."

"But there are no more able-bodied Easterners left west of the—" Gregory shook his head as he connected the dots, but William nodded. "Nu-uh. You can't be serious. The free folk hate the gangs—and there are so many of them. How the hell will we get them on our side?"

"Free folk?" Kubler asked. "You mean the Highlanders? In Prayer's Passage?"

The rifle of the Tokali clicked as he pulled back the bolt behind them. "Time to go!"

"Please, Billy," Gregory said, shaking his head as he pulled William aside, "you have to reconsider. Let's just talk about all this when you get back, please. It isn't worth it, and you need some time to, you know, just …"

Raising a hand to Gregory's shoulder, William silenced him before standing tall and pointing a finger at his chest. "I know exactly what I'm doing, Gregory."

"It will be well worth it," Kubler said in a serpentine whisper from behind William's ear. "The Enigma will be so pleased with you."

Before William could turn back to the Tokali, Gregory gave the priest a dirty look and lunged forward, pulling William in for a hug. "Goodbye, brother. You be safe."

After an awkward pat or two on Gregory's back, William let his best friend go. Backing away from his comrades and toward his captors, William raised his palms. "Find a way."

*

"Latera." The whisper Latera heard was icy, shrill and drawn out, and yet, it soothed her. It was also becoming clearer each day. No longer a faint echo. "Latera. I see you."

Racing through passing visions, she reached out and grabbed onto one: Walter Keagan's men from the Hold who had chased them into Fayette prior to their capture of William. They were at a campsite now, slumped around a fire, with their pins glowing in its light. It appeared they were taking a break from retreating to their leader as she had ordered them to.

A thin man with a thick moustache took a sip from a flask, and an ensuing belch escaped him. "Running at a girl's command? This is some bull if I ever sniffed it."

For a few minutes, no one replied.

"A familiar scent in your case, I'm sure," another man said, his voice much deeper and a bit muffled given that his lower lip was full of chewing tobacco.

The others laughed at the first's expense.

"Who do y'all think Walter's gonna blame for William getting captured, huh?" the first man asked. "That's right. He's gonna blame us. And y'all are sitting around giggling like it ain't shit."

The deep-voiced fellow spat a mess of brown. "What is it with you and shit?"

"Walked right into that one," another said.

The thin man stood up and tightened his belt. "Oh, hardy-fucking-har. Real funny. Let me tell you what—we're all walking into something. Going back to the Hold with the news we're meant to deliver? There won't be no mercy for the messenger."

Another spit. "Well, what do you think we should do?"

"We take him back. How are we gonna call ourselves Keagan men if we just retreat with our tails between our legs? And from a young, ragtag group of them filthy savages, no less."

"If any harm comes to William—"

"What story sounds better to you: the one where we just ran away and let him get captured, or the one we might come up with if he goes down in a fight? And, hell, maybe we'll get to keep our heads for it too. They sure as shit won't be safe as far up y'all's asses as they appear to be."

The others looked around, each about to burst.

"Don't none of y'all say it!"

Silence.

"You'd like the sight, though, wouldn't you?" one finally had the nerve to ask. The group exploded into laughter as the thin man went after the perpetrator.

"Enough," the deep voice said, still sitting in his spot by the fire. "Get some rest now, all of y'all. The little turd is right. In the morning, we go huntin', and we bring our boy home."

As cheers followed, Latera snapped out of the vision and, realizing she had been in a dream, woke up with a jolt. Her eyes adjusted to the darkness as she panted for air. Leaving her tent, she reviewed the grounds on which her group and their captive, William Keagan, rested. After traveling through the day since taking him, it appeared everyone was accounted for. There were also no alarming sounds among the typical owl hoots and cricket chirps of the night.

"Latera? Is everything all right?" Hammond asked from behind her, causing her to jump.

"For the sake of the Mother," she said in a whisper, bringing a hand to her chest.

Hammond approached her and placed a hand of his own on her elbow; at his touch, a smile escaped her. It took her back to the moment of their kiss under the stars. "I am sorry. I did not mean to startle you."

"Do not be. It is okay. But why are you awake?"

"It is nothing."

Aware that it wasn't, she gave him a sidelong glance.

"I … I just worry, you know?"

"I do know, Hammond," she said, pulling her elbow back. It wasn't her intent to mistrust him, but considering the history of her dealings with Elan and their people, she couldn't help but keep up her guard. "I worry too—constantly. And you know each reason why I do."

"I do. It is just …" He paused. "My people will not leave the Hold when we arrive with William. I know the others wanted you to include them in the deal—the safe return of William for the release of *all* the natives. But while your people will run north as quick as lightning, I know the Tokali will not leave. They do not think they are captives. Even after their difficulties prior to our escape. They have been sold the Keagan vision."

Doubt was replaced by empathy as she recalled her own miserable time living within the Hold's walls and walking its streets. Hammond's concerns were real and pure of heart. "And you worry about living as a part of that vision when you return."

"No," Hammond replied to her surprise, his previous nerves turning to icy sternness. "I hate them, of course. But I worry much more about living in a place where you are not, Latera."

Her heart swelled. She raised the palm of her hand to his cheek and held it there for a moment before pulling his lips to hers. After a few seconds, she broke the kiss and searched his eyes, which she could just make out in the dim, fading campfire. "Are you real?" she asked with a smile.

"*You* are asking *me* if I am real?" Hammond's lip curled up. Then he brought his arm up as if to observe it. "Hmm … maybe … but how can we be sure?"

Latera grinned but decided to reply seriously. "You do not have to stay in the South with your people if you do not wish to, Hammond. There is plenty of world out there—especially in this territory."

"Your people though—will they be okay with a Tokali among them?"

"I am the chieftess, remember?" Latera said with a wink, glad he had understood her implied invitation. "They will do as I command them to."

"Well, if they truly will accept me … then are you telling me I *am* real after all?" he asked.

With a laugh, Latera shoved him. "Stop it."

"At long last someone has confirmed it for me!"

For a moment, Latera froze as she acknowledged how happy Hammond appeared to be. Thinking again of the peaceful nature of their camp, she recalled her dream.

My dreams are not dreams.

Her smile faded. "We need to wake the others. Now."

"What? It is the middle of the night. Have they not earned their rest?"

"When my people are freed, only then may we rest. For now, we fight."

Latera was a seer now, which her V'ahani comrade, Mika, had confirmed for her. And as his wife and her best friend, Winona, had suggested, she'd need to use her abilities and take any advantage they could get.

*

With the campfire reignited and the spears they'd fashioned the evening prior jabbed into the ground around it, everyone stood together at her request. Most sagged with heavy eyes and contagious yawns, and though she couldn't deny feeling a hint of the same drowsiness, Latera fought it to project the urgency of the situation. "The group of Keagan men who were after us before have decided not to return to the Hold as we ordered them to. In the morning, they will be after us in an attempt to retake their leader."

Observing William to see how he would react to the news, she noted he was sitting on his knees with his tied hands bound in prayer, paying little attention to her words. His silhouette was lit by the glow of the flame, and it haunted her, in a way. She rubbed her fingers together, wishing the unsettling feeling gone.

"How can you be sure of that?" Elan asked, snapping her out of her trance.

"I just—"

"Mika and I overheard them talking before we departed Fayette," Winona said, jumping to her defense.

She had requested that Winona and Mika keep her newfound abilities to themselves—a V'ahani secret. Much to her appreciation, they took the request seriously. "Yes, they did. And earlier this evening, in calling to the wind, we confirmed their path has reverted north in our direction. We will attack first."

"But they have twice the men we do," Shelton said.

Latera nodded. "This is true. But in these lands, we have hogs. And if one falls, we have hundreds more."

"Is our training advanced enough?" Warrick asked, casting a nervous look toward Hammond, who at this point had only controlled a hog twice for a brief instant to stop it.

Near the fire, Winona ripped a spear out of the ground. "Ready or not, Tokali, we have no choice."

Once the Tokali gathered their things, Latera had all the natives but Mika call to the wind to search the area for the exact whereabouts of the Keagan camp. Seeing as Mika wasn't a fighter and couldn't control the hogs as the Tokali could, she knew he'd be better suited to keeping watch of William. She also trusted him more with William than any of the Tokali. Although Winona was no warrior either, she had a key role in training the boys to control the hogs and would be a needed resource in supporting them in the fight.

The reconnaissance team sat in a circle, finding their birds of the night one by one. They each snapped into their respective creatures' mind as if taken into a deep trance. Latera hoped the search wouldn't be long since she knew their enemies were close. She soon found an owl to answer her call, and in an instant her eyes were in the sky.

The owl's vision in the darkness was better than her own, but the images were still blurrier than her sight in the daytime and were without color. Trying hard to focus on the landscape, she found it difficult to match what she had seen in her dream. A quick movement below had the owl craning its neck down and to the right, but it turned out to be some form of scurrying wildlife. Though Latera could sense the owl's hunger, there was no time to stop for the potential snack. An hour or so passed, and still nothing more was seen in the rolling hills of the southern Murrieta.

A sudden disturbance caused Latera's link to the owl to loosen.

The owl shook and lost altitude as Latera snapped out of its mind. Breaking a connection always caused momentary confusion for the animal.

"Latera—Latera, we found it," Winona said, shaking her shoulders. "We have found their camp. It is not far, but we must hurry if we want to reach them before they are given the chance to wake."

Rising to her feet without hesitation, Latera was ready to be off. "Who saw it?"

"I did," Shelton said.

Gannon, Shelton's sharpshooter brother, raised a hand. "We *both* did, Chieftess."

"All the better. Lead the way, then. Both of you."

The brothers led the group through the dark of night, each taking the occasional pause to call to the wind again and regather their bearings. They bickered about what they'd seen along the way, but since both of them claimed to have found the gang members, Latera trusted they'd converge on the right location.

After another hour of travel, Elan approached the brothers at the front and whispered loudly. "You really do not need to call her that, you know."

"Call who what?" Gannon asked.

"She is not your chieftess."

Latera couldn't believe her ears, yet at the same time, she wasn't surprised in the least that he would say such a thing.

"Oh, leave it alone, Elan," Hammond said with a groan.

"I was talking to Gannon."

"Sure you were."

"I was. Look, soon our people will be released, and I guess we have her to thank for part of that—so no offense to you, Latera— but it is not like the Tokali and V'ahani of the Riverlands will be happy allies once we release them all from the Hold. We are Tokali, Gannon. She is not our chieftess. So we do not need to address her as such."

Latera had no response for him and took the offense she knew he was trying to give her, no matter how much he might deny it. In making the point in front of her, he was establishing that he did not consider her worthy of the title or the level of respect.

"They can address her however *they* see fit, Elan," Hammond said. "*You* are not our leader."

Elan stared hard at Hammond for a moment.

"And do you really think the Tokali will leave the Hold?" Hammond chuckled. "You think our people want saving?"

Elan made a sarcastic, guttural noise as he shook his head. "Yeah … obviously."

"I am not so sure either way, but we will all just have to wait and see," Warrick said, clearly wanting an end to the brewing argument.

From within the tall grass they had been wading through, they came upon a beaten path. Gannon's pace slowed. "Is this what you were talking about?" he asked Shelton.

"You mean the trail you tried to tell me I had imagined? Yes. This is it."

Gannon made a face at his brother and loaded his rifle before turning back to the others. "Be silent now."

Shelton too waved them on. "They are close."

The path led up a hill with some trees. Once they entered the tree line, Latera felt the scene was familiar. Though she hadn't paid close attention to the Keagan men's surroundings in her dream, she recalled an open area in the woods. Sure enough, with her eyes long past adjusted to the darkness, she could see the tents. Raising a hand to the others, she waved for them to retreat out of sight and earshot. Once clear, she beckoned the group toward her and whispered, "It is time. Tokali, form your ranks and summon your beasts."

As Winona and she had taught them in their training, the five young men took to a knee to call upon their hogs. With her arms together behind her back, Winona waded between them as they focused. "Your gifts allow you to control one hog at a time." There was a calmness in her hushed tone, and she paused after each sentence. "And each hog may not be massive. But this land is filled with them. They are stronger than their size, and they are rabid with the vengeance of the Mother. Know that She makes no mistakes. Now place your hands to the earth and summon as many as you can. Order them one by one to surround our enemies. Ask for Her gracious permission to speak to them. Ask with all the gratitude you can offer."

Latera recalled the voice calling her name in her dreams and shivered. "And we shall utilize these beasts only in the defense of Her children," she said, in part to snap out of it and in part to lead.

"Look," Winona said to her, pointing in the direction of the path from which they had come.

Between the trees, Latera could see a pair of white, glowing eyes coming toward them. It spooked her at first, causing her to remember her vision of the hog from when she had been training

Hammond. But when three more appeared, she couldn't help but be proud of Winona and herself for the job they had done in preparing the Tokali. Once the first round of hogs had settled off the perimeter of the camp, the process repeated until there was what appeared to be a hundred—each commanded into as much silence as possible by their masters. Understanding the difference between command and control was one of the vital teachings Latera and Winona had given the Tokali prior to capturing William. She was proud to see it put to action.

"That is enough. Let us move closer and prepare to attack," Latera said. Winona nodded and instructed the Tokali forward.

Once they reached their positions, they heard a rustling in the camp. A yawn followed—it seemed one of the Keagan men had woken to relieve himself. Latera recognized the scrawny, moustache-sporting man from her dream. He sauntered with a drowsy lag in their direction. Latera could feel her heart beating out of her chest. She swiped at the beads of sweat escaping her hairline and, ignoring the summer heat, took a deep breath.

Looking to the others, she raised a hand again. Before she could wave it to order the attack, though, she noticed Hammond looking at her with a worried frown. It hit her then—when the Tokali had summoned the hogs, only four at a time had come: one each for Shelton, Gannon, Elan, and Warrick. In the darkness, she couldn't tell if his cheeks were red, but Latera was certain Hammond was too embarrassed to share his struggle. Though she felt for him, she wished he'd have said something sooner. She couldn't deal with it now.

"What the hell?" the Keagan man said to himself in the middle of unbuckling his pants. It was clear he must have heard the hushed snorting of the hogs. There was no time to waste. Latera waved her hand down, and eight eyes glowed as the snorting loudened into intense wailing. "Oh, crap. Fuck me." The skinny man tried to redo his buckle, but the hogs leveled him, one staying behind to dig a tusk into him as the others continued toward the camp. The cry he emitted rivaled that of the hogs, and his companions soon exited their tents at the commotion. Yelling was followed by gunshots. With each shot and fallen hog, the respective Tokali gasped, losing control, and they were slow to get it back. They were so slow, in fact, that the second wave of hogs was shot down before it even reached the tents.

"Do your best, tribesmen," the deep-voiced man from Latera's dream called from his cover. "We ain't scared of y'all's pets. Plenty of bacon for the morning."

The thin man continued to moan. "For fuck's sake, I'm still out here. Be careful where y'all are shooting."

"Latera, four at a time is not enough. They need to release them sooner," Winona said once the third round of charging hogs were sent off.

"What do you mean?" Latera asked.

"The hogs are rabid. Once they are directed toward their enemy, full control should no longer be necessary with only enemies present. Even after they follow through with the command, they will do what they naturally do. We need more to attack at once."

The logic hit her hard and fast: since the V'ahani required men to fight beside their grizzlies, which were less numerous in the North than the hogs were in the South, maintaining control over the wild beasts was crucial to ensuring effective combat measures. However, there were no allies in the path of these hogs, so the more erratic they behaved in this case, the better. Realizing the brilliance of her friend's plan, Latera nodded as gunshots rang through the air. "I will tell Hammond and Warrick, you take the others."

Latera darted to Warrick's side first to shake him out of his trance, explaining Winona's idea once he was aware. He appeared fatigued, panting and sweating, but he nodded and got right back to work on his fourth hog. As Latera made her way to Hammond, she could already see the effects of the plan. More and more hogs charged, their sheer numbers allowing them to reach the men at the camp.

"Listen to me, Hammond," she said, shaking him too, despite knowing he was only pretending to be in control of a hog.

He still waved his head and blinked his eyes as if he had been, which would have made her chuckle if not for the circumstances. "What is it? Why are you stopping my—?"

"Hammond, I know you are having trouble, and it is okay."

"No, I—"

"You do not have to pretend. We are still proud of you either way. I am proud of you."

He shook his head and studied the ground. "I can do this, okay? I need to."

Placing a hand on his shoulder, Latera nodded. "I know you can. Just remember, you must be at ease."

Hammond's hand met hers before he closed his eyes and put his other hand on the ground. Despite the horror she had felt during their training, Latera stayed with him again. As he strained and muttered to himself, she tried to be there with him, praying to the Mother to guide him. The more she concentrated, the more the whispering voice came back to her.

Latera.

Her breathing became heavy as she was drawn to the voice. It grew louder in her mind.

Latera.

Hammond was still whispering, which meant he wasn't in control of a hog. Her focus on him redoubled over the voice.

I see you.

Latera's eyes burst open, and before her she saw herself, with her eyes rolled back into her head. In utter shock, she looked down to see a hand was on the ground before her, only ... it wasn't *her* hand. It was Hammond's. Jumping to his feet, she was mortified to see herself still kneeling and realized she was controlling him. Latera was controlling Hammond, her new love, just like she would any grizzly in the Riverlands. The involuntary scream she emitted was much deeper in tone than she was used to, but it was cut short as a pair of tusks emerged from the black forest before her. The hog they belonged to squealed, and before she could react, it charged straight for her—just like when she had tried to help Hammond before.

She raised a hand at it. "Ease! Ease—"

Now lower to the ground, she was racing toward Hammond in the body of the hog. She was controlling its movement—or he was—or she was, through him—she was lost to the logic. The hog continued right past Hammond, whose eyes were also rolled back, and rushed into the camp in a fury.

There was something different about maneuvering the hog compared to a grizzly. To steer its movement was more difficult, as if it were inebriated in its rage. All sight was a chaotic blur, intensified by the more chaotic campsite. A mess of crying hogs rushed left and right after desperate, cowering men. The deep-voiced man stood surrounded with his back to a tree, and Latera's beast rushed toward him along with three others. With a pop and a bang, two of the hogs were shot down, but on the third his pistol clicked empty.

"Oh, goddamn, son of a bitch," he said as he twirled and clawed at the tree behind him, trying to climb it.

An ear-piercing sound ripped out of the hog's mouth, which captured the vitriol both it and Latera felt. Her target found a branch to cling to and was soon off the ground, forcing the pig to break its pace. It howled in a chorus of others at the Keagan man and all his weakened allies.

"All right, enough, y'all. Please. We surrender," he called out. "Back these fuckers off, and we won't give y'all no trouble."

Recognizing the need to end this without anyone noticing both her and Hammond were under, Latera released her control as best she knew how. When she did, she was Hammond again, so she relinquished her grip on him next as soon as possible. As terrified of the entire ordeal as she still was, she was flooded with relief to see him standing before her.

"Hammond, are you—?" she asked, interrupted by dizziness and a dry gag reflex. Though her violation was accidental, she couldn't help but feel guilt and prayed he would be more ignorant than she was about it.

"Did you see? I did it. I controlled the hog! But I do not know why I ..."

Does he not know what I have done?

"Yes, I saw," she said, wiping her mouth. "But you do not know why you ... what?"

"Before. I stood up and I shouted. I do not know what came over me. But you were ... your eyes. Are you okay?"

He does not know. How is this possible?

A shiver rolled up her spine, and she reached out to touch him but stopped short. Part of her hesitation was to ensure that she was herself again. However, a greater reason was how afraid she was of what she might do to him, if touching him would lead to controlling him again. She was so unsure of what she was capable of.

Looking at him, she replied, "I do not think I will ever be okay again."

CHAPTER 3

THE VIRIDIAN RALLY

Old allies, allied again.

Henry couldn't believe Jimmy Keagan was sitting before him. He couldn't believe Jimmy Keagan was the father of New Berkeley's Fraternal Forgotten—the union of labor forces organized against the city's massive, growing industrialists to fight for the fair treatment of the working man. It was an especially shocking fact given that those very industrialists had been established in large part by Jimmy's deceased brother and former partner, Leonard Keagan.

His eyes still were adjusting to the small and bleak room Jimmy's men had abducted him to. He guessed this building was some sort of hideout, as Forrest's control over the city must have required. As for Jimmy, he was dressed much simpler now than he used to be. It appeared he had traded in the fine tailored suits of his gangster days for a worn overcoat and garments just loose enough to tell the people he was one of them. What had always separated Jimmy from the rest of the Keagans was his softer-spoken nature, a trait Henry knew to be reflective of his low place on the totem pole of Leonard's business in the past. Henry's wife, Maria, had always told him she thought Jimmy's son Walter's rough edges were due to a resentment of this moderation in his father.

"Is that really you, Jimmy? I mean … of course it's you. But how? It's been, what, three years since you up and vanished?"

"It's been almost five years, actually. And I could ask you the same question." Henry opened his mouth to respond, but Jimmy—who wasn't *all* class—interrupted. "But, for now, I won't. Because I know you deserve better than whatever it is you got. We're all just fractured forms of who we once were, it seems—for better or worse."

Jimmy's sudden banishment from Leonard's organization had been an obvious, unspoken truth back in their gangster days. At the time, Henry—and many others, for that matter—had known it was best to feign ignorance about it. But with this comment from the man whose misfortune he had once looked past, Henry's cheeks warmed, a tinge of guilt nagging at him. "Look, Jimmy, I … if I'd known what went down with you and Leonard, if I'd known you were going to be disappeared, I swear—"

"Don't," Jimmy said as he waved a hand.

"No, honestly. And after the fact, he said it was family business, so I figured it best not to ask questions, you know? But believe me, the lack of explanation for it … it got me thinking when it was coming time for me to retire."

Jimmy's dark brows raised. "Did it?"

"Oh, you bet. Maria was a wreck about it. It's why we went along with everything Leonard said." She had been a wreck at the time of Jimmy's displacement, but it being a factor in their decision to leave later on was a complete lie—one he hoped might earn him some favor points.

"Tell me—how are my children doing in the *new world*? Can't imagine what ten years over there might do to a person, but it's like I told them when Walter said they were going: we all need to find our way in our own way. What do you think, though? Would I even recognize them anymore?"

As if he were transported back there, Henry's shoulders sank, and he looked down at the table, where he rubbed his palms together. "Things haven't been easy for any of us—the Murrieta is a wild place—but they're doing okay. Walter's Walter last I saw him, and Donna and Blanton have obviously grown a lot since they left here."

"She still do that thing?"

"What? Oh, you mean Donna's habit of only talking after Blanton does? Yeah, she does."

"Hm. Man, if I'd have only known then how much I'd come to miss those twins." Jimmy shook his head. "Their little ticks used to get to their mother and me then, you know? So I don't blame Walter for taking them. But since they've been gone and she passed ... those are things I hold on to the most. What about Leonard's sons, though? They good too?"

Henry scanned the room again. On two of the four walls was a printed list with the title, Code of the Fraternal Forgotten. He was much more interested in that than Jimmy's current line of conversation, so he read through the so-called Code of the Fraternal Forgotten while answering. "There's nothing good about what those boys are going through. But they're surviving."

"I really wish I could've been there to help William with his deal. We'd talked about it before him and the others left for the Murrieta. I was supposed to be there in Leonard's ear when he returned, supporting the unification of the sprawling East and the wild West. What a thing it would've been, huh?"

The failed journey came back to Henry's mind. "You and me both. But, yeah, things haven't exactly gone to plan."

"They never do." Jimmy grinned. "But we adjust, and we find ourselves where we find ourselves. We'll get you caught up on where that is, though, like I said."

"Again, hopefully sooner than later. Especially if I'm gonna take on the role of this Emory Wallace persona I've managed to create for myself. I need to know who *he's* to be fighting alongside and why."

"What? Do you not feel like you know me?"

"To be honest with you—no. Five years later, I'm not so sure I do know you," Henry said, tapping the table.

"And is our enemy not apparent either?" Henry's eyes narrowed at the thought of Leonard's lifelong best friend, Jackson "Forrest" Hayes, the man Henry currently hated most in the world. Before he could spit fire, though, Jimmy stood up and retreated to the door, opening it and gesturing for Henry to follow him. "Ah, but of course he is. Come on, let's take a walk. There's something I need to show you, and after all you've been through of late, I'm sure you could use some air."

Following Jimmy's lead, Henry exited the room. He expected the lighting to improve, but it didn't by much. The entire compact building was dimly lit. Within it were women and men at desks, sifting through envelopes by candlelight. Jimmy explained how the letters consisted of an array of insider correspondence, messages of support, and submissions of small fees that the Forgotten requested of its members. Though the funds were modest, Jimmy told him, they kept the Fraternal Forgotten afloat, and thus, morale remained strong. The code from earlier was plastered all over the walls here too, which he was told helped reinforce the rules, values, and loyalty that the union lived by. Henry was amazed at how well it was all organized.

The busy atmosphere, which in a way reminded him of a less messy version of Leonard's office, was charged with energy. At the exit door and each corner stood tall men draped in dark, long trench coats and funny-looking hats. They too seemed reminiscent of Leonard's operation, appearing to be fashioned after his henchmen, though they took up less of the room and were much more disciplined in their stillness. Though there were differences between the nature of the Forgotten and Leonard's organization, the similarities made Henry wonder about the scale and potential of what Jimmy had here.

Jimmy stormed through the room toward the exit, neither the busy workers nor the frozen guards paying him much mind. It seemed odd and almost bothersome to Henry that they didn't acknowledge the presence of their leader. But his anxiety overtook the annoyance when Jimmy swung open the doors, letting in a burst of sunlight, and walked out onto the street. Forrest's mafia had always run the city, and word darted along its cobbles quicker than the rats. But Henry wasn't a coward, so he swallowed the nerves and followed Jimmy, who was wandering ahead of him with a merry skip through these unfamiliar streets.

Henry looked around, searching for clues to his exact location. While the bustle was reflective of New Berkeley proper, the buildings here were shorter and simpler in design. He noticed right away that those around them also seemed to be walking along without a worry, all as carefree as Jimmy. Passersby even exchanged greetings—an unheard of occurrence in the city he remembered. It was as if they were in a different place altogether.

Where must we have gone wrong for this to be so strange— neighbors behaving neighborly?

That is what made him love the simpler countryside on the outskirts of the city where he used to live—though it saddened him to recall how those areas had been urbanized and developed. Henry gazed in fascination at this place that seemed to revive that way of life.

"Afternoon, Mr. Wallace."

"Whoa," Henry said, startled by the sudden call of a fellow walking in their direction and tipping his cap at them. The man seemed shaken by his response, as did the woman whose arm was locked around his. "Oh, excuse me. Good afternoon."

Jimmy smiled and nodded at the couple, who returned the same tenfold, each shaking his hand. "Please, excuse my friend. He's not yet accustomed to how we do things here."

"No problem at all, Mr. Keagan," the man said.

The woman laid a hand on Henry's arm. "We were just so happy to see you're okay. It was very brave what you did at our protest, and we can't thank you enough."

If the touch didn't do it, the words made him swell with pride. Before replying, he remembered to kick back into his fake accent and made a mental plan to continue with it at all times so he wouldn't slip up. "It was nothing, y'all, really. Any brother or sister of the Forgotten would have heeded the call."

"It was an above-and-beyond display," Jimmy said as he faced the couple. "Will I see you both at the rally this weekend?"

"Of course, Mr. Keagan," they said in near unison.

"Glad to hear it. Until then."

With a pleasant nod, the couple scurried off, and Jimmy marched for a few more blocks until he came to a busy roundabout. Henry's curiosity in his surroundings had become a need for explanation. "What is this place? How can Forrest allow y'all to walk so freely in his city?"

Jimmy came to an abrupt halt before him and turned with a satisfied look. "Oh, this isn't all his city anymore. No one's learning it faster than him either." He arched up his head at a two-story building beside them. "We're here. Follow me."

They entered a hall with rows of benches lined up before a platform on which a podium sat. It looked like a large church-type setting, but there were no Cereb holy icons or crescents or references to the Enigma anywhere. Off to the side was a stairwell, and they used it to ascend to the second floor, where there was a much less dramatic office. The office had a balcony that overlooked the roundabout they'd seen outside. On all corners of the street stood the uniformed guards of the Forgotten. However, their gray coats were more like camouflage here; they blended in with the townsfolk, who were all fluttering about in conversation. Some discussion seemed casual, while others appeared to debate or barter with each other. As far as Henry could tell, though, all interactions were cordial. It was clear that these were one people, each individual helping and engaging with others toward a common purpose.

Their numbers didn't seem tremendous, but he could picture it on a much larger scale. He could picture the ultimate goal.

Whatever the secret is to this sanctuary of a community, why couldn't they spread it? Why couldn't all of New Berkeley adopt it?

"The people are starting to see," Jimmy said as he appeared next to Henry. "Forrest can't touch us here because he knows the power we have over him. All the wealth in the world won't protect him from revolution. And here we show the people they have that power at their fingertips. Our numbers aren't ideal in the city, so we go and protest when we can. But we've made a home here. A safe place with law, fairness, and transparency."

"But Jimmy ... where is *here*?"

"This, my dear Emory, is your new home. This is the Viridian District."

*

The Church of the Humble Followers was silent, other than the whispered prayer of Mary-Claire Norvell. Gregory sat several pews behind her front-row seat, impatiently awaiting the arrival of Father Kubler for the late-night sermon he had requested that Gregory attend.

A day had passed since William's departure, and they needed to discuss next steps regarding William's "recruiting" plan, but Kubler insisted he sit through the sermon first. Though Gregory was a faithful Cereb, he didn't like what Kubler had promised William or the influence he had over his friend. In fact, Gregory didn't much like Kubler at all. Part of him wanted to ignore Billy's request and stay far away from the priest. Yet, at the same time, there was no

55

one else to help him. And, truth be told, he'd take all the help he could get with the tall task requested of him—he had no idea how they'd even secure a conversation with the Highlanders, let alone win them over. If he had to work with the priest to accomplish that, so be it.

The whispers stopped, prompting him to turn his attention to Mary-Claire. In the candlelit dark he could see her lifting her palms to the sky and craning her neck back.

What the fuck? Is she having an experience or ... ?

Her arms started to shake.

Oh, yeah, she's definitely having some kind of experience. Why the hell am I here again?

Light footsteps echoed through the church. "Is it not a marvel— that we find ourselves here on this night?" Kubler asked as he appeared near the altar like the moon from behind a cloud, looking right at Gregory.

Wait, did he hear me?

No. That's impossible. Get it together, Gregory.

"What an evening He has granted us, Father Kubler," Mary-Claire said. Her hands were down by her side, and she sat upright like her little moment had never happened.

"Gregory," the priest said with his arms extended out toward him and a warm smile, "I am overjoyed you could join us."

Without a word, Gregory returned an uncomfortable wave.

"I would like to begin tonight's service with a hymn. If you could all please open your hymnal to 'The Fifth,' we will begin with the first verse in C."

Though he wasn't against singing at church, Gregory found

himself not in the mood. However, he did open his hymnal to the requested page, out of respect.

Kubler stood up straight and lifted his arms again. "Let us begin."

"Later on, when the crescent shines," Kubler and Norvell sang in unison. "A dancing star in the dead—"

"Ah-ah-ah," Kubler interrupted them with a wave of his hand. "Gregory, is everything all right? Why are you not joining us?"

"I was, Father. Did you not hear me?"

"Gregory. It is not me you are attempting to fool when you lie in the house of the Enigma."

If he hadn't been trying to be polite, Gregory would've rolled his eyes at the comment. "Of course, Father. It won't happen again."

"Perfect. Now let us start from the beginning."

Come on.

"Later on," Mary-Claire and Kubler sang.

"… when the crescent shines," Gregory joined in with them. "A dancing star in the dead of the night. Is it chance or a promise of light? The Father's gift, our worlds are right. Mother, she said to 'live for Him. Behold His mercy, let your heart swim.' Her words were heard, now I am freed. Walk or run, He will guide me."

The others dragged out the last *me* for longer than he was willing to hold the note. When they finished, Kubler took a deep breath. "Thank you, my precious flock. It is no mistake that I brought your attention to the Fifth in these late hours. While our numbers are small, as they tend to be during our evening services, I would tell you not to be disheartened."

"Never, Father," Mary-Claire said. The whine of her voice made Gregory squirm.

Kubler gave her a nod, to which she began toying with her hair as if her presence had been acknowledged in a tremendous crowd. "I would tell you not to be disheartened because there is power in faith, and our power will serve as a light. With it, we will become the crescent and the dancing star. We will illuminate the path out of the darkness of this territory. And we will guide its lost souls so that their hearts too may swim. In the process, our Cereb family will be allowed to grow more than we ever imagined before. For He will guide us, and we will be free."

While he was impressed with how much the priest was able to relate the hymn to their situation, Gregory grew impatient. "But, Father, how might we secure this growth? Or ... what must we do?"

"Was this not clear in what I said?"

"I thought it was clear, Father," Mary-Claire replied.

Oh, get over yourself, kiss-ass.

"Perhaps, if you could just elaborate a bit?"

"Faith, Gregory," Kubler said.

Gregory thought there had to be more, but no more came.

"Faith?"

"Yes, of course. Faith." Mary-Claire pivoted on her bench to face him. She was nodding as if it all made sense and Gregory was an idiot.

This is what I get for asking a practical question in the middle of a sermon. She doesn't even know what we're talking about.

"That's our whole plan, though?" Gregory asked, ignoring Mary-Claire and focusing on the priest.

"The Enigma provides many signs within our worlds—hints,

if you will," Kubler said as he stepped down into the aisle. "I knew William being brought to me was one of my signs. When the time comes, He will show us the way. As long as we have faith."

Crack!

Gregory whipped around at the sound, and his stomach dropped. Standing in the entryway of the church was Clovis. The doors were still reverberating from how hard he'd flung them open. He looked like a wreck as he marched in with his right-hand man, Devin Turpin.

"There you are, Gregory, you spineless ape!"

Gregory shuddered. *This isn't good.*

"Clovis? You're back already?"

"What in the fuck are you doing here praying when Billy's in danger?"

"Excuse me," Father Kubler said, but his calm voice was a mouse compared to Clovis's roaring lion.

"It's complicated. Please, just let me explain," Gregory replied, fearing for his life as he always did around Clovis. But Clovis only kept storming toward him.

"Maria already told me everything I needed to hear. Come here, you son of a bitch."

Clovis grabbed him by his collar and threw him onto his back on the bench. Despite Gregory's size advantage, Clovis's sheer rage outmatched him. Knowing that if he responded in kind, a full fight would break out, Gregory sat up and began to slide away. "Stop this, please."

"I can't even fathom it!" Clovis shouted in his face. "Losing him to a few natives? Even for a worthless fuck like you, that's—"

"Enough!" Father Kubler shouted with such a boom in his voice that everyone froze. Before continuing, Kubler straightened out his robes and returned to his characteristically calm demeanor, albeit with a sprinkle of frustration. "Yes, William has been taken. No, he is not lost. Yes, we will get him back, but we will do it together or not at all. Clovis, the Enigma provides us with signs in our worlds. Just stand down for a moment and hear what we have to say. I believe your talents may be crucial to our efforts. I believe … you could be our sign."

These words were the very last Gregory wanted to hear. He wanted nothing to do with Clovis's "talents" or with any plan that held Clovis as a "sign," but even with his disdain, he knew he had little choice.

He looked up at Clovis and Father Kubler, who stood facing one another, eyes locked. Then Clovis followed the priest's example, straightening himself out. A dark, yellow-toothed smile crept across Clovis's face. "Devin, go fetch Billy's tribute, Charles, and run the bastard down south to my sweet brother like we discussed. As for you, Mr. Priest, let's you and I talk more about my talents."

Inwardly, Gregory cursed the Enigma and wondered what horrible things he must have done in his previous world to deserve this one. This place was hell, and before him stood both its devils.

*

Though the night had swept in, the bustle remained in the Viridian District; members of the Fraternal Forgotten whom Henry had seen earlier in the week filed into the hall. The time for their rally had come. In a back room behind the stage, he waited and watched the crowd with Jimmy, who was peering into a mirror and making some last adjustments to his appearance. It was a larger bunch than Henry had expected, which he couldn't be happier about.

As the audience took their seats, Henry wondered why the rally was scheduled behind closed doors and not out in the streets for all to hear, but it wasn't the first aspect of Jimmy's process he questioned. In the days he'd spent observing everything he could about the Fraternal Forgotten, he'd often thought the same thing over and over: the scale of his renewed comrade's thinking wasn't big enough for him. The murder of his daughter, Judith, and the man who gave that order, Forrest, were constantly at the forefront of Henry's mind. He needed Jimmy to think bigger.

No less than all of it—the entire operation. Find a way—any way—whatever it takes.

As he repeated his oath to himself once again, the question Henry had wanted to ask Jimmy all week bubbled up inside of him and refused to be pushed back down. "You know, you don't ever have to tell me what happened between Leonard and you if you don't want to. But, Jimmy, I need to know what you have against Forrest."

Jimmy turned away from the mirror to give him a fierce look.

Just then a whistle blared, and a woman could be heard addressing the attendees from the podium, trying to settle down the commotion. But Henry kept his eyes on Jimmy.

"Well, he's a conniving, possessive piece of shit to put it mildly," Jimmy said.

"A what?"

Straightening himself out as he rose to his feet, Jimmy grimaced. "A crooked fucking vulture."

"Yeah, but I don't—"

"Brothers and sisters, the father of the Fraternal Forgotten, Jimmy Keagan!" the speaker said to thunderous applause. Henry thirsted for the details he knew he would have to wait for.

"You don't, but you will," Jimmy said as he passed him. "And I'm gonna ask you to say a few words, by the way," he added quickly. "That all right?"

Henry made no attempt to restrain his excitement at the opportunity. "I'd be thrilled."

Jimmy nodded and trotted onto the stage with a wave at his audience. Henry followed.

Whatever Forrest did to Jimmy must've been quite the number. An addition to a long list of crimes. We must bring his operation all the way down.... And there is no time to waste.

"Thank you, Forgotten. Please, be seated," Jimmy said over the noise. On cue, they sat, and Henry followed their lead, sitting in his own chair on the stage. "I want to get right to it tonight and tell you that we have a special guest. This is someone each of you might know, either by having seen his incredible display of courage firsthand or by hearing about it through word of mouth. He won't know it yet, but we do very much like to talk here, don't we?" As the crowd hooted their approval, Jimmy took a moment to smile at him. "And we only say good things about each other, too, so you shouldn't have anything to worry about … at least, until we get to know you better. Then you'll be fair game like the rest of us."

More easy laughter, but Henry was unamused; he was still fixed on his mission and somewhat bothered by Jimmy's flippancy. His mind raced from point to point, looking for the best strategy to improve their strength—to increase the influence of the Fraternal Forgotten and bring about the downfall of Forrest Hayes.

"In all seriousness, though, please join me in welcoming, for a few words, a man who stood up for those in need when they were at their most vulnerable. He is the embodiment of what it means to be a member of the Fraternal Forgotten and is a model for how we should all strive to be. Friends, without further ado, please give it up for Emory Wallace."

Jimmy rushed over to shake hands with him as Henry rose to his feet. Those in attendance let out an intoxicating roar. Once Jimmy let go and took the same chair, he approached the podium and inhaled. Though beads of sweat clung to his forehead, his hands were steady. Their cheers filled his lungs, and a charge ripped through his body—it was his time. Yet despite the joy he felt, he made every effort not to show an ounce of it. He decided they needed a leader, not a cheer captain with a toothy grin.

Once they quieted down, he continued to say nothing but maintained an intense stare. Silence filled the hall. Pulling his hands behind his back, he stepped off the podium and paced all the way to the left side of the stage. Scanning the crowd before him—a pitiful but big-hearted assortment of New Berkeley's struggling poor and lower-middle class—he saw their uncertainty setting in. On their faces was an uncomfortable yet razor-focused tension, which was exactly what he was after. When he was sure each and every eye was centered on him, he pivoted and marched one slow step at a time to the other side. Once there, he stopped again; a good two or three minutes had passed since his introduction.

"Em—"

"As Jimmy mentioned, my name is Emory Wallace," Henry said, interrupting Jimmy, who he was sure had been about to check on him. He was and had been in full control, however. "I'm the man y'all have heard about—and sure, those stories are about me. But I'm not here this evening to be honored, nor do I find myself deserving of any such honor. My true purpose for being here tonight is to tell you the most important thing I've learned so far in my short time among your Fraternal Forgotten. You see, brothers and sisters, what I've come to realize is that we're all Emory Wallace."

A fist raised in the air. "Here, here!"

Another. "Damn right!"

"There would've been no rescue at that factory without the unity and kinship y'all had on full display," Henry said with increased vigor and animated hands. "It inspired me beyond comprehension. It taught me that together, and only together, can we be so bold and so strong. And so I tell y'all now because it's never been clearer … the days of rule by the barons of ruthless industry are coming to their end. The day of the Forgotten—and one day of a unified New Berkeley—is only just dawning."

The response was a swift roaring cheer. Jimmy stood, clapping and approaching him as if he were finished—but he was only just getting started. Before the audience members had the chance to come down from their roaring high, he continued. "But there is much ground yet to be gained. We cannot afford to be complacent when so much is within our grasp. So, if y'all will hear me, I'd like to offer some simple ideas on how we might take this next step. May I share my thoughts with y'all?"

Before him, the fervor continued. Behind him, Jimmy slowly

returned to his seat, lifting one eyebrow in question. Henry ignored him. "Fantastic. Thank y'all kindly for the support. Now, there are two things missing in this city: written laws and law enforcement to uphold those laws. For too long the market and its victors have been free to dictate who's protected and under what circumstances."

A whistle. "Far too long!"

"That's right. But no more. The corruption and moral ambiguity needs to end with us," Henry said as he nodded and wagged his finger at the person who had chimed in. "As you've seen in this very district, under the code that Jimmy's set forth, fairness is possible. It's about time we reclaim our city and share this equity with all people. Now, does that sound like the future y'all would want for our children—to give them better than the filthy factories they slave away in?"

Powerful cheers resounded through the hall in response.

"And are y'all not tired of having your own safety confined to this one district?"

Scattered applause answered him.

"Good. Y'all should be." He paused, staring down the crowd for a moment, allowing the tension to build before he went on. "But to get there will require three measures. The first is sacrifice. Each one of us must continue to be willing to give to the cause more than ever before, socially and financially. Only with your support can we build the other two measures, which will be designed to ensure we're lifted to prosperity. The second measure is to establish an elected law-making body to expand the code and represent all people of our city. Though this will start small with the Forgotten, we'll extend our reach and provide enforcement of the code and the official law through the third measure: a well-organized police force." On saying those words, Henry lifted his hands toward the back of the room, where the gray-coated guards lined the wall, protecting the door. They wore the same uniform as those he had seen throughout the Viridian District and stood just as still. "These men have been modeled after the cronies of our enemies. No longer. They're better and will be respected as such. We will train them so that their justice is swift and their prosecution feared."

More applause broke out among the crowd, and Henry took a deep breath to calm himself and his tone. Before he began, he looked to Jimmy as if addressing him. "Forrest Hayes took everything from me, just like I know he's done to some of y'all. To be transparent … he took someone very special from me. But let me tell you what. This isn't just about vengeance—it's about justice … about family." His arms extended again as he faced the audience to show them he was one of them. "So I leave y'all with this: to earn the comfort we seek in our lives, we must first be ready and willing to bask in austerity. To win our war for peace, we must stand firm on this knife's edge." He froze to let his words sink in before giving up his stage. "Thank y'all for your time."

An uproarious chorus of support filled the hall as every member present rose out of their seats and clapped. Jimmy joined in again, though this time a bit more reservedly, and brought a hand to Henry's shoulder. Beside himself, Henry waved at those before him, dreams of Forrest's demise dancing through his mind.

Perhaps I am cut out for this.

Some activity at the far end of the hall by the door caught his attention. When he squinted, he could see a scuffle of some sort with the guards.

The four culprits were wearing black coats.

Only Forrest's men wore those coats.

Cries split the air as the butts of rifles connected with the faces of the resisting guards. Members of the Fraternal Forgotten began to panic, particularly when Forrest's thugs aimed their guns at the crowd. The guns had short barrels but large drums and were unlike anything Henry had seen before.

"Everyone stay calm," Jimmy said, shouting at the top of his lungs over the commotion. "They wouldn't dare shoot here. Isn't that right, boys? So how about you cower home to daddy and stop ruining everyone's night?"

The doors swung open, and Henry's blood boiled as Forrest, the man he most hated in the world, entered. "No. They won't shoot you *here* unless I tell them to. And whether I tell them to depends on your next move, *boys*, because daddy's come to take back what's his."

CHAPTER 4

NORTH STAR

The night of the attack on the Keagan men was a sleepless, solitary one for Latera. She didn't want to be around anyone; she didn't want to be whisked through dizzying dreams; and she didn't want to hear any voices. All she did want was silence—to be alone with her own thoughts in her own mind—and to bask in this moment of peace for as long as she could.

While the others slept at the camp they had commandeered from their retreated enemies, she sat cross-legged, meditating through the night with her back to a wide tree. Both arms rested on her legs, the pointer fingers and thumbs of each hand rubbing together as had become her steadying habit. The bark of the tree was rough, but in a way she needed the feeling to balance her tranquility with the true nature of the world. She was focused and clear at once.

As she dove deeper into the recesses of her mind, she came to the Riverlands—oh, how she missed her home. She could still feel its chill race up her neck, and suddenly, clear as day, she saw the River White before her. She sat on the frosty bank. The wind whistled through the trees alongside the rushing river. Only the sounds of nature saturated the air. This had been the peace she'd been searching for. Latera took a deep, extensive breath into her nose, filling her lungs with the scent of pine, before releasing it from her mouth. She took another. A cloud emerged from her mouth with each puff.

For a brief moment she thought of what was missing: her people. A faint rumble sounded then. As the wind and the current picked up, so did the beat of her heart. The sky darkened.

"Latera." The voice from her dreams echoed her name in the intensifying storm. With each passing gust, it repeated and grew louder.

From her seated position, her eyes shot open, and she stood up as the voice's tenor rang through her bones. With her hand raising up into the sky as if to reach for it, she recognized she was still by the River White. "What do you want from me?"

"Everything."

The scene descended into dark, stormy madness. "Everything?" she asked.

"I will find you."

Lightning streaked across the sky, striking a tree beside her with a fiery crack. Burning embers exploded from the tree in a burst of smoke. Thunder roared as the tree snapped at its base and started to fall in her direction. Backing away in a frantic crab crawl, Latera did her best to shake herself out of the nightmare. It didn't seem to be working. The tree free-fell, and she raised her arms for cover, bracing for an impact. When it was about to land, her head jolted and collided with the tree behind her. She was at the camp, still sitting with her back to the same tree. Her profuse sweating and the surrounding early-morning darkness told her she was awake and in reality.

There was something pinching her shoulder now, though. Remaining frozen in place, she turned her eyes to the side as far as they could go without moving her head. The shape was black. Craning her neck the slightest bit, she saw a crow stared straight at her.

"Latera," it hissed.

She shrieked at the top of her lungs, diving away from the crow as its wings fluttered in her face. Even after it perched on the ground, she retreated in the same crab-crawl as in her vision; the world around her began to spin, and her skin heated up.

"Prepare yourself."

"No!" she cried, desperate and hysterical. "Please. Go away. Please just go away."

The bird's head craned sideways and stayed that way as Latera's tears mixed with the sweat on her cheeks.

"I can't do this anymore," she said with a sniffle, her words a mumble now. Was there never to be any peace for her again?

The crow hopped once toward her, and she jumped. Another hop caused her to back away. Before she could take another breath, it darted forward, causing her to scramble farther back still until she ran into another tree. Once she stopped, it landed on her raised knee, its beak right before her face.

"I can't do this. Please."

The crow's head craned once again before turning upright, and it locked its gaze with hers. "You can and you will."

A moment later, it flew off like lightning, all trace of it gone in an instant.

Two weeks of tracking took their toll. Though Dominic's body was as taxed as he was sure Daniel's was, the mental drain was much worse: they came up short at every turn. Dominic's ceaseless longing for the stage didn't make the situation any easier. He spent his days in mental rehearsals of the three acts of every trick in his arsenal: each pledge, each turn, and each prestige. It was becoming stressful to be kept away from his passion and his life, and feelings of resentment were creeping in.

As for the task at hand, Clovis's trail seemed to snake with intentional irregularity. This wasn't surprising in the slightest but was disheartening nonetheless. One thing they were confident about was that Fayette had to be a stop on Clovis's escape south.

Dominic sighed as he climbed atop his horse again at the beginning of another day of tracking. They'd just finished a quick breakfast of plump rabbits over fire and were ready to set off.

The dawn came soon after they began their ride, and with it came an overcast thick enough to block out the sun. It was there, though, hiding in some unknown place. The clouds were pale without a hint of stormy gray. Mornings like this were Dominic's favorite. In a way, he believed it was nature's own performance to keep its inhabitants guessing.

Will the sun break through? Will the rain wash away our troubles? Will a storm come and change our course?

"Ugly ass day," Daniel said, snapping him out of his distraction. "Appropriate for our arrival."

With his focus away from the sky, Dominic had a chance to

mind his immediate surroundings. The path had been changing from the wooded terrain of the Riverlands into the sweeping hills of the central Murrieta. "Arrival?"

"We aren't an hour out of Fayette now … like we should've been days ago."

"You're really gonna go there again?" Dominic asked with a groan, unwilling to restrain his frustration anymore. They'd argued about the best route to take in pursuit of Clovis, and Dominic had pushed them to go for the longer, safer option.

"I'm just saying." Daniel wouldn't look his way, squinting ahead as if the town were in sight.

"Well, do me a favor and save it. If we'd have gone direct, he could have flanked us, and we'd have been fucked. I'm not trying to die in whatever sick fashion your brother can think up."

"You escaped him before, magic man."

While Daniel did look over this time and grin, Dominic's blood boiled. The familiar name he'd been taunted with in the past still stung, though Daniel wouldn't know it was disparaging. "Do *not* call me that."

"Sensitive subject—noted," Daniel replied.

Their horses plodded along for a few minutes in quiet.

"Look, I'm sorry for giving you shit, okay? I just don't want them to get to Billy before I do, is all. He's in a vulnerable place. Clovis would manipulate that and then … well, I just gotta get to Billy first."

Dominic rotated in his saddle to look at Daniel. "Understand this, Daniel: I'm here with you to kill Clovis so I can finally go *and stay* home," he said. "Because I've accepted that that's what it's gonna take to get back to living the life I had before you and your brothers took it all away. Anything beyond that is your business and not my priority."

"Yeah, man. I get it. And I want that for you, for Harran—hell, for me too. But I worry that, in a way, there ain't no going back for me. And as I've already lost one brother ..." Out of the corner of his eye, Dominic saw Daniel sigh. "I just don't want to lose them both."

Dominic remained stone-faced and opted not to reply, though on the inside his defenses had fallen a bit.

The rest of the hour-long ride went without a word; only the chirping and crying of the birds overhead broke the silence. When they reached Fayette, the first thing to come into view was the mansion Daniel had told him about. It was as big a home as he'd ever seen, painted in colors Dominic didn't believe mixed well.

Beside him, Daniel ensured his revolvers were loaded and slid them into their hip holsters. Dominic followed suit, and they dismounted their horses before finding a hidden place to tie them off. Not knowing how much impact Clovis already would have had on those left in town, they needed to be stealthy and unseen. If he was there, the capture would have to be quick and efficient.

Their first move would be to observe the mansion. For a few hours they sat and waited to see who came in and out. The only person of significance was a man named Gregory, who Daniel described as a friend of William's. He appeared to be returning from town. A few minutes after he'd entered the mansion, Daniel shuffled in place. "How long will we wait here?"

"We should give it just a little longer. There's no need to rush." An uncomfortable sweat patch was forming on Dominic's upper back as they waited, and he wriggled to try to keep the fabric from sticking to his skin, but it clung to him nonetheless. A tiny fly started pestering his face too—and soon another joined the obnoxious fun.

Daniel also looked uncomfortable, but that wasn't a reason to move before they should. "Why? If he's inside, we could confront him right there. We need to end this and get it over with."

The idea of his journey being over so soon was certainly appealing. Reconsidering his position, Dominic took a deep breath. They should still be smart about it. "Is there a back way in?"

"Of course. Do you see the size of the place?"

All it took was a nod for Daniel to jump up and lead the way. They snuck across the field they'd been spying from to the side of the house.

Creeping along the exterior, he saw Daniel brush a hand along the paneling where two bullet holes had impacted. "What the hell happened here?"

"We'll find out, but—" Before Dominic could finish his whispered response, Daniel was rushing around to the back of the house. Dominic chased after his partner, furious that he'd put both of them at risk. "Daniel! Slow down!"

"Billy?" Daniel asked up to the windows in a half call, half whisper. "Billy, are you there?"

Having reached the corner, Dominic stopped and called out to Daniel in a hushed tone. "What the fuck are you doing? Get back here. You'll get us killed."

"Daniel? Is that you?" a deep voice called from above.

Daniel spun around to face the second-story windows. "Gregory! Yes!"

"Stay there. I'll come let you in."

"Locking the doors now, are you?" Daniel asked.

"Had some incidents here recently. Be right down."

When Gregory disappeared, Daniel gave Dominic a look as if to tell him to come out of hiding. Putting a finger to his mouth, Dominic declined.

Unable to see around the corner, he heard the door crack open. "Dan—"

"Incidents?" Daniel asked, cutting Gregory off.

Though Daniel already knew the story of William's kidnapping, thanks to the message Hanzah had received from his sister, Dominic had told Daniel to act as if he were unaware. It was a way to ensure whether or not he was getting the truth from his associate—a test. And Gregory did tell the truth, reciting the same turn of events that they'd been told.

Daniel released a deep breath, a sound of satisfaction. "Listen, Gregory, I don't blame you for what happened."

"I appreciate that."

"But I'm not just here to check in on the home front." Daniel paused. "Things got complicated up north."

"I know."

"You know?" Daniel asked, hesitation creeping into his voice.

"Clovis has already been through here, Daniel."

"Gregory, whatever he said, it isn't the whole story—"

"I figured." Gregory cleared his throat. "I've known all three of you a long time, Dan. I know you'd never betray Billy like he's suggesting. But I wanted to warn you: not everyone will feel the same."

"I knew I could trust you, Gregory," Daniel said. "You said he'd been through here? As in, he's gone?"

Gregory leaked out a laugh. "You think you'd get such a casual greeting if he weren't? He was here, but only for a short while. Once I told him what happened with Billy, Devin and him up and left. Said they were going straight after him, straight to the natives down south. Not before they gave me my scolding for it, though."

"You okay?"

"Yeah, I'm fine. Used to it from him by now."

"You're sure that's where they're going—the Hold?"

"I'm sure. It's why they took Charles."

"Well, then, there's no time to waste." Dominic could hear some backslapping and guessed that Daniel had embraced the man. "Thanks for all you've done to take care of this place while we've been gone, man. Especially being there for Billy—you're a Keagan brother in all but name as far as I'm concerned."

"Thank you, Daniel. But please … Billy's not in a good way, and I'm not sure how much more he'll be able to take. Please find him and help him. Only you can now."

"I will."

Dominic figured it best to remain hidden at this point. It'd be better if everyone in Fayette—anyone that could come into contact with Clovis or his men at any point—thought Daniel was traveling alone. It gave them a small advantage. So, after Daniel's goodbye, Dominic prepared to slip away unnoticed. When Daniel's eyes cut to him, he indicated silence and for him to leave alone. He'd followed stealthily, and they'd reunite outside of Fayette.

One thing was clear: there really was no time to waste. If Clovis was heading south toward William, Daniel might get his wish after all. It would be a battle of brothers, and one they needed to come out on top of for the sake of the entire Murrieta Territory.

*

Beyond the Keagan mansion, Daniel was beginning to fade into the horizon of the hills. Gregory stood watching by the back door as Daniel departed the home. There he remained, rubbing his wet palms on his pants without pause until the moment Daniel all but vanished from view. Once he did, Gregory darted straight back inside and up to Henry and Maria's room.

"There, I did it. He's—"

"Gregory!" Maria said, interrupting him as she wrenched from Clovis's clutches and ran into his arms.

Clovis stood still, for a moment peeking out of the bedroom window where he would have been watching to ensure Gregory's lie to divert Daniel had worked. Though Gregory had been forced to deceive his friend, he took solace in knowing Daniel truly was Billy's best hope. At least some good might come out of his falsehood.

"Finally," Blanton Keagan said from the bed, where he sat with his sister, Donna, as well as Francis, Florence, and Henrietta Abigale. The Abigale children sat cowering behind the young Keagans.

"Can we go now?" Donna asked Clovis, speaking only once Blanton had, as her habit dictated.

Clovis's gaze snapped to his cousins. "Y'all are Keagans,

understand? Now, I gave y'all a simple-enough order in watching those brats for me, and I was pleased to see you do so. But being a member of the Keagan gang is a privilege—one y'all will learn to appreciate in time."

Blanton's somber, hazel-brown eyes locked with Gregory's. The bond Gregory shared with the young red-headed boy had strengthened since they met, and from their conversations he knew the struggles Blanton faced. In some ways, they weren't so different from his own. "What if we don't want to be in the Keagan gang?" Blanton asked, causing Gregory's stomach to drop.

"What did you just say?" Clovis asked in a deep, menacing tone.

"He just misses Walter, is all. He worries being part of the gang means being apart from family all the time." Donna said. "Isn't that right, Blanton?"

As Blanton's lip quivered, he nodded; still Clovis stared him down.

"Blanton, Donna, how about you take the Abigales downstairs now?" Gregory asked, turning next to Clovis. "Daniel's gone, and they did as you asked, yeah? What do you say we get them fed?"

"Take them to the kitchen," Clovis snapped at the twins, beckoning them toward the door.

The kids jumped off the bed and filed out of the room on their merry way. Maria gave Gregory a brief kiss, her relief and gratitude apparent. When they pulled apart a moment later, Gregory saw Clovis hop down from the windowsill out of the corner of his eye. "I gotta say, you done good with Daniel, buddy boy. Well done, indeed." Gregory moved to put a little more distance between himself and Maria; they still were uncomfortable flaunting their indiscretion. But as he began to do so, Clovis's hands came to each of their shoulders. "Oh, please, don't stop on my behalf, y'all."

With his stomach turning, Gregory squinted and shook his head. "That's ... okay."

"What? Is it because I threatened her? Is it because she's a married woman?" Clovis removed his hand from him and snaked behind Maria, wrapping his arm around her shoulders. Gregory stopped his reflex to push Clovis away. "You know, with Daniel turning into the monster that he did, it isn't easy for me to know who I can trust." Clovis's hands moved to grip Maria's waist. Maria cringed. "Can I trust you, Gregory?"

"Yes—yes. I did what you asked, didn't I? Now, please, let her go."

As Clovis released her one finger at a time, she only tensed up more. Gregory pulled her close the second Clovis let go and backed away to the door. "Bye, now," Clovis waved with a toothy grin before slamming the door shut, leaving them alone in the room.

As soon as Clovis disappeared, Maria eased gently away from Gregory.

"I'm sorry for that, love," he said as she marched across the room. "It won't happen again."

The silence cut to the bone. She refused to look at him or even acknowledge his words.

"What's wrong, Maria?"

"It's nothing," she replied, shuffling around in a dresser drawer by the bed.

He watched as she began to pull articles of clothing out of the drawer and place them in piles on the bed. Dread swept over him. "Maria."

"What?"

"I told you before, I have everything under control," he said.

She tilted her head and raised a doubtful brow.

"What? You don't believe me?" he asked, equal parts offended and upset.

She didn't respond but simply maneuvered toward a closet, from which she pulled out a suitcase, hurling it open onto the bed beside the clothes.

"What are you doing?"

"I'm taking the kids and going back east."

Horrified at the prospect, he took a careful step toward her. "Back east to what? To Henry? After all the nights you've cursed his abandonment? I swore to you I'd be there for you."

"No, not to Henry," she said, still looking down. "I don't know where yet. Maybe I'll go right past New Berkeley and we'll settle somewhere sunny. Maybe Alvenika."

He continued forward and placed a hand on her shoulder. She finally stopped moving. "Please. You don't have to do this. Not with all we have together. It's something special, and I ... I love you, Maria." She looked up at him upon hearing these new words between them. "And I promise I have this under control, okay? Once Billy sees the truth, everything will be good, and we'll be able to just focus on us and the kids."

For the first time, she squared up to him, rolling her eyes at the mention of William. "That's just it, Gregory. William can't see. You tried to protect him from his father; you tried to protect him from

Clovis; you tried to protect him from Father Kubler. But you need to face it: he's lost."

His body shifted away in denial. "No. He's—"

This time she pulled him back. "Yes—he is. Listen to me, baby: he's lost, and it isn't your fault, okay? The same way you've told me Henry isn't my fault. My poor Judith and I were buried by the ambitions of broken men. But you aren't like them. You've done everything you can for everyone but yourself. For once you need to do what's right for you and understand that your destiny is yours to make."

Her words impacted him like a punch in the gut. Gregory sat heavy on the edge of the bed. Maria sat by his side. She leaned her head on his shoulder, and he draped an arm over her. The more he thought about it, the more he realized he had never really considered what his own destiny might be. All he knew was that ever since he'd entered the Keagan gang, he had been among friends—best friends—who had given him a place in the world when he had nowhere else to turn. But Maria was right. Billy's mindset was shifting, and it was getting harder for him to tolerate the risk to her and the children. They were in the range of an increasingly probable fallout, and he'd never forgive himself if anything happened to them.

"Give me two weeks," he said.

Maria sighed and stood up. "But why? Two weeks for what?"

Clutching her hand in his, he rose up beside her. "So I can do what's right for me. Please. And then, if you still want to go, I won't stop you."

With a frown, she gave him the eye for a moment before she

subtly nodded. "All right. Two weeks. But that's it."

"Thank you, darling." Grateful for the concession, he gave her a kiss on the cheek. An infectious grin crossed her lips. "Alvenika, huh?" he asked. "Never took you for a beach girl."

As she opened the door, she turned to him, shaking her head. "I'm not."

With Maria gone to tend to the kids, Gregory sat alone for a while to think. The following morning he'd travel with Clovis and Father Kubler to Prayer's Passage. Expanding the Keagan gang would be one of two things he would need done to bring Billy back to sorts—the other he accomplished by sending Daniel southward. But this wasn't just about Billy anymore. Like he told Maria, this was a task he was doing for himself as much as for anyone else. Once Billy came around and their gang was expanded, his loved ones would all be safer. He needed to prove to himself that this life was one where he could provide for them, where they could prioritize their family. Gregory wasn't sure if he was any different from Billy or Henry, but he intended to find out if the life they'd built together was still the life he himself wanted.

*

A scream snapped William awake.

A girl—the girl—Latera.

His captors, also jolted awake by it, abandoned their tents in a panic.

"Latera?" the other female V'ahani, whose name he didn't know, shouted. "Where is she?"

"Sounded close," one of the Tokali said.

Another ran straight into the trees, calling her name. All the rest followed suit but for one, who stood behind, scratching his neck in a sulk, appearing somewhat upset. William remembered this one. His name was Elan, and he was the son of respected Tokali Malik and Adila, who carried out the mission for the Keagans to lure the V'ahani of the Riverlands to the Hold. The young man's parents had been William's main points of contact with the natives of the South as well, since his gang had overtaken them.

Kubler's request. The girl is going mad. I'll start with Elan.

William smiled to himself.

It won't be long now, my Judith.

"Some look in your eye," William said, attempting to insert Father Kubler's calm into his tone.

Elan's eyebrows shot up in surprise. "What about it?"

"I didn't mean any offense by it. I used to have a similar one. It's the look of a fellow who ain't where he belongs."

"How can you tell?"

"Because I've been through it, you know. And it's a tough thing—it's like something familiar's missing, but how to get it back still eludes you. Stays hidden like a raft in a fog." Elan stared down at the ground. William decided to beckon him closer. "Come sit with me for a minute."

Elan approached the tree he was tied to and sat before him cross-legged. "Can you really see that in my face?"

"Ah," William said, pausing for effect, "were you hoping you'd hidden it better?"

Elan sighed. "I suppose so."

"Well, I'm sorry to bear the news, then. But you'll find your way again. You come from a good stock; those parents of yours are smart ones."

At the mention of his parents, guilt flashed in Elan's eyes, which was precisely what William was hoping for.

They sat in silence for moment. "Are you mad at me, Mr. Keagan?" Elan asked.

"Mad at you for what?" He knew the answer but wanted to make Elan feel he was a friend.

"For helping the V'ahani escape. If I would have stopped them, you would not be in this situation."

"Nah, man." He raised his hand and shook his head. "I couldn't fault you for following your heart. Neither would your parents, I'm sure."

The guilt further etched into Elan's features—again, as William had intended.

"Perhaps I let my feelings get the better of me."

"Yes, we do outrageous things for love, don't we?" William asked nonchalantly.

"What? No. I—I did not ..."

"Hey, there's no use trying to put it past me, buddy. I saw you looking Latera's way at the mansion. Your eyes were stuck to her like mosquitos to a vein. Plus, it's always about a girl—in one way or another."

William paused. *Now for the trap.*

"You can talk about it if you like. I'm sure it's been tough to have no one to talk to, given how she favors your friend."

When Elan sat up straight, William knew he had him. "Hammond," he spat. "He does not understand anything. If things had not gone as they did at the Hold, this would be different. There would be no need for any of this."

Finally, some real information. "What do you mean?"

"Well, at the Hold, Clovis and your men started to improve V'ahani living conditions before we left. But in order to do so, they displaced some of our people from their homes. And to be honest ..."

"Go ahead. And don't you hold back."

"Well, it angered us. We thought the Keagans were on our side. When we came to our agreement, you promised us unity in the Murrieta."

With a smile, William raised a brow. "Now you know I haven't been to the Hold since before the V'ahani arrived—haven't had the chance yet. But with all those people in one place, it sounds to me like making things fairer for all of them would amount to the very unity we promised y'all. Am I wrong?"

"When you say it this way ... I see it differently. Have I been selfish?"

"Nah. Anything but. You were influenced by your friends. And the girl, too, perhaps?"

"Yes, her too."

The smile returned as William waited. He knew silence was his friend here. Elan would feel compelled to fill it. He didn't need to wait long.

"The truth is I have had feelings for her since I led her people south. As we got closer to the Hold, though, and I realized how betrayed she would feel by me, I distanced myself again. By the time we arrived—"

"Our plan had already gone and fucked over your chances." With a genuine sigh, William couldn't help but think of Judith and of what it would've been like if something similar had gotten in the way of them. "Well, shit, I'm sorry to hear that. Hate to feel like I've gone and damaged a young heart. Your journey took a ton of bravery, though. You should be damn proud."

The chattering of hectic voices sounded from the trees as Latera appeared at the campsite with the others flanking her. When they lifted their heads, she stared them down with a fire-spitting gaze.

"Latera, speak to us, please," the other native woman said. "What happened out there?"

"I am going into my tent now." Latera pointed straight at William. "When I come out I want him off the tree with his hands bound behind his back. Beside him, waiting for me, should be the sharpest spear we have at this camp."

"Please, talk to us."

"No questions, Winnie. Not now."

Latera stormed into her tent after her sudden outburst. The others at camp were slow to react following the spectacle, and William wondered over it. He wasn't worried—he couldn't be less afraid of death at this point and knew she needed him alive anyway—but he was more curious about her instability than anything.

They're breaking, Judith. And guess who's gonna be there to put them and everyone else in this territory back together? Just like you would want. We might be together again sooner than I originally thought, baby girl.

With the others staring at him, he shrugged and bowed his head, praying loud enough for them to hear.

"I will handle her request," Elan said to his sleepy-looking comrades, speaking louder to be heard over William's prayers. The group accepted his offer and went to sit together around their campfire.

Once they were out of earshot, Elan came behind him to untie him from the tree. "I'm glad it's you," William said, pausing his prayer. "Here's hoping your woman doesn't decide to impale me, though."

The rope loosened around William's hands, and Elan broke into a whisper. "When I get these off, you should run, Mr. Keagan. I will distract them."

I've truly got him if he's offering to help me escape. But that's not what I need.

"What? Run where?"

"I do not know. Back to Fayette. Or to the Hold. Just not here."

"Listen to me, Elan. I ain't running." *That's not what the Enigma needs done. I need converts.*

"What? Why? I want to help you."

"Because I ain't got no need to. And *I* want to help *you*." With his wrists free, they rose to their feet together, and he spoke in confidence with the tree as cover. "What if I told you that you could have another chance? That if you and your people were to live with faith in certain basic principles, y'all could be granted everything y'all seek in this life and every life after—with each one *better* than the last? For starters, you wouldn't be put in a position to have to sacrifice your love again."

There was a moment of pause before Elan spoke. "You have proven to make good on your promises to the Tokali before. For this, you have my utmost trust and faith. I am sorry I ever broke it—that I distrusted the Keagan plan. I would be honored if you would share with me these principles."

"Good. Very good," William said, remaining outwardly stern despite his heart racing in excitement. "Now tie my hands up like she asked."

*

Time had passed, though Latera didn't know how much. It was still dark outside her tent when she opened her eyes. The inside was bereft of tranquility despite her attempt to sit still and calm herself. All she was sure of was that something was wrong, and at times it seemed everything was wrong. It no longer felt like a privilege to be a seer. She couldn't confide in any of her friends about what she was feeling—she couldn't even make sense of it in her own mind, much less put it into words.

She recalled the trauma of being at Walter Keagan's mercy in the Hold—the teeth-grinding agony of being tied down to a chair, with his wretched voice in her ear. While his wasn't the voice in her dreams or of the crow, she wondered if they, too, were a threat, just as he had been. And if not a threat, then they at least seemed like a warning. But a warning of what?

Yet, at the same time, a part of her felt drawn to the voice. So she'd sat in her tent, considering all the various sources of her unease, and they each led her back to the look William had given her when he had been captured at the mansion. For one reason or another, it haunted her, and she needed to confront it—or rather, him—and to do so alone. If William was hiding something, too, all the better. At least she'd understand what the warning was about. And if she could know that, she might be able to make sense of the rest.

With determination, she stormed out of her tent. She found everyone sitting around the campfire; some even had fallen back asleep there.

On seeing her, Winona and Mika jumped to their feet.

"Is there anything you need from us, Chieftess?" Winona asked. The question awakened the others.

"Only to stay here and to not follow us under any circumstances. I cannot be distracted," Latera said as she marched over to William and lifted the spear leaning against a tree beside where Elan was guarding him. His wrists were bound behind him as she had requested. "I will be back shortly."

"You will or *we* will?" William asked.

Pointing the spear at him, she nodded her head at the trees. "We will soon find out. Now get marching."

Off he went, and she followed close behind with her weapon in one hand and a torch Winona had lit for her in the other. It didn't matter where they went, so she let him lead. They just needed to go far enough from camp. She didn't know yet what she needed to do and didn't want the others to interfere.

A dim fog hovering over the ground thickened as they marched on. William tripped but caught himself. "How much further, madam?"

"Do not call me that. We will go until I say *stop*."

"As you wish."

He continued forward. A few more minutes passed with William always about five steps ahead of her. They were in dense tree cover now.

This will do. "Stop."

With a sharp halt in place, William craned his neck up toward the sky before spinning around. "Where'd we go wrong, huh? I mean, what are we doing out here? I told you I'd have your people released."

At his mention of her people, her veins iced over. Finding some soft dirt, Latera dug her torch into the ground and tightened her grip on her spear. "You lie."

"Lie about what?"

Taking her spear in both hands, she edged toward him. "Who is watching us, William?"

"Watching you?"

"Who is coming?"

Appearing unphased by her menace, William stood tall and took a step forward of his own. Once again, his expression fell into one she struggled to understand. Confidence and uncertainty and darkness combined in one awkward glance. "You're missing something, aren't you?"

"I am," she said, pausing her own advance as she stared down her demon. "I am missing the truth. And you will give it to me."

He grinned and chuckled as he came closer. "We've got more in common than you may think. You've done some impressive things. So have I. And we've both come a long way."

"Tell me the truth," she said, aiming her spear at him with light, steady hands. The pace of her breath picked up, and her neck started to ache. Once again, her thoughts mixed with dreams, and both rushed through her mind. A stinging pain was left in their wake. William's presence was all that kept her from begging out loud for the overwhelming anxiety to stop.

His approach didn't cease, forcing her to pull back the weapon to keep from sticking his belly with it. He was right before her now; she stared into his eyes and lowered the spear in defeat. She couldn't kill him—it would give her no closure or answers, and she'd lose a hostage. She didn't *want* to kill him either. She just wanted this heavy sense of dread and warning to clear. Maybe she was wrong to bring him out here. Maybe he couldn't provide her any clues, let alone answers.

"You *are* ready for the truth, aren't you?" he asked. "I didn't think you would be so soon, but maybe I was wrong."

Hope bloomed in her chest. Perhaps he did have a secret— something that would shed light on her feelings. "I have *been* ready."

"Good. You are being watched, Latera. You're being watched over every day by a mighty god called the Enigma. He sees you, and His spirit is coming. It'll come to fill you up and reunite you with your people. In this world and, when you leave it, in your next."

Latera grinned, and suddenly, inexplicably, she felt clearer in thought. "Is that right?"

"Yes, it is! You're looking for something to believe in, and if you live with faith in Him, He'll bring you closer to what you love every single day."

Unable to hold it in any longer, Latera burst into laughter. In no time at all, it was like the phantom—the shadow over him—had vanished from before her. If this was his secret, there was nothing to fear. It must be something else, which meant she was wasting her time out here with William.

William frowned. "What's so funny?"

"Thank you, William, really. Somehow I knew this would help."

"Well … good … because it's the truth. I can show you the way, too, and—"

"Oh, no, please stop," she said, chuckling again. "Do you actually think I would believe such nonsense?"

"What? Yes. I mean, no, it isn't nonsense. The Enigma's real."

"Let us just get back to camp. I have gotten what I was after."

"No, you haven't. We aren't done here. Are you trying to tell me the Mother isn't nonsense?"

"William—"

A faint rustling sounded to her right, but she could see nothing through the fog.

"Did you hear that?" Latera asked.

"Hear what?" Branches cracked, and a shadow darted by. "What the fuck?"

"Who is there?" Latera asked, raising her spear. "Show yourself."

"Clip my binds. Please. I'm useless to you like this."

Ignoring him since there was no time to oblige, she raised a hand to back him up with her, one step at a time. Through the haze, she could make out the shadow shooting straight for them.

"Oh, shit!" William exclaimed behind her just as black, fluttering wings swept at them, lifting just in time to rise over William's head. He ducked out of the way but lost his footing, unable to balance with his hands tied. Latera left him on the ground and followed the bird. The torchlight revealed it to be a crow, perched atop a tree branch above her, staring down.

"I am here," Latera heard it cry.

"Oh, come on, not that fucking cawing again," William said from behind her as he regained his footing. "Where is she?"

"I see you," Latera said to the crow in the Mother's tongue, locked in on its dark eyes. "What message do you bring for me, child of the Mother?"

"I knew it was you," William said as the sound of more crunching branches came from behind her. "Didn't think I'd be seeing you again, Nova."

Without a moment's hesitation, Latera whipped her attention to him.

"What did you just—?"

Latera fell silent as the silhouette of a woman materialized out of the fog. The crow, now behind Latera, flew over her head toward the woman. As the woman got closer, the details of her appearance emerged: hair in a crown braid, icy blue eyes, and a youthful glow, so similar to her own. No longer were Latera's breaths heavy—now they simply weren't coming at all.

"It cannot be."

"Hello, Latera," the familiar voice said.

Her spear fell out of her hand and clanked to the floor. With tears in her eyes, she choked out one word.

"Mama?"

CHAPTER 5

JNHERITANCE

The mist sat heavy around them. In a way, it seemed to have thickened even more with the appearance of Latera's long-lost mother. After all the years and time it had taken Latera to come to grips with losing her, now, somehow, she was here—alive and looking as if she hadn't aged a day.

Thinking it had to be another dream, Latera rubbed her fingers together. When nothing changed, she dug the nail of her pointer finger into her thumb. Despite the pain, she kept pressing harder, but still her mother stood before her.

Nova appeared to understand Latera's uncertainty because she slowly crept forward with her hands raised and a gentle smile on her face. "Yes, Latera. Mama sees you. Mama is here."

"But—" Latera said, unable to breath as the shock hit her. She began to hyperventilate. "You—you cannot be. I do—I do not … where have you been?"

"William, would you mind?" Nova asked.

Latera hadn't even noticed that William had gotten to his feet. Briefly she wondered how her mother knew William, but she was too overwhelmed with the fact that her mother was alive to truly process the thought.

With a brief nod to Nova, William headed back in the direction from which they had come.

"Mama, where have you been?" Feeling out of control again, she wondered if she'd lost her entire grip on reality. It was too much. She fell to her knees and let out a hysterical cry.

Nova was much quicker to come to her side once she hit the ground. Her mother's arms came around her, one hand lifting her chin up so that their eyes met. The sight broke down Latera all over again. She sobbed.

"What is wrong with me?"

"It is going to be okay, my love."

"No," Latera cried, distraught. "Nothing is okay."

"I know how difficult it has been … what you are going through—"

Latera retreated from Nova then. "How could you know? All this time you have been gone. And yet, you were alive and—and well. You cannot know what it has been like. You abandoned us."

"Please. Be at ease, my love. You do not know the truth yet. But you will."

The lack of answers was turning Latera's shock into ire. All the reasons her mother might have voluntarily left her rushed through her head. None of them were good enough. White-hot anger shot through her.

"Apparently it has been some time since I have known the truth. But I wonder—was I the only one? Did Father know? Hanzah? Did any of your *family* in the Riverlands know why you left us?"

"No one knew. Because no one *could* know."

"Well, now I *must* know. Tell me why you left, why you allowed us all to believe you dead all these years."

"I will. But you must remain calm. Can you do that for me?" Nova asked, with a look to ensure the request be followed.

Latera's stomach tightened as she nodded, afraid of what her mother might say.

Looking down, Nova paused and lifted a clump of dirt and leaves in her hand. The deep breath she took as she shuffled the debris around her fingers made it clear to Latera that her mother would have as hard a time spitting it out as she would hearing it.

"My dear ..." Nova finally said, opening her hand up to the sky, "I am the Walking Widow."

For a moment Latera froze and contemplated what she had heard. As she struggled to process that the legend could even be real, doubt pulled at her. Her mother, the Widow? Even if it were possible, it didn't explain to her why Nova would abandon her.

Shaking her head, she protested, "I am not a child anymore, Mother. I know the Widow is a myth our people have passed around. Do you really expect me to believe you?"

A smile showed on Nova's face, but it seemed misplaced. "Trust me, I am well aware you are not a child," her mother said, raising a hand to her shoulder. "The voice in your dreams calling your name—who do you think it belongs to?"

"What do you know of my dreams?"

"I know what it is like to have dreams of the past. And while it was not my voice, Latera, I do know what She said."

"She?"

Sweat trickled down her forehead, and her heart beat out of her chest as the voice returned to her thoughts now. It was clear and calling her name as it had been for weeks.

"What are you saying?"

"I am saying the Mother once called my name the way She now does yours. She once spoke to me and guided my path so that I could carry out Her Call."

The phrase *Her Call* caught Latera's attention; it echoed off her mother's tongue and into her mind. The voice that had been whispering her name began to repeat it in a pitch that caused her to shiver. "Her Call?"

"It is Her will to uphold the balance of Her domain. It was my duty to help Her in doing so in whatever way She asked," Nova said, her eyes wide, as if memories were being projected upon them. It was the nature of those memories that Latera felt a burning desire to understand. "I was Her vessel to watch over these lands and to ensure Her children knew Her word. Our Mother had given me the abilities you are only now starting to realize. So I suppose, in a way, I misspoke before. The truth is, I am not the Walking Widow— not anymore. My Walk has ended, Latera, because yours has just begun. I have come to you to tell you that you are the Widow now."

Latera's mind raced, but she admitted this would explain all the changes she had undergone. It gave her some answers at least, which was comforting in a way. A warmth pulsed through her bones; she studied her palms. Still, so many questions remained. She struggled to fathom it—*her*, the Walking Widow of legend. It was too much to process. "I do not know what to say."

Nova let out a deep breath and stood up before extending a hand. "Follow me?"

Accepting the help to stand, Latera nodded. An immense

sense of relief swept over her. For the first time since leaving the Riverlands, she could relinquish the heavy weight of leadership and responsibility for her people. Now her mother was guiding her. At least for a little while, she could be the follower. It made her feel like she was a child again. And in her mother's presence, she thought, perhaps she always would be.

*

It was difficult for Gregory to leave Maria behind at the mansion. It echoed too much of when Henry had done the very same. The lack of care from her husband was what drove her to Gregory in the first place, and he didn't like the comparison.

Day by day he was falling harder for her and growing closer with her three children too. They knew they were beyond a fling now, though when Maria failed to say *I love you* in return, Gregory worried that perhaps he was more invested than she was.

Leaving her now probably wasn't the best way to secure her love, and that was his ever-present worry as he sat atop a strapping Appaloosa riding toward the dangers of Prayer's Passage. But there was no alternative. She'd given him two weeks to accomplish what he felt he needed to do. And so he needed to make the best of the time he was granted.

Beside him, on horses of their own, were Clovis and Father Kubler. While he felt out of place beside them, he knew he needed to represent William's interests until his leader returned. Winning over the Highlanders would strengthen the Keagan gang and, in turn, increase stability in the Murrieta. Once this mission was done, life would be safer for his loved ones. This was his primary objective, and he needed to find a way to keep these insatiable men focused on attaining it.

He recalled again what Henry had told him about William's revelations during their trip to New Berkeley: how William had regarded the extent of Clovis's cruelty in their expansion, and his wishes to somehow rectify the issue. Judith's death and Clovis's subsequent manipulation had prevented William from focusing enough to act on what he'd learned. However, Gregory would not let him forget and would do his best to somehow remind William of what was important. For now he needed to monitor the situation and lift William's spirits by achieving what was asked of him.

"I don't know how much you and Father Kubler talked about it, but I'm guessing you know what we're aiming to do here, right Clovis?" he asked.

"Oh, we talked all right," Clovis said with a grin on his face that made Gregory's stomach turn. "We talked plenty."

"Right ... so yeah, we need to—"

"Recruit the Highlanders." Clovis's face was expressionless as he stared straight ahead, slouching in his saddle.

"That's right." An awkward silence followed. In it, he became worried he'd been left out of the loop somehow. "So ... do we have a plan here, or ... ?"

"Did you forget already, Gregory?" Kubler asked with a sigh.

Squeezing his lips together in frustration, Gregory remembered the priest's call for faith.

"Don't you worry," Clovis said, beating him to a reply. "I'll do the talking."

"Okay. But out of curiosity, what do you think you'll say to get them to listen?"

Before Clovis could reply, Kubler interjected. "Forgive me, Clovis, but bringing people from different walks of life into a way of thinking is my job. With respect, perhaps I would be best suited to this task."

"I thought I made myself clear when we spoke before, Priest. Tell me, how many people from different walks of life were there in your church the other day before I showed up?"

Gregory was beginning to wonder what the aforementioned discussion between these two had entailed. It was difficult for him to imagine.

"At the time it was Mary-Claire, Gregory, and myself," Kubler replied a moment later.

"So three? Well, shit, consider me sold on your ability to sell your vision." Despite his efforts to fight it, Gregory couldn't subdue a chuckle at the sarcasm laced through the words. "Look, I've done this plenty of times before. These wild folk are dim as dirt. They're sheep in need of a shepherd. And you best believe I'm the one. Because I decide who walks this land and who'll be led to the loam."

"I will have you know our church is growing." The priest's voice cracked as it raised in tone, which Gregory assumed was because it was not used to such a change.

A deep laugh emanated from Clovis's gut. "Well, if Gregory was new, then, yeah, from two humble followers to three *is* technically growth. I'll grant you that."

This time Gregory stifled his grin, hating the idea of giving Clovis further satisfaction.

The priest sighed again and kicked his horse forward, turning it to the side in front of theirs to halt them and command their attention. "Listen to me, please. To win them over, we must encourage their faith."

Not this again.

Neither Gregory nor Clovis responded. Kubler's current defensiveness made his youth apparent in a way that Gregory hadn't noticed before. "To encourage their faith, we must give them some reason to believe. These people want freedom above all else. What better way to promise them freedom than through the Enigma, who provides us worlds more suited to us with each noble life we lead? Whether you believe or not, you must admit, selling is giving a person what *they* want, even if they don't realize what that is yet."

"But, Father Kubler," Clovis said in a mocking, childlike voice, "I do believe."

"Might you be serious for a single moment?"

With a sniff, Clovis shut off the act, and his face turned to stone. "I am being serious. I more than believe."

"Is that right?" Kubler asked, sitting up straight.

"It is," Clovis said.

"Well, then, why not spread the good word of Cerebism, Clovis?"

The priest's naïveté was silly to Gregory; he knew there was no way Clovis could be a Cereb. But Kubler's desperation to believe he was indicated just how badly the priest sought converts.

"All right, we must be crossing into Prayer's Passage soon. What do you two say we quit this bickering and continue on now?" Gregory asked, tired of the debate.

"Certainly. As soon as Clovis answers this last question." Unsurprisingly to Gregory, his plea for a cease-fire was ignored.

"To be honest with you, Priest, I can dig your angle—it makes some sense that they might react to it. But there's one thing you're gonna have to learn just as well as them if we're gonna be on the same page: in this world your Enigma's granted you, Father, gods walk among men." Clovis kicked his own horse forward and right at Kubler's, forcing the priest to retreat. Trying to play them down, Gregory ordered his steed on past them. When he saw Clovis lean toward Kubler and poke him on the nose, though, the hairs on the back of his neck stood on end. "And I'm one of them. I'm the fucking Almighty, let me tell you."

"I do not—"

"Oh, but you do. I know what you're after. You just ain't gonna get there without me, and you know it."

Two tiny silhouettes appeared in the distance ahead. Gregory squinted, but he couldn't make out what they were. "What the hell is—?"

"I do believe you are ... my sign."

"You're goddamn right I'm your sign," Clovis said in a rabid cheer. "I'm the fucking shepherd sent here to offer my swift judgement. You want to see the flock grow? You can go ahead and spread the good word: Clovis Keagan's come to bring this world the deliverance it thirsts for."

Turning to them for the briefest instant, Gregory noticed a dainty, awkward smile on Kubler's face in reaction to Clovis's sick statement. Suddenly, he was much more terrified of what was occurring between the two men and what it might mean for his plans as a whole than he was of the figures he spotted in front of him. Still, he didn't feel like dying today.

"Keep quiet," he said in a loud-enough whisper. "Both of you."

Before Clovis could protest, Gregory pointed forward. The shapes were clearer now, and he could make out two large hats and bandana-covered faces—one bandana black, the other red. They had been traveling southwest, intersecting the northeast trajectory of Gregory's lot. One of the riders stared in their direction and rose a hand, causing the other rider to freeze in an instant. Both sides were locked in a several-hundred-yard stare down.

"What do we do?" Gregory asked.

With a slow clacking of hooves, Clovis brought his horse to Gregory's side. The clicking of a revolver came next. "Time to bring the herd to pasture, y'all."

"No. Wait—"

Pop!

Clovis fired a shot into the air, right beside Gregory's ear. An intense ringing caused him to grab at his head for a moment in shock. By the time he looked up, the chase was on. The Highlanders doubled back from whence they came, and his companions raced after them. It took him a few seconds to recover, but he soon followed, knowing he had to at least try to control the now-volatile situation.

With his steed pounding along the dusty, barren patches of dirt and weeds at full gallop, he felt as if he were in flight. His horse and he were one as they tore across the terrain, closing ground on the others. A shallow tributary soon came into view up ahead. It slowed down the Highlanders; Gregory could see one of the riders was shorter and appeared to be less proficient with their horse.

Having closed the gap between him and Clovis and Kubler, Gregory noticed Clovis had his gun aimed forward and an eye closed.

"Stop! They won't shoot back," Gregory shouted over the sound of the gushing wind.

The gun pointed to the sky. "How do you know?"

"The one on the right—it's a kid."

Squinting ahead with a grunt, Clovis spat. "Better hope you're right. Surround the bastards." Without more warning than those words, Clovis veered off to the left at a much quicker pace.

Gregory shrugged at Kubler, but the priest grinned and veered off to the right. He assumed it would be his job to race straight at the duo, so he did. The first to cross the stream was Clovis, who was gaining fast. By the time he had crossed, Gregory had reached the water as well. He hurried his ride over the river, warm water kicking up onto his exposed forearms and neck. When he reached the other side, he could see Clovis's pistol raised again.

Bang!

Before he could say something to stop it, the shot was off. Dirt popped into the air where it hit the ground. To Gregory's relief it was well ahead of their targets; it caused the Highlanders' horses to freeze, then rear in hesitation. The warning shot had worked. Clovis darted forward and pulled up alongside the larger rider, just as the pair spurred their horses onward again. Gregory rushed to reach them.

"Don't y'all make this difficult, or I will," he heard Clovis say to the Highlanders as he kept pace with them. Galloping at full speed, the larger rider glanced at Clovis, remaining silent, before angling forward again. But the horse he rode seemed to be tiring, its pace slowing.

"Oh, okay. So this is the game y'all wanna play, huh? Sweet deal."

One unsteady move at a time, Clovis attempted to gain his footing atop his saddle. Before Gregory could acknowledge what he was seeing, Clovis launched off his horse, tackling the Highlander off of his own and slamming them both to the ground. The two sung out together, Clovis in a maniacal howl and the rider in painful agony.

When Gregory caught up, he felt the urge to ask if Clovis was insane. Having already known the answer, he decided to focus his efforts on the young Highlander, who was sitting astride the horse, looking conflicted about whether to ride on or stay.

To the side, Clovis had the Highlander man pinned. Though he must have been in pain after the hard fall, he resisted. "Please! Don't hurt her! Don't hurt my daughter!"

Kubler arrived. Gregory cut him a warning look to not do anything rash.

"It's okay," Gregory said with a hand up to the young girl as he dismounted his horse. "Everything's going to be okay. We just want to talk." The girl trembled slightly without a word. Seeing an opening, he approached. "How about you come down from there so we can get you back to your daddy? What do you say?"

The horse stayed still as he approached it. Recognizing she might not be able to get down on her own, Gregory reached up to help her. The moment her feet touched the ground, she ran to her father. With a sigh, Gregory followed behind. Father Kubler was already squatting beside them, whispering comforting assurances in their ears as if he hadn't just chased them down.

"What do we do now?" Gregory asked.

Clovis came back to his horse and scanned the terrain. "Now we build a fire and make damn sure they see the smoke."

*

The sun's rays were beginning to bring color to the dark sky as Latera followed her mother. The fog dispersed around them just as they left the tree cover. They exited out into the open and found themselves marching through a hilly basin.

"Where are we going? My friends are back there, and they will be worried about me. I am sure Winona and Mika would be more than happy to see you again too."

"To both a familiar place and an unfamiliar face. Unfortunately, your friends will not be seeing me."

"What do you mean? Why not?"

Her mother spun toward her, her blue eyes gentling as a nostalgic smile spread across her lips. "I, too, was filled with questions for my mother during my transition, you know."

"And did *she* have answers for you?" Latera asked with some frustration.

In return, she received a snort. "My, how you have grown from the reserved, agreeable little girl I raised in the Riverlands. I would ask what happened to that girl, but I have seen her transform myself."

"Well, *I* would ask what you mean by that, but I know I will not get—"

"Answers," Nova said. "Yes. I am sorry, this moment is just such an easy one to get lost in after so many years. So, where to begin? I suppose I can start with the name. The Walking Widow is named as such because she does not physically age once she transitions into her inherited role. This is why I look the same as you remember me ... for now."

"So you are telling me I will continue to look young while others grow old?"

"The favorite trait of every new Widow. Yes, until your Walk reaches its end. Once it does, you will age as we all do—as I now do again. But there is a price to all good things, my love. Now, I have a question for you: when about would you say your newfound abilities began?"

It took a moment for Latera to recall what all her abilities were as they'd been dizzying her brain for a while now. They began with the dreams, though; she was certain of that. "My first dream occurred right around ..." It hit her like a pile of bricks, and she wondered how it hadn't before. "My twenty-first birthday."

"Yes, the V'ahani celebratory turn into adulthood is more than a formality, for a Widow at least. When she reaches this mark, she shall become one with the Mother until her firstborn daughter ages to take her place. It was a tradition started by a past Widow and maintained throughout the history of the clan."

"So the Walking Widow is V'ahani?"

"No, child. She belongs in spirit to neither clan, and our ethnicity has been mixed evenly through the years. Only in the time before and after her Walk does a Widow exhibit abilities exclusive to a single clan. This is why prior to your transition day, you were able to speak to the grizzlies and not the hogs. Your father is who made you a grizzly, as did mine for me. My mother, on the other hand …"

"She was Tokali?" Latera asked with a twinge of disgust. Though she had never met her grandmother, Nova had told her stories about her … stories she now guessed must be untrue. Hearing she was a Tokali helped make sense of why they'd never met.

"Yes, she was, and I can tell you more about her another time. But now … now you are not limited. As the Widow, you can speak to all creatures of the Mother's domain, as I am sure you have found out by now."

"Including … the people of the clans themselves?"

Nova nodded. "So you did come to it on your own. I had to be told of the ability before I realized it."

"You mean it is natural?" Latera asked with a gasp. A shiver crawled down her spine at the thought of controlling another person again. "How do you get used to such a thing?"

"You must be careful with this responsibility, my dear. When power such as this goes unchecked, the consequences can be dire. I do not think I ever got used to the feeling myself. But we have no choice other than to take the greatest of care in our choices," Nova said.

After a moment of pause, her mother gave her an admiring look that remained as they trekked through the hilly basin. It made Latera's cheeks lift and ripen with warmth. "What?"

"You know, it is a curious thing. I have been away from you for so long, yet I have seen you grow more than I would have if I had never left."

"What do you mean?"

"Your dreams—you know they are real now, yes? You have seen moments from the past with omniscience—seen them in ways your own lone memory could not itself fathom?"

"Yes."

"Good. But you will see it is not only your experience you may draw from. Your dreams contain a full history of this great territory, Latera. It is how I know all about your journey and have been able to watch you grow through these many years. Hanzah too. I have been so proud of you both."

Distracted by her reflections about the nature of her dreams and their significance, Latera didn't recognize the grounds they had come to until Nova slowed her pace. She took a minute to observe the flat earth beside a large rocky cliff. It hit her that this was the cliff she had scaled on her initial journey to the Hold. It was near where her father's councilman, Castor, had soon after committed suicide. A "familiar place," as Nova had put it.

When her mother nodded her forward, suggesting they climb it together, she began up the steep slope once again. This time, though, she did not fall or slip or scrape herself as she had done before. This time, her mother was there to help her, step by step, until they reached the glorious top.

And there they sat, beside one another again, staring out at the endless landscape. Latera's breaths deepened without any effort. They simply came and went like an ocean tide. The colors she saw also became brighter, and she felt the weight of her role in the environment. As miraculous as it was to her before, Latera viewed this setting in a whole different way now. The elevation was no longer an escape for her from the issues she faced in the Territory.

Instead, she realized she was a part of it and always had been. "I still do not understand why you left us."

"Part of this role is making difficult—and at times, impossible—decisions," Nova said, running her hands down her pant legs. "Because when the Mother provides us with our Calling, we must rise to complete it in Her name."

Assuming this referenced the voice in her dreams, Latera sat up straight. "When will She provide it?"

"As I told you, it is our purpose to execute Her will in bringing balance and faith to the Territory. Depending on the state of things, some Widows have been given a Calling several times during their Walk. The timing of the Call is different for everyone."

"So … the Mother needed you to leave?"

Giving Latera a somber look, Nova huffed and shook her head. "I was V'ahani for a time in social title alone, and only because we must blend in with the environment we inhabit. This is the most important rule of being and remaining a Widow: no one can ever know of your Walk, Latera. If you are discovered, the Mother will be forced to find a replacement, and this is not advisable. I have seen it in my dreams—cases of former loose-lipped Widows going insane when they revealed their standing prior to the transition of their daughter. After you serve, it is okay, but it is still not wise, and you will not be accepted for it. The clans have never been kind to those who make such claims without the ability to support them. She makes certain of this, I am sure."

"Sounds more than a bit unfair." And it did. She found it hard to believe that her deity, one she had so long looked up to, could be so cold, especially to a Widow.

"Do not repeat those words ever again," Nova snapped. She'd gone from urgent to angry in an instant, her voice like a whip. "In fact, tell me you know the Mother's two objectives."

"I do," Latera said, rolling her eyes.

"Well? What are they?"

Latera crossed her arms and looked away.

"Faith and balance, Latera. Burn those words into your mind. We must not reveal our status because doing so could lead Her children to worship Her Widow rather than have faith in the true Maiden. We must not reveal our status because under the wrong influences, our abilities may be exploited for tyranny and disrupt the balance She seeks to maintain. Do you understand?"

"Yes—yes. I understand," she said, taken aback by her mother's intensity.

"You must, because this is the price we must pay for Her gifts. Always live with nothing but gratitude for them. There are much more terrible fates we could have been granted."

Castigated, Latera was unable to pick her eyes up right away. They sat a moment or two in silence, and into it she launched the question on the forefront of her mind.

"So, when you left, I guess you were at risk of discovery? And was it part of your Calling? I am confused."

For a beat, her mother said nothing. Latera nervously picked up a smooth pebble next to her and rolled it around in her hand.

"I will stay close during your journey south, so let us finish talking about my departure another time," Nova said, rising to her feet. "I am sure what I have told you must sink in, and I would recommend you meditate on it heavily in the coming days.

Connect with the Mother as much as you can."

"No," she replied, remaining seated. "Please, tell me about your Calling. I need to know."

"I will, child. I promise. But you should get back to your camp soon, and there is one more thing I need you to see before I do—an unfamiliar face."

This answer did not satisfy Latera; she knew her mother was putting off the issue. No matter how uncomfortable it would be, it was of the utmost importance to her to know the truth, to know the why. She did not know how to express the need to her mother just yet, though. She rubbed at the pebble as she responded.

"Very well. But one more thing. Since my dreams have begun, Mika has told me my abilities would suggest I am a seer. He said—"

"Oh, Mika—as intelligent and curious as he has always been, he is so very wrong this time. This term *seer* is one of many developed by Widows to hide their true nature. These terms have been passed around as rumor, which naturally turns to lore, which naturally turns to assumed fact. People tend to believe what they hear from loud, enthusiastic voices. But no, there is no such thing as seers. Does that answer whatever you were going to ask?"

"It does." Latera replied as she threw the pebble over the edge of the cliff.

"Good. Now let us depart."

While they descended, Nova called up to the wind. Latera wondered who her mother was communicating with, but her curiosity didn't trump the feeling of being upset with Nova. It wasn't a mood she wanted to be in so soon after reuniting with her mother, but she was unable to shake it. Reaching the bottom well before Nova, Latera spotted a horse with a small figure atop it riding her way. Turning back, she saw Nova give a reassuring nod. When the horse reached them, a young boy who appeared shy of ten years old hopped down and came to her mother's side.

"Latera, this is Kai. He is my son—and your step-brother."

The news felt like a punch to the gut. She wanted to cry right then and there, but wouldn't. "Hello, Kai," she said without emotion or movement.

How could this be her Calling? Why would the Mother do this?
She wouldn't.
Would She?

"Hi."

As cute and innocent as Kai seemed, neither of those traits registered in a significant way for her. All she knew was that Kai was the love child of the mother who had left her, who had abandoned her, and who had allowed her to grieve her supposed passing for years. Even if it was the will of the Mother that she see this new family Nova had created, it devastated her—she simply couldn't accept it. She couldn't accept that the Mother would sanction, let alone request, such a thing.

"May I go back now?"

"If you—"

Unable to hold in her anger any longer, she spun back in the direction of the camp. "I am going to go back now."

"Latera, please wait—"

It was too late. She was off and running, once again seeking the solitude of her tent.

*

Tensions ran thick in the hall as the rally attendees remained on edge, silently staring down the barrels of the guns pointed their way. Henry, on the other hand, breathed easily. There was no fear or nervousness in him, only a white-hot fury. If he were armed, he'd take the shot. Despite the distance and all the people, he'd take the shot.

"What are you taking back precisely, Forrest? You've abused our bodies in your factories without a care. You've taken our spirit and buried it in cement. What more could you take from us?" Jimmy asked.

"Well, first of all, how about an invitation?" Forrest asked, moving up the aisle toward the stage with his strange, distinct swagger, all the while surrounded by his armed guards.

It was a sickening sight for Henry. If he were to have it his way, this devil would not be permitted to step foot in the Viridian District, at a minimum. He'd be sure to rectify this error soon.

"You people seem to think this city belongs to all of us—so why shouldn't I be allowed my share of the festivities?" Forrest asked with a slight chuckle.

"Laugh while you can," Henry said before Jimmy could respond.

"Oh … oh, no … Jimmy, don't tell me… . First you went and lost your balls, and now your stage's been taken too?"

"His stage is—"

"Save it, Emory," Forrest said with a dismissive wave. "You think I don't know who you are? Maybe you and yours aren't aware of this in Alvenika, but Leonard Keagan and Forrest Hayes run this town."

It was odd to Henry that Forrest still included Leonard in his claim. "You keep telling yourself that," he said. "Emory—"

"Oh, I'm gonna have some fun with you," Forrest said, interrupting Jimmy and wagging a finger Henry's way. "It's about time, too, because I was getting bored of these ants."

By now Henry was a bull who had seen red. In his mind he was kicking back the dirt, getting ready to charge, when Jimmy placed a hand on his chest and eased him back. "Stop this. Let us carry on with our discussion in peace. We'll return your men by the morning, Forrest."

"So you do know why we're here!" Forrest said, as Henry wondered what they were talking about. "But, look, you know I'm not a patient man. It's already taken a week to find out and confirm where my boys up and vanished to. I ain't gonna wait another minute. So go ahead and bring them to me now."

"They were about to massacre a group of peaceful protesters, Forrest," Jimmy replied, shaking his head. "I think it's fair they be held for another night."

Before Henry's eyes, Forrest was walking all over Jimmy, and given the casual way in which Jimmy allowed it, he had to assume this was always the case. It wasn't the only thing frustrating him, though. When the Forgotten first rescued him from Forrest's men, Henry had heard Jimmy's associate tell him that the attackers were "taken down." Now realizing this didn't translate to them being killed pushed him to intervene. "*That* is the minimum? Their crime warrants no less than a life sentence. And y'all are talking no more than a week's detainment?"

"We aren't talking detainment at all," Forrest replied. "Jimmy, I've had enough of your dog for the night. Now be a man and send him to bed."

Shaking his head in disbelief, Henry gazed out at the Forgotten, who had been championing him just minutes before. "You're lucky you even have the opportunity to see those men again."

"Psychopaths!" a woman shouted. It was one-half of the couple who had approached him on his first day in the Viridian District. He nodded his gratitude to her.

Murmurs moved through the crowd.

"Emory," Jimmy said, "I can handle this, please—"

"Did you just suggest bringing harm to one of my boys?" Forrest asked, interrupting Jimmy again.

"Come now, he doesn't—"

"No. How fucking dare you." Forrest lunged his way, but his own men restrained him. "This is my city, you hippy fuck."

"Yeah, you mentioned that." As a giddy Henry stepped forward in response, he too was intercepted and held back by Jimmy.

"Don't *any* of you ever forget it either," Forrest threatened, redirecting his look toward the audience. They responded with jeers despite the menace of the weapons they stared down. Forrest ignored them. "Leonard Keagan's cement built New Berkeley tenfold. We've provided a place for your *spirits* to inhabit and work. But do you people show us gratitude? No. Instead you infest it with your communal dreams. Well, guess what? That's all they'll ever be—just dreams."

"Fraternal Forgotten, rise together above this fiend," Henry cheered as adrenaline took over. "Y'all will be silenced no longer.

Let y'all's tormentor hear your cries for justice!"

The crowd roared, and as they became aggressive, Forrest and his men crept back toward the doors in a defensive posture. Ecstasy overcame Henry. Even with their weapons, they were far outnumbered, and they knew it. Perhaps Forrest's four would have been an adequate force to control Jimmy's Forgotten, but this was no longer Jimmy's Forgotten.

This was the high Henry had been waiting for since the moment he had lost his daughter. And with one hit, he was addicted.

"Everyone stay calm, please," Jimmy said in fruitless desperation.

"Jimmy, you hear me?" Forrest asked, shouting over the riled hall. "You have till noon tomorrow, you worthless shit. If I don't see my boys by then, I'll give you a fucking massacre. You better believe that."

"We'll see you in the streets, you maggot! Bring your best. No guns!" With Henry's last shout, Forrest and his goons departed the hall. It was a win recognized by all—led by none other than Emory Wallace.

"This is only the first victory, my brothers and sisters. But it is the most important. And it deserves a celebration in the streets the likes of which this district has never seen. We will make New Berkeley hear us tonight, and they will envy our family. Fraternal Forgotten, let them hear you!"

The resulting cheer was deafening. Joyous faces hollered and flooded out of the doors. Joining the tail-end of the crowd, Henry was instantly met with frenzied support from all around him. There was no way he could remember all the names introduced to him, but he would remember their enthusiasm.

On the streets in the heart of the district, people sang a mixture of the Forgotten labor chants, Cereb hymns, and other upbeat ditties. As sparklers and their smoky residue lit the sky, more and more Forgotten approached Henry. In the middle of one conversation, he spotted Jimmy, who must have been the only sorry-looking person in the whole district, standing off in a corner alone.

Whatever. He should be thanking me.

Two men approached Jimmy and forced his solemn stare away from Henry. Within a few minutes of conversation, Jimmy pointed the men his way.

That's right. You know who they're after now.

He noticed they both had a stocky build, though one's skin was white as snow and the other's dark as night.

"Terribly sorry to interrupt," the darker-skinned man said, addressing the follower Henry had been speaking to. "Might we have a moment of your time, Mr. Wallace?"

With a nod, Henry said his goodbyes and gave his gratitude to those he had been talking to before huddling in with the strangers. "What can I do for y'all?"

"Name's Nathan Hawley. This is my brother, Terrance Hawley," the same man said. "We—"

"Y'all are actually brothers?" he asked out of genuine curiosity.

Terrance rolled his eyes. "We have the same last name, don't we?"

"Well ... yeah. Of course, my apologies."

"Oh, please, don't worry yourself—we get it all the time. We come from two different fathers but were both blessed with our mother's eyes, as we like to say." Nathan gave him an easy grin, but Terrance remained stone-faced. "Anyway, we shouldn't be in your hair too long. We're new to town—just arrived two days ago from the Murrieta Territory—and we're searching for a friend by the name of Henry Abigale." Henry's breath escaped him. "So far we've come up empty. But we were able to find out Jimmy Keagan was alive, which led us here. And now Jimmy has pointed us to you, Mr. Wallace."

So they don't know. Thank the Enigma they don't know.

"Know anything that can help us?" Terrance asked.

Leaning in to avoid being heard, he kept his voice down. "Who sent you?"

The brothers exchanged a look, and Nathan nodded. "William Keagan," Terrance said.

"Prove it." The brothers reached into their shirt pockets and flashed him their Lion's Paw pins. "Smart thing, y'all keeping those hidden in this city."

"William sent Terrance and me here to report on Mr. Abigale's progress on the Forrest Hayes front. Should we find Mr. Abigale, we are to help him in any way possible. Might you be able to lead us to him, sir?"

Grateful William had finally woken up from his miserable state, Henry was thrilled to have outside help. Keagan gang members loyal to William would have enough skin in the game to be useful assets. Guiding them back over to Jimmy, he promised them answers and requested for Jimmy to put them up somewhere close for the night. A meeting was also planned between the four of them for the morning. He didn't want to reveal his identity out in the open like this, where he risked anyone overhearing them. No, he'd share it with them in the morning, in private.

Once he said his goodbyes, he ventured off into the night. The first place he visited was a local saloon. From wall to wall, it was packed with song and cheer and drunkenness. Within an hour or two, he was fully immersed in all three. As his vision became hazy, he decided to return to the streets. Wandering had always been a by-product of intoxication for him. Next thing he knew, the crowd was thinning.

Is this still the Viridian District?

Everything was much darker and dirtier here. The people walking in and out of the back-alley joints were shady at best. He approached the next doorway he came upon, and the sign in the center of the door seemed in his drunken state to be moving. All Appetites, it read.

A brothel.

His palms sweated as he shuffled on his feet. "No, H—No, Emory," he said aloud to himself, a hiccup following the words.

But as he put his hand on the doorknob, the rush he had felt in the hall raced through him anew. It was like his youth was being returned to him. Only the thought of Maria could temper it—or was she taking it away? He couldn't decide, but thinking of her bothered him in some way.

Being here was necessary for their family's protection, he reminded himself. Otherwise, he'd never have come back. Maria didn't understand all he did for her and their family.

He glanced at the sign again.

But this … I swore I wouldn't go back to this.

With one last look up at the sign, Henry let out a deep sigh, dropped his hand, and turned away. But before he took a single step, he stopped. Scanning all around to see if anyone was watching, he noted the coast was clear and entered.

The inside was dark and empty except for one slender middle-aged man, who sat at a counter and didn't look up when Henry walked in. His outfit was rather messy, but he sat perfectly upright in his seat, which was surprising since he appeared to be reading with only a small candle for light. On either side of him were two doors; the one on Henry's right had a small sign that read Gals, and the one on the left had one labeled Gents. Behind him appeared to be a coatrack, with a line of twenty or thirty jackets of varying quality. On the left half of the rack, Henry noticed a fedora hat with a red feather sitting atop one of the high-end, dark jackets. He burped as he squinted at the feather, the lushness of the contrasting hue hypnotizing him.

"Welcome to All Appetites," the man at the counter said, snapping him out of his trance. He noticed the fellow was still looking down. "We cater to all appetites. What's your preference?"

Still shy about being in this space again, Henry chuckled at the rehearsed intro. "Uh," he said, scratching the back of his neck. He squinted at the doors again to recall which was which. He pointed at the right. "Gals, please."

"Have a jacket?"

"Yeah, I—" He stopped as he looked down and saw that he didn't. His cheeks warmed as he wondered if the man noticed his error. "I mean, no sir." A burp rose in his chest, and he lifted his fist to his mouth to cover it. "I do not."

"Great. Well, feel free to go inside and take your pick."

"Thanks."

"And remember, here at All Appetites we guarantee you'll get your fill or that you'll do the filling—whatever you're into—" the desk attendant said, still not looking up from his book, "but either way, no refunds. Here we have taste, and we ask our clientele to be tasteful as well."

"Okay, sounds—"

"And if you do want to taste, that's extra."

"Noted."

"But encouraged."

"Great."

"So enjoy your stay and remember—"

"You cater to all appetites?"

The man's head snapped up, and he focused on Henry for the first time, causing him to jump. A thousand-mile stare pierced his soul, and he felt like prey in an open field.

"Tasting is extra," his predator said, much less enthusiastically than before.

"Oh. Ok. So. Can I, uh?" he asked, pointing to the door.

"Enjoy your stay."

The attendant buried his face in his book once again, and Henry stumbled toward the door on the right as fast as he could. It opened to a dim hallway similar to those he'd entered before and long thought he'd never enter again.

CHAPTER 6

HE SAID, SHE SAID

After accepting Nova's request for his departure, William felt dizzy. Once out of sight of the pair, he stopped to lean on a tree and get his head straight. His conversation with Latera had confused and disheartened him.

What if she never hears the message? What if I can't convert any of them? What if I fail? Will I never see my Judith again? I can't fail. I can't fail. I can't fail.

The dizziness morphed into a pounding headache. He tried to push the negative thoughts away with a deep breath. As he inhaled through his nose, he grew aware of his solitude. Under any other circumstances, he would use this opportunity to escape, but he knew doing so would mean there'd be no chance whatsoever of seeing Judith again. Exhaling, he shook his head.

"Mr. Keagan."

"Shit! What the hell, kid? Where did you come from?" William asked, nearly having a heart attack when Kai materialized from behind a tree.

"My mother says I am to bring you back to camp and then circle back with her. I may be small, but you should not underestimate me. I will have my eyes on you. So no funny business."

The boy's determination was commendable. William nodded and headed back, glad for further incentive not to run. Perhaps it was a sign from the Enigma, or perhaps it wasn't—he just didn't know. Figuring out the verity of the priest's talk of signs was harder than he thought it would be.

The return trip went without a word from Kai, who stopped when the camp came into view. "This is where I leave you now." With a sigh, William continued on. "Wait. My mother told me to ask one other thing of you. I do not remember what it is, though. Please give me a moment to think."

After a few seconds of observing the boy, who peered up at the trees in strained thought, he remembered the time at the saloon when Nova had mentioned her need to be secretive, even to Kai. Considering he had yet to repay her for helping him through Prayer's Passage twice, he figured it was the least he could do. Also, it'd be ideal not to give the other natives any other reason to believe in their so-called God, when his goal was to convince them of the Enigma's higher power. "If it's about not telling anyone—"

"It is about not telling anyone at the camp you have seen her. Also, to let them know Latera will return in due time. That is all. Thank you. Bye."

"You're … welcome," William said to Kai's back.

When he returned to the camp, the others were waiting. Seeing him alone, they were quick to surround him. Turning around to show them his still-bound wrists, he pleaded for them to listen to him: their leader was safe and would be back in her own time. Their questioning was as frantic as could be expected. However, they soon understood that he couldn't have done much to her even if he had wanted to and that he wouldn't have returned if he had.

While the others fretted, Elan volunteered to retie him to the same tree he had been imprisoned to before. He was glad to get the young Tokali alone again. He decided he'd need to push him harder this time.

"Did you tell them the truth?" Elan asked in a quiet tone from behind the tree as he fastened the rope. "Did she really send you back?"

"Now that I know you've got feelings for the young lady, you think I'd hurt her? Never, Elan."

"*Had* feelings."

"Elan, I thought we were going to trust each other from now on?"

"Yes, Mr. Keagan." Elan paused. "I may still have feelings for her, but I am not certain."

"Well, the best way to figure it out would be talking to her about it, don't you think?" William asked from his seated position. He cared little about the romance between them, except that if it were to blossom, and if Elan became a believer as William intended, convincing Latera of the power of the Enigma might be easier. "And call me William. We're equals, you and I, both of us striving towards the same goal—a better life for the Murrieta."

Now crouched in front of him, Elan smiled and bowed his head. "Yes ... William. And, William? Can we have our talk now? When she took you, I worried we would not get the chance. And I would very much regret not hearing your principles for the better life you say we can earn."

William took a deep breath and tilted his head back to contain his excitement. In doing so, his attention fell on the other Tokali at the camp. "We most certainly can, buddy. But if you would like to become a follower and beneficiary of Cerebism, there's two things you gotta do. Without them, the Enigma, our God, will not grant you a better world in your next life. Quite the opposite, in fact."

Elan now went from crouching to sitting cross-legged. Rather than clarifying, William purposefully made the Tokali thirst for the answer.

"What are the two things, if you do not mind my asking?"

"First, you must set aside time to pray to the Enigma—to thank Him for His gifts."

"So the true God is a 'He'? The V'ahani are wrong?" Elan smiled.

"Yes, they are. Very much so. Before I get more into it, though, I should tell you the second rule is that we must bring as many nonbelievers to the light as we can. Do you think you'll be able to handle this responsibility?"

He tried to hold eye contact, but Elan looked down and lifted a twig at his feet, breaking off one piece at a time. "Our people trust you at the Hold. I am sure they will listen once we return, as they have before."

Leaning down trying to catch Elan's eye, William shook his head. "We're alive *today*, Elan. When you know what it is you gotta do, there ain't no such thing as tomorrow."

"You are right. I will … go get Warrick and Shelton? They might be more open at first than Gannon or Hammond."

"Perfect. The Enigma will be pleased with you for helping them find the truth."

Laboring to his feet, Elan made his way to the others. William wasn't yet clear on which faces corresponded to which names, but he was pleased to see the first young man Elan approached was the one sitting alone and writing. His solitude would make him an easier sell. The second, on the other hand, was with the rest of the group, sitting around a fire. To his surprise, Elan and the first split up, and Elan returned to William. Before he could ask what happened, William saw the first Tokali approach the second.

"A leader delegates. Smooth," he said to Elan.

"Yeah. Warrick is the kindest of us—"

Warrick—the loner. Shelton—the short one.

"—so I told Warrick I needed help with something, knowing the others would not think it strange that he would assist me. He is asking for another hand from Shelton now."

Second-guessing his pleasure at Elan's move, William began to worry. He was depending on Elan's influence to gain favor with the others. Was Elan not their leader? "Do they not trust you?"

"I mean … they do not distrust me."

"What does that—?"

"Hey, Elan," Warrick said, approaching with Shelton. "What did you need our help with?"

Elan plopped down again and patted the ground at his side. "Take a seat, please. William has something he would like to share with us."

Well, shit. Time to show Him what you're made of, Billy.

Warrick and Shelton paused, but then Warrick dutifully sat, although Shelton remained standing.

"Should the others not hear what he has to say? I can go get them," Shelton said.

"They're worried about their friend at the moment, and rightfully so," William said, gesturing with his head for Shelton to sit. He didn't. "She's going through a lot right now, that one. We all are. But she's the one y'all look up to, so it's gonna take a toll on them, too, when she's down. Now, look, I know y'all have come to see me as the enemy. I get it, okay? I do. Integration is a tough thing. But the Tokali decided to follow the Keagan gang for a reason. And my intentions are nothing if not pure here, so I hope you might hear me out for a moment. Because I believe in our common vision to unite all the people of this territory. I can see that somewhere along the way, our separate identities blurred that vision. But I'm sure we can get it back by sharing a common faith."

After a pause, Shelton took a seat. "Your people have never spoken of the specifics of your faith before."

"Neither have yours. The Tokali have been no less agnostic than we have been. And this is our problem. By committing to the Enigma, our God who provides you with this world you see around you, we can come together behind a system of values."

"Tell them what you told me, William," Elan said, shuffling closer, "about what can come if we follow His principles of Cerebism."

"But I thought the Mother was our God?" Warrick asked. "Was it not through Her that Latera taught us to connect with the hogs?"

All eyes burned into William, including Elan's. His throat felt dry with panic, but he pushed forward. "Uh, no. It's …" *What is it?* "Your control of animals is just another part of the world the Enigma has chosen to grant you."

While writing, Warrick glanced up. "But are you not a part of this world?"

"Of course I am."

"If we are all part of the Enigma's world, why can you Easterners not control them too?"

"Yeah, I wonder the same," Shelton said with a nod. "Also, why could there not be two gods? Would a god of the land and a god of the mind not make more sense?"

The migraine from earlier returned, and William felt dizzy again.

No more questions, please. "We cannot question His will."

"But we must ask questions if we are to understand it, no?" Shelton asked.

Why won't they just listen? I just need them to listen.

"If you were to understand all of it, there would be no faith," Elan said, getting defensive.

William appreciated the point from Elan because, for a moment, he became frustrated with the task Father Kubler said the Enigma needed of him. William wasn't a priest; he didn't have the way with words that Father Kubler had. This was so much more difficult than expected.

But I can't fail.

"Yes, you must have complete faith in the Enigma if you want to be given that which you seek," William said, trying his best to inject some of Father Kubler's tone into his response.

"Well, it is difficult to have faith without a shred of evidence," Shelton said. "At least the gifts of the Mother are clear. They sound more significant too."

Warrick put his notes down. "And why would we ignore those gifts at the request of a god who offers us none?"

His face red with embarrassment, Elan turned to William for an answer. It was clear then that William had lost them all. They insisted on their faith in their Mother deity. Just like Latera.

"He'll give us what we seek. He has to. It has been promised. Please. We just need to believe. I just need y'all to believe. Please."

Shelton stood up and helped Warrick to his feet as well. "But, Mr. Keagan, do *you* believe?"

The question struck him like a comet crashing to earth. It played over and over in his head—only it was him asking himself. Each time he did, he felt Judith slip further away.

Next thing he knew, Shelton and Warrick were gone.

"I am sorry, William," Elan said, also rising to his feet. "I tried. And if it helps, I still do trust the Keagans." William could not utter a reply. "I will give you a moment."

And so Elan left him. And once again, he was ever aware of his solitude. Judith was gone. He didn't have the priest for answers, and he hadn't seen his brother Daniel in months. All he had now was the hope that he would be reunited with Judith and that Henry and the Hawley brothers would be able to handle Forrest Hayes.

But just then, Latera returned to the campsite, reminding him once more of his failure, and the chances for either of those outcomes felt slim.

Once the hope vanishes altogether, what will become of me?

*

The will of the Mother—the Great Maiden of the Territory—whose word Latera had followed and supported since she was a child, was not what she expected. At the same time, her own mother wasn't as she remembered either. As she redefined all she had known to be true, the past changed for her.

The Nova she saw this night was not her mother—she couldn't be. And yet she was, illegitimate son and all. The mere thought of it made her sick to her stomach. The boy did nothing wrong—she knew this—and still she hated the thought of him. He was a symbol of Nova's abandonment of her family. An abandonment that was only committed in fear of God, who had always been described to her as just, caring, and generous. None of those words felt true to her now, as she marched back through the trees toward the camp. This version of God instead inspired words like *obedience, pain,* and *sacrifice.*

When she finally arrived at the campsite, her friends swarmed around her. But their concerned words went right through her.

"I am going to go to sleep for a few hours," she said, not in response to any particular question. "When I awake, we continue to the Hold and finish this."

"Are you not going to tell us what is going on?" Elan asked, though the others moved to appease her request for space.

Winona scoffed, and her hands met her hips. "No. She has no need to."

"But we will need clear heads to negotiate with the Keagans at the Hold."

She sighed, then took a deep breath to perk up. The sensation she felt was strange. Before she discovered she was the Widow, she was a leader, both of this group and the V'ahani of the Riverlands. But this new responsibility felt like so much more than leadership alone. Something Elan said made Latera not see him as a pest anymore, but a disciple. The feeling was all-encompassing and overwhelming. She couldn't even begin to fight it.

Walking toward him with a smile, she placed a hand on his shoulder, which made him first flinch, then settle into stillness. "I am clear, Elan. So very clear." She scanned the confused faces all around her. "Understand this: these are not negotiations. We will not compromise."

With a nod, Winona returned her smile before she sought out her tent. Mika followed suit. Slowly, the rest turned away as well.

"Latera," Hammond said, catching her arm from behind. "Do you have a minute to talk?"

"No." His voice startled her and caused her heart to race. She pulled away, causing the hand on her arm to drop. "I mean—not right now, sorry. It has just been a long night, and I need some rest."

"Oh … okay. I understand. Whenever you have the chance, then."

It was difficult to look him in the eye, but she did. "Of course. I will find you, okay?"

With a nod, Hammond walked away, and she entered her tent. As she lay down, she realized that the news her mother had brought her worsened the situation between her and Hammond. Not only did she have to deal with the uncomfortable feeling of having been in his body, but she also held a new secret she could never tell him. The worry plagued her, and she squeezed her eyes closed.

Would she become an actual widow if she stayed with him, as the title would suggest? Would it be inevitable? Or could she have a daughter before she needed to leave to maintain her secret? Was she ready to have a daughter soon? She had so many questions, but they all brought her back to her mother's choices.

"Latera."

The voice called from the dark void surrounding her. It was Her. Latera could feel it now.

"How can I know this is real?" she asked. "Please show me."

Like her dreams from before, visions passed by in rapid succession until she was whisked into a scene of her mother standing by the River White. Though Nova looked the same, Latera knew she was actually younger, since it was a vision of the past. Again, the past as she knew it was changing, only now it was doing so before her eyes.

She watched as her mother marched to the river to fake her own drowning. By the time her father, Arkouda, arrived at the scene from wherever Nova had sent him off to, she was gone, the evidence planted. Along with his councilmen, he stood there in shock and devastation.

"No more," Latera said, unable to behold either Arkouda's sorrow or the consolation of the same councilmen who would one day come to murder him. She had never seen her stoic father in such a state until now, even when they had mourned her mother's loss together. The darkness flooded her mind once more, and she cast her questions into it. "Why would she do this? I still do not understand. She did not need—"

Without warning, she was whiplashed into another scene, further south down the flowing river.

"Behold, my child."

Washed up on the bank lay Nova, soaked, her face covered in tears as she clawed at the dirt to pull herself from the rushing water. "Why did you have to choose me?" Nova panted in between her hysterical cries. "Latera, I am sorry. My baby ... I am so sorry." Clasping her hands together to pray, Nova rolled onto her back. "Please ... oh Mother ... oh Maiden ... do not let my daughter know this pain. Do not ask of her such a cruel Calling as you have asked of me. Allow her Walk to be on level grounds. It is all I seek in return. Please."

The youth Nova maintained started to take on a brand-new meaning for Latera. Rather than seeing it only through the lens of time, she now recognized how similar her mother and she looked. As she watched her mother at her lowest point, she saw herself. From her struggle to act when her father died, to her difficult time at the Hold, to her recent barrage of newfound stresses, she never stopped worrying for her people. Nova thought of one thing when she washed ashore: her daughter.

"Latera? It is me." Jolting awake, Latera saw her mother beside her. "I am sorry to wake you. But I could not wait to tell you how sorry I am, and—"

Latera launched herself forward and wrapped her arms around Nova before anything more could be said. Burying her face in her mother's shoulder, she whispered, "I love you, Mama. Whether the ground beneath us is level or steep, I will always love you."

Nova squeezed her tightly, and since she was the only person alive who could understand what she was going through, Latera imagined her mother's arms wrapped around her as her armor.

"She wanted to study them," Nova said, her voice cracking as if she were haunted by the memories. "She called upon me to get close to the Easterners so She could understand them."

"What did they do to you?" Latera asked as she backed out of her mother's arms, her thoughts centering on her own tormentors: Walter and Clovis Keagan.

"I did not go through the bad to make anyone else worry about it—least of all you."

Though she didn't like the answer and showed it, Latera nodded. With how little she enjoyed sharing her own struggles, she understood it had been Nova's experience to endure.

"But it was not all bad, either, as you have seen with my sweet Kai," Nova continued.

Upon hearing the favorable mention, Latera loosened her grip on her demonization of the boy. But a moment later, what her mother had said sank in. "You had him with ... one of them?"

With no obvious confirmation, Nova's gaze fell to the floor. "Their migration from the East began right around the time I reached my twenty-first year and became the Widow. Some forty years ago, as hard as it is to believe. They only trickled in at the time. But as they kept coming, my dreams started to center on them. The real disruption began in Prayer's Passage, but it spread west until Tokali settlements were coming under threat by wanderers and the sprouting of the first gangs. This is when She had seen enough. She needed to figure them out."

"But what of our allied Easterners in the Riverlands? Could you not study them?" Latera asked, remembering Adonis Morrell.

"I did. In fact, it was my first Calling and what brought me to your father. I actually contributed to our securing a formal alliance with the people of Harran perhaps more than he did. Even he took convincing at first, despite the inroads he had been making with them. And this is also why you must always have gratitude for the Mother no matter what She asks of you. Because She provides us greater gifts than we could possibly imagine. In that case, She brought me you." Again, Latera connected the dots between her mother and herself. Even without the recognition, her mother was a leader all the same. "However, it was their worst who were the greatest threat to the Territory, and their worst seemed repelled by the North's winters. On the other hand, there were also other things She needed to grasp about her power over them—things I could not carry out if I had stayed where I was—things like the impact of mixing the bloodlines. This is what led me to leave and, eventually, to Kai's father. It was my Walk's second and final Calling."

"So what did She find? And how will She respond?"

"She will show you what She found when the time is right. And as for what comes next, I cannot know," Nova said as she took Latera's hands in her own. "But I know it will fall to you to answer Her Call. And I know you will do it, daughter of mine."

Though she had faced pressure and adversity before, Latera could fathom nothing as significant as being called upon directly by the Mother. The moment, the responsibility, and the consequences of it would all rest on her shoulders even more than they had in the past. With the Territory's conflict building, she wondered how she could carry the weight.

*

Latera was able to get a few hours of sleep after her mother left and before the sunrise. Before departing, Nova had promised she'd remain close by, if out of sight of the others. Now Latera needed to concentrate on moving her group south. Despite yearning to catch up more with her mother, she had no time to waste in the quest to free her people at the Hold.

So the group carried on without much spoken. Her followers went as their leader went, and since no one knew what was behind Latera's recent behavior, her silence spurred theirs. The only consistent speaker was Elan, who seemed to be muttering to an unresponsive William. Latera noticed a change in William—certainly since the mansion but also since they had last spoken. His skin was pale, and at times his hands appeared to shake. Knowing what he'd been through, some part of Latera couldn't help but pity him, though his feelings remained the least of her many concerns.

When the sky began to darken after their long day of riding, they found a place to make camp. The Tokali confirmed they would reach the Hold in another two days. Exhaustion from their travel kicked in fast, and all were asleep soon after eating—all but Latera. Once the snoring and heavy breathing began, she crept out of her tent. Unsure of where she should go, she decided to sit a moment and wait for a signal. As the wind whistled, she thought of Hammond and looked at his tent with a frown. How she wished she could tell him everything she was feeling. But not even her brother, Hanzah, or best friend, Winona, could know. What it would mean for their future, she wasn't sure.

A fluttering swept in from behind, and a crow landed on a rock beside her. Recognizing it from before, she sat up. "Hello, there." The bird twitched and tilted its head without reply. "Where is she?" The crow lifted its wings and darted to a tree to the north of them. When Latera jumped to her feet and raced to catch up to it, it stopped and craned its neck again. Just as she reached it, a rustling came from the camp. Her heart pumped, and she froze in place. The sound seemed to be one of the others turning in their tent. A moment of silence passed before the bird flew off, and Latera went after it again.

The black crow was difficult to see in the night, but it didn't take more than a few minutes before Latera could make out her mother's lone silhouette beside the cover of a rocky cliff. They embraced as the bird disappeared into the sky. "You and your friends travel fast."

"Will this be necessary from now on, Mama? I understand the need to hide. But it feels like I have been reunited with a ghost."

"My mother used to say we should be sure to trust our feelings. There is always some shred of merit to them."

"Are you saying you are a ghost?"

Nova chuckled and sat, crossing her legs and resting her hands on her knees. "No more than you are now. Sit with me." Following her mother's lead, Latera sat and mimicked her position. "Tell me, because I can see it in you: what still troubles you?"

It wasn't easy for her to put words to it, nor was she eager to jump right into telling her mother about the things she'd been experiencing. It had been so long since they'd spoken in this way. She stared at the ground as if what she sought might be scrawled into it.

Her mother's fingers gently lifted up her chin, forcing Latera's eyes to meet hers. "Latera, I am appreciative of the forgiveness you afforded me earlier, but you must tell me what you are feeling. No one else may hear it."

"During your Walk, you said you watched me, yes?" Her mother nodded. "So you know they call me their chieftess now. It is my duty to lead them, by promises I have made to them and to myself. And beyond this, I also have other responsibilities and have built … friendships."

"With Hammond?"

"Mother! Tell me you did not—"

Nova laughed out loud, but Latera was unamused. "No, no, dear. I did not see anything materialize before my Walk had ended. But a mother knows."

"Do you swear? How can I be sure?"

"Goodness gracious, calm yourself," Nova said as she cackled with a snort the way Latera remembered she used to.

"How can I calm myself?" she asked, a smile escaping her before she pushed herself to get serious. "This thing—this burden we have—it forced you to leave us behind. But there is so much here for me now, so much to turn my back on. Must I one day abandon everything and everyone I have fought for in order to complete my Calling? Can that really be Her will?"

Rocking in her seated position, Nova shook her head. "Abandon is a word you should never use. It is not what we do as Widows. We move on for the sake of those we love, not at their expense. To tell you the truth, if I were in your shoes, I would finish this rescue mission and leave your people once they are saved. There is so much you will need to learn, and you are not ready to birth your heir. Not yet."

"Am I not ready? Must I leave them, then? Is that my fate? Mama, I feel as if there is no way I could ever do that."

"Oh. No, child. I am sorry, I should not have said what I would do. There is nothing you *must* do except to follow your own path. Please, if there is one thing you understand, let it be this, okay?"

However uncertain and confused she felt, Latera nodded in acceptance of the basic tenet.

"Close your eyes for a moment and breathe," her mother said. The order sounded too good to pass up in her stressed state. She took a long breath in through her nose and out through her mouth. "Good. Now hear my voice. But also, hear Her voice—as I know by now you have. Do you feel Her with you?"

Latera had always been spiritual, but the energy she felt now was deeper than ever before. The voice from her dreams echoed her name in her mind. As she inhaled, she felt her own presence and its place in the world around her. Each exhale evidenced the existence of her soul. "She is everywhere. But … why could I not see it so clearly before?"

"Do not be troubled by it, my love. You simply needed to be shown the way, as we all do. And this is why I have returned to you now—so that on your Walk you are equipped to show Her children the way, as all Widows have done before you. Because to help others to prosperity, we must first walk the path ourselves. As we have discussed, this is the first objective of all Widows. It is something I know you learned to some extent even before you took my place, yes?"

A cool evening breeze blew on the back of Latera's neck. It sent an uncomfortable chill up her spine. Pondering her mother's words, she reflected on her journey. "But I have experienced things and— and done things that have haunted my dreams. Things that have not made me feel prosperous or good." She thought of the kettle of vultures she had summoned to feast upon the councilman's body after his suicide, and her eyelids shut tight. No matter what Castor had done, even if he'd helped betray and kill her father, her actions had surprised her then and felt unbecoming of a Widow now.

"We must first touch the floor to have any real sense of how high the ceiling is or might come to be. Sometimes the way to do that is to fall face-first. For many, it is the only way. But how high you have come since, Latera. Now look at me for a moment." Latera opened her eyes and saw Nova was shaking her head. "You are not close to finished. Whatever decisions you make during your Walk, know that you make my pride swell. Whether I can watch you anymore or not." Nova winked, and Latera couldn't help but smile as the weight of the world seemed to lift off her a bit.

The sound of pattering footsteps approached from behind them. "Mother, one of her friends is coming," Kai said, appearing out of nowhere before Latera could react. She saw him in a different light since the truth had been revealed. Though the manner in which he came into existence would remain difficult to accept, she knew it wasn't his fault and felt bad about having been cold before.

Nova rose to her feet and held a hand up to Latera before she could do the same. "One of whose friends, Kai?" Nova asked in a cute way, as if she were seeking an answer she'd already given him.

"A friend of Latera's—my big sister."

"Good boy." Nova winked.

"Aw. Were you keeping a lookout for us?" Latera asked. "Thank you, Kai. That is awfully brave of you."

"Yes, he was, and yes, he is," Nova said, wrapping an arm around the boy. "Now let us make like ghosts."

"But wait. Mama, now that … things have changed," she widened her eyes, assuming Kai didn't know that his mother had been the Walking Widow, "can you still not be seen? We can come up with a story or whatever it takes. Our people would welcome you home. And Hanzah, he would be so happy to see you again."

Nova studied the ground. "Reflect on our talk as you continue on, dear. I will do the same."

"I hope so."

Off they sprinted, around the cliff and into the darkness. Once they disappeared from her sight, Latera closed her eyes to meditate again. With so much to consider, she wanted to take advantage of what she'd learned with every passing minute. An owl hooted overhead—whoever was coming from her camp was searching for her. She was determined to make every attempt to put it out of her mind until the person arrived. In the darkness she felt light. The pressure of her fingertips on her knees, the bend in her back, and the weight of her thigh on the rocky ground were sensations she appreciated.

"Latera?"

She was surprised to hear it was Elan behind her, but she wanted to be certain not to let any past frustrations return to her. "What can I do for you, Elan?"

"I love you."

Her eyes shot open. "What?" she asked, unwilling to turn around and face him if she'd heard him correctly.

"It is true."

She sighed, and her face fell into her palms. What utter nonsense. "Please, turn back and put it out of your mind."

"No, Latera, it is true. I cannot let go of these feelings I have for you. I have not been able to say it or show it, but after speaking to William, I am sure it is how I have felt since our journey began," he said, approaching as if he hadn't heard her. "He is really wise, you know. A uniter, like you. I believe you could work well together if we hear him out on what he has to say."

She fought to find a way to be kind in response to his declaration, which he didn't seem to see was more about the Keagans—and getting her to "work" with them—than about any "love" he might have for her. Didn't he see how William Keagan had clearly manipulated him in an attempt to soften her? Likely he had not. Which meant that, at this point, Elan was as lost as his vile mother, Adila, and perhaps even more clueless about social cues.

Latera took a breath. "I am well aware of your confidence in the Keagans, but you do not understand what love is."

"We treated you all wrong when we were at the Hold—I can see that now. But I know we can do it right next time."

His hand came to her shoulder. She fought against visibly jerking away, especially once she had processed what he had said. "Next time?"

"Yes. There is no need for your people to leave. We can still be together." *Lost and delusional.* "And I can give you some time to think about it. But I needed to tell you ... because when you know what you need to do, there is no such thing as tomorrow."

Lifting her head from her hands, she looked up at him and placed an open hand on his. "I do not love you, Elan. I appreciate your contributions and your honesty. But allies is as much as we will ever be. Now let us move past this and get back to camp, okay?"

"Are you serious?" Elan asked.

Out of the brush ahead, Hammond appeared. "Latera?"

Her hand slid straight off Elan's. "Hammond."

"I was looking to see if you were okay, but … I will go back to camp now."

Latera's heart beat out of her chest and splintered as she saw Hammond start to turn. She didn't want him to leave—she couldn't allow him to, not with what he must be thinking, with how this must look to him. Time seemed to freeze. She looked up to Elan and placed a hand on the earth. Whispering to the Mother, her thoughts converged on Elan. The familiar process ripped her from her body.

Now in control, she observed how her own motionless body sat below him.

"Did *he* help your people south? Did *he* save your life? No. Of course not. And still you choose *him*? Selfish bitch!" she made Elan say loud enough for Hammond to hear. Through him, she shoved her body to the ground.

"What did you—?" Hammond came running back toward Elan. "Do not touch her!"

"She has ruined everything," she replied, bracing for Hammond's impact. The blow took the air out of her, and the fall to the rocky ground was sharp. Once she had taken those impacts, which she felt she in some way deserved for this transgression, she released her control.

Now back in her own mind, she lifted herself up off the ground and raced over to them to split them apart. "Hammond, it is okay. I am okay."

Though he didn't resist her efforts to separate them, Hammond remained furious. "It is not okay. He has been harboring his senseless hatred for too long. Now it is out in the open, and it needs to stop, Elan."

When she didn't hear a fiery reply from Elan, she noticed he was shaking and that his stare was empty.

"But I ... I do not know why I ... I did not mean to ... to say those—" he stuttered.

Blood dripped from Elan's nose, which didn't seem to be the result of his scuffle with Hammond.

"Elan?" Latera asked in a panic.

Elan reached up to touch the blood and stared at his red finger before falling to a knee. She and Hammond raced to his side as he did. Taking an arm around each of their shoulders, they helped him up as he gasped for air until he passed out.

Hammond rose to his feet and hoisted Elan up. "He is still breathing. Let us get him back to camp."

Unable to find any words, Latera followed Hammond's lead. The crushing force of fault returned again. This was her doing—it had to be. How quick she was to disregard Nova's call for responsibility. How she hoped to the Mother that the consequences would only affect her.

CHAPTER 7

CARDINAL

Henry woke with a blistering headache. Though the sheets of his bed felt crisp and clean, his person felt like a ball of filth. A terrible taste sat in his mouth as well. He rotated onto his side and groaned at the state he was in. Squinting his eyes open, he assessed the weak sunlight peeking through the window curtains. It was still in the early hours, which wasn't surprising. Sleeping in never seemed to be an option when alcohol was involved, however much he desired to.

The memory of what he did last night after the rally was hazy, but he remembered he had visited a brothel. His eyes snapped open. Scanning the room, he relaxed. He was back in the hotel he'd been staying at in the Viridian District. Part of him prayed the whole thing had just been a dream—he had no recollection of how he got back to his room.

As he sat up, he raised his hands in the air and stretched with a long, drowsy yawn. Rising to his feet in another starfish stretch, he recalled Forrest's men were supposed to be released today at noon. He felt confident it wasn't near the meeting time yet, but he needed to ensure he retained control of the situation before Jimmy could give up their bargaining chip without any return.

He spent the next half hour or so making himself presentable.

When he finished and exited the room, he paused a moment by the Code of the Fraternal Forgotten on the hallway wall and read it again.

The Code of the Fraternal Forgotten

I am Forgotten. But this is not my burden. It is my honor and my privilege.

Because inherent in me is a strength that no one may take away.

So to my fellow Forgotten, I say: I shall.

I shall:

- *Provide my valuable labor to acquire the resources necessary to better my community.*
- *Give what I deem I can to my brothers and sisters in need.*
- *Not steal, nor accept, when offered, more than what is fair.*
- *Use my voice first in our fight for better working conditions.*
- *Live according to the righteous will of the Enigma to ensure a better next world for myself and for each of the Forgotten.*

And to those who would threaten my fellow Forgotten, I say:

Fair work for all or the towers will fall,

Because when they drag us down, the Forgotten heed the call!

Jimmy really had been onto something when he had crafted this code, but he'd taken it as far as *he* could. Henry knew he could be the one to take it further—to fulfill its potential.

His mind drifted back to last night, to the high of the rally and to the hazy aftermath. He still didn't know whether he had stumbled his way back from his time out or if someone had picked him up. Either way, he knew he needed to be more careful if his power grew.

After descending a flight of stairs to the lobby, a bellhop informed him Jimmy was in the hotel's private dining room with the Hawley brothers. Furious he was missing out, he stormed ahead in that direction. The side hallway leading to the door seemed longer than it was because of his headache, and the rug rolled out on it was like quicksand. Finally throwing the doors open, he saw the others sitting at one of three tables in the room, with a chair in between Nathan and Jimmy waiting for him.

"Nice of you to show up, Emory," Jimmy said in a sarcastic tone Henry didn't appreciate.

"Look, I don't want to hear it." The chair he pulled back made an obnoxious shriek as he dragged it along the floorboards. It wasn't the first time he had been unintentionally careless in this condition. "And without further ado, boys—I'm Henry Abigale, the man you've been searching for."

"Well, then, it is a pleasure, Mr. Abigale," Nathan Hawley said, rising to shake his hand, not missing a beat. "You'll have to forgive us for not recognizing you. The beard and bald head make for quite the disguise, I gotta say."

"Good to hear. Let's be sure to keep my identity quiet too. As far as everyone around here is concerned, I'm Emory Wallace."

The brothers exchanged a look, a habit he had noticed in his last interaction with them as well. It was as if they were conversing without words.

Henry caught Jimmy rolling his eyes. "Yes. Emory Wallace: politician and womanizer."

"Now just where do you—"

"I get the idea from your actions alone, Henry."

He knows about last night, then.

"Do you realize how dangerous it is for you to be slithering around outside the district?" Jimmy asked, pausing to give him a hard look. "You have all these apparent plans, and yet you don't seem to be able to control your own self, let alone an entire city. I certainly won't be babysitting you while you attempt a coup in the organization I founded. I hope you understand that."

Henry decided it was best to ignore the reference to his vices and indiscretions.

"Is that what you think this is? A coup?" he asked, feigning surprise, though deep down he appreciated the categorization. "We're on the same team here, Jimmy. We're all on the same team. And I hope *you* understand that. Now tell me, what did I miss?"

"Well, sir, we were just discussing the Murrieta and William's plan for uniting the East and West before you walked in," Nathan said. "Mr. Jimmy seems to share our excitement to revive talks once we're in a place to do so here in New Berkeley."

Though he could have dropped his accent in his current company, Henry didn't really want to. Best to always stay in character to prevent future slipups.

"To be straight with y'all, it'd be my great pleasure to never deal with that territory again. So, in my opinion, it's a secondary concern at best. And if Leonard was right about one thing, it's that there's no controlling the place enough to do any kind of business there." He paused for a breath. "On a more important note, though, I've thought a bit on it, and I want you Hawleys to head the police force we're gonna be developing here in the coming months."

Again, the brothers eyed each other in indecipherable fashion.

"Is that so?" Jimmy asked.

"Yeah, it is." He looked directly at the brothers. "Y'all think you'd be up to it?"

Nathan stroked his naked chin with wide-eyed uncertainty. "Recruiting, training, and operations? We'd be in charge of everything?"

"Jimmy and I will be here to help you in whatever way you need."

With slumped shoulders, Jimmy sat forward in his seat. "Will we now?"

"Yes. And essentially, yes, y'all will be in charge."

Nathan and Terrance exchanged yet another look, then faced him. While Nathan remained still, Terrance gave a definitive nod.

"We'll need your ranks to be formidable and established in say … six months' time. By then, New Berkeley will be holding its first mayoral election—which'll be on us to organize, Jimmy." A now-open-mouthed Jimmy said nothing. "First, we'll spread the word of a vote through the press. Then we'll ratchet up support for our ticket. I'm talking constant, vigorous campaigning. We'll inspire the people to action and unity. And then, once we seize power, we'll use every law and resource at our disposal to burn Forrest and his enterprises to the fucking ground. It'll be our war, and for the first time the playing field will be level because the people will be on our side."

Leaning back in his seat, Jimmy smiled and toyed with a fork, brushing the tip along the tablecloth. Once he'd recovered from his shock, he'd become smug. It irked Henry. "Fantastic. You've really thought this through. Taking Forrest down should be a walk in the park."

"Never said it'd be easy. Not once." The strain of his hangover returned to his head. To distract himself from it, Henry twisted his neck with a crack, rolling the bones one by one. "But just because you couldn't handle him on your own doesn't mean you gotta bitch at me about it. I'm coming up with solutions that'll save the people from a man motivated by nothing but greed."

"Sure you are, and that's your problem—you don't have the slightest clue what motivates Forrest. I've been living in his orbit since before I was ousted, and I promise you it's never been greed. If you don't understand what really makes him tick, you'll never get what you want from him."

Henry noticed Nathan shifting in his seat and Terrance repositioning his with a squeak. The brothers clearly were uncomfortable with the lack of a united front.

"I don't want to *get* anything from him," Henry said. "I want to *take* everything from him."

"Listen, I'm not opposed to some of your ideas, all right? The people of New Berkeley want fairness, and like you, I want him to hurt along the way too. But I've played the long game all these years for a reason. Because we're dealing with a wild, cunning animal—a predator who is part of this ecosystem, whether we like it or not. If you try to just rip his meat away from him, he'll bite your fucking arm off, and there isn't any need to take those hits when you can train him to accept smaller meals instead."

Uninterested in Jimmy's claims that Forrest wasn't disposable, Henry rolled his eyes.

"I'm serious, Henry."

You're not man enough. That's what you are.

"Henry," Jimmy said again, clearly wanting him to bend to his point. He refused.

"Well, what is it, then?"

"What is what?"

"What is it that motivates him?" Henry asked, picking up the knife on his tablecloth and twirling it between his fingers. "Seeing as you know him so well."

Jimmy laughed and folded one leg over the other. "You wouldn't believe me if I told you."

"Try me."

A sigh came from his counterpart. They stared each other down. "All right … it's love, Henry. Love and vengeance."

Looking up at the ceiling, Henry rubbed his forehead in disbelief. "Bullshit."

"It's the truth."

"What the fuck could he know about love?"

"Didn't I say he wouldn't believe me?" Jimmy asked the Hawleys.

They remained silent.

"Well, sorry, but I'm not buying it. Look, you never asked what brought me back here after him, and I appreciate that. But this is a man—" His accent dropped as he recalled Judith's head, so he paused and covered his mouth. "He had my daughter killed … and in the worst possible way. You can't even imagine it, and I can't bear to repeat it. So forgive me for refusing to acknowledge his capacity to love."

Jimmy sat up, all signs of contention removed from his posture.

"Henry, I am … so sorry to hear that. I had no idea."

Henry shook his head and waved a dismissive hand as the pain of the memory flared.

"It was Judith, wasn't it?" Jimmy asked. "Good God—so that's the reason William sent you two."

"Aiding and assisting Emory is our primary objective, yes, sir," Nathan said.

"And I'm sympathetic to that, okay? I am." It appeared Jimmy was addressing them all now. "But like I said, what we need is not to overreact. If we do, it'll only be at the expense of those we represent. What we've been striving for here in the Forgotten—and should continue to strive for—is a system in which organizations like Forrest's are checked, not undone. I mean, think about how many people his factories employ. Those are our people, guys. When operated with fairness, those businesses could provide far more than they take. And as for our need for vengeance, it'll also be way worse on Forrest's psyche if we slow-bleed what he and Leonard built. Trust me on that."

Unwilling to accept any further talk of half measures, Henry stood up from his seat. "Sure. We done here?"

"As long as we're all on the same page," Jimmy said, also standing, then buttoning his open jacket. "For now, we need to get these hostages delivered to Forrest, so let's fetch them and get to it before the man has a tantrum and orders the district demolished."

Fully prepared to do more negotiating than delivering, Henry followed Jimmy's cue. "Let's," he said, giving a wave for his associates to join him in departing the dining room. Together the four walked until Jimmy exited the hotel and the Hawleys stopped in the lobby. With the coast clear, he joined the brothers, raising three fingers. "Police force, campaign, election—I want continuous reporting on your progress toward those things. Understood?"

The brothers nodded. "Your ears only, sir?" Nathan asked.

Henry was impressed. "Y'all are fast learners," he said as he gave each of them a handshake. "Now what do you say we not waste any time?"

In a few hours, they'd be facing down his mortal enemy once again, and once again he'd have some type of advantage. It was a position that provided him with pleasure the likes of which could only be rivaled at the brothel. Who knows, he thought. If their talks went well, maybe he'd reward himself with another trip there tonight.

*

Two days had passed, and no one had come for the Highlanders captured by Clovis, Father Kubler, and Gregory. Clovis assured them the others would attempt to collect their brethren, but Gregory was getting tired of waiting. The dried-up lands of Prayer's Passage in the summer heat didn't help, either—not in terms of keeping them all fed or focused. Even Kubler, who seemed more smitten with Clovis's allure with each passing day, suggested ending the waiting game. Though he found the priest's plan to have the two hostages simply escort them to the rest of the Highlanders particularly insane, he did think anything would be better than starving to death or succumbing to heat exhaustion.

Moreover, he admitted to himself that the priest's plan was also the only solution he could fathom for carrying out William's plan, despite the captives' refusal to say a word to them and the uncertainty of any organization at all within the ranks of the free-ranging Highlanders. An overbearing sense of guilt that both Judith's death and William's capture happened under his watch still ate at Gregory so badly that he was willing to do damn near anything to get this done. His best friend had given him so much at this point, and he needed to repay him in some way. Other than keeping Maria and her children safe, it remained his top priority.

With the midday sun hovering straight overhead, beating down on his scalp through his stubby hair, the perspiration was once again getting bothersome. His partners in this miserable endeavor lay prone in the distance and, using the cover and vantage point of a hill, watched the fire they'd lit and relit to ensure the smoke stayed fixed in the sky. While they waited there for any sign of life, his responsibility was to stay farther back and keep an eye on the captives. The exposed Highlanders sat dejected underneath a lone tree since Clovis had forced them to remove their customary bandanas and hats. The tree provided only a sparse pocket of shade, but it was the best available cover.

"I know you have your reasons to hate us, so I get why you haven't been responding to anything I say," Gregory said to them. By now he was long past bored and didn't mind essentially talking to himself. Drawing faces in the dirt to pass time got old fast. He shifted in his cross-legged seat and tried again. "To be honest with you, it hasn't been easy for me to understand why Billy thought an alliance with your people was possible. Doesn't seem like we have much common ground on the face of it."

The father sat silent and unmoving, with his hands on his knees.

His daughter huddled on the side of him opposite Gregory as if she were hiding. Their gaunt frames and cheeks told a story Gregory knew he needed to understand.

"But the more I think about it, the more I realize we're the same."

The man's neck pivoted like an owl's, and his squinting glare centered on Gregory. For the first time since their capture, he had their attention.

"You don't think so?" he asked, pausing for a moment and hoping for any kind of response. Still, nothing. But whatever ability he had in him to sell pressed on—nevermind that, to him, their similarities were few and far between. "Well, I do. In fact, I know it—or rather, I learned it at some point. What it comes down to is this: we don't like strings."

Again, he stopped and waited. This time, though, Gregory didn't continue. He averted his gaze as if he hadn't said anything.

Then, out of the corner of his eye, he could see the man shake his head in confusion.

"You're the member of a gang." In his proud internal jubilation, Gregory noted the slow, deep, almost lazy voice of his counterpart. It slid off the fellow's tongue like molasses. "There is a pin on your chest you wear to symbolize your place in this gang. It represents your pledge of allegiance to follow the orders of its leader. To put it mildly … you sir, like the rest of them, are infatuated by these 'strings' you claim to dislike."

Before replying, Gregory waited a few seconds. He wanted to ensure the man's speech was done and that he wouldn't be interrupting. He also needed to choose his words carefully to keep the discussion going.

"I am a member of a gang. And your assessment isn't far off. But what I said was we don't *like* strings. I did not say we don't need them."

The Highlander laughed himself into a wheezing cough. "Well, if you think we need them, then maybe we really don't have a thing in common."

"With all due respect, why the hats and bandanas, then? Why refer to yourselves by the title?"

The man's previous amusement was replaced by reddened cheeks and a hardened look of resentment. "We don't. We didn't create the name. It was given to us, and we adopted it."

"Then—"

"And we did so," the Highlander spoke over him, "only to identify with those who share in our cause. Our symbols do not represent a denial of our own free will as yours do."

"So are you not tied to your cause?" Gregory asked.

"No. This right here." The man pointed at his daughter. "This is the only thing I am tied to. Family."

With a sigh, Gregory scratched at his head, finding himself considering and agreeing with the counter. Perhaps he wasn't a great salesman. Turning over to his sack, he pulled out a can of beans. Once he cracked it open, he rose to his feet. His large frame towered over them, covering the bits of sun that peeked through the tree branches. He reached out, holding the can in front of the girl. She cowered behind her father.

"If I could prove you're wrong about me, would you let me?" Gregory looked to the girl and back to the father. "Honestly, sir, can you afford not to?"

The man's expression was both hesitant and open as he nodded at his daughter in encouragement. Her bone-thin arm reached out toward Gregory, who tried to provide as welcoming a smile as he could. As soon as she grasped the can, which appeared much larger in her hand than in his, she retreated back behind her father and began scarfing down the contents.

"While I appreciate the gesture, it will take more than a meal to—"

"Tell me: does she know the way back to wherever you came from?" He checked that Clovis and Kubler were still in the same position with their backs to him. He untied one of the horses from the tree.

"What are you saying?" the man asked.

"Is there a singular place you come from? Or others like you she would know how to find?"

"She knows her way home. But why?"

Pulling one of their horses up alongside them, Gregory gestured for her to take it. "Because, in a way, you're right. It's about time I made a choice of my own. And even though it's against my current orders, the Billy Keagan I know would agree with me. Home is where she belongs. Children shouldn't be hostages."

With a nod, the Highlander helped his daughter onto the horse. Though she was visibly anxious and borderline resistant, he whispered his reassurances to her, and she seemed to settle down in much shorter order than Gregory would have expected of a child. It was clear she was far more accustomed to the dangers of Prayer's Passage than she should have been. Before she left, Gregory gave her another can of beans for the trip.

As her horse stormed off in a cloud of dust, Clovis and Kubler realized what Gregory had done and were far too late to do anything about it. Gregory and the girl's father watched her escape with a glint in their eyes. Seeing her go made Gregory think of his passed son, Leroy. He hoped that by setting her free he was honoring Leroy's memory in some way. In that instant, he recalled Maria's wish for her own family to be afforded the same freedom and understood it in a deeper way than he had before.

"Thank you, Gregory," the father said. "Once she has had a few hours to safely flee, I will take you and your men to my people. If it is your wish, the Highlanders will hear what you have to say."

*

At noon sharp, Jimmy led Henry, the Hawleys, their captives, and twelve of Jimmy's men to a street on the northwestern corner of the Viridian District. A dreary arch overhead announced an entrance to the district in fading letters. The sight made Henry curious about what long-term Forgotten membership growth had been like under Jimmy—he couldn't imagine it had been high. Lining the perimeter of the entire district was a faded, splotchy-white painted line that separated the district from the rest of New Berkeley. He wondered which side had drawn it. Judging from the way Forrest had marched right in on their meeting last night, Henry thought his lack of respect for the movement was evident. To him, the wear of both this border and the sign suggested that such disregard was regular—or at least that respect wasn't cultivated or prioritized.

At the entrance to the district, Jimmy had two of his men haul Forrest's three off into a shop behind them. The sacks over their heads were tied at the neck, and their hands were bound before them. They were all drenched in sweat. It brought Henry great joy to see the men who had come close to massacring his soon-to-be followers in such a predicament. Witnessing Forrest seeing them this way would be an even greater treat.

Just as Jimmy's two disappeared through the door with the bastards in tow, a line of tall men appeared on the street's horizon. Those out and about in the city dispersed from the path of the fifteen or so thugs Forrest led through the streets. They were without their customary black coats, and the sleeves of their undershirts were rolled up. Each was young—Forrest the exception—and wore some type of hat atop his greasy head.

The road between the two groups was long, which gave Henry plenty of time to observe their walk. There was a swagger in the step of Forrest's men. It was familiar to Henry from his days with Leonard. Actually, every part of this scene was familiar to him. Except that he now stood on the side that had always lost in his day. No more, though—with him here, things would change. And though he felt in some ways his youth was revitalized, he was more than ready to fight the same brand of thugs that his younger self had thrived alongside.

When Forrest and his goons were within a block of Jimmy, Henry, and their small party, they slowed. No one else was around now, though some curious faces peeked out from behind the window curtains of the worn-down buildings on either side of the district line. In the initial moment of silence, Henry noticed a red-ribbon-wrapped fedora atop Forrest's head. Upon closer inspection, he could see a red feather on the side of it. He remembered this piece, though he hadn't registered it before. It had been atop Forrest's head during their first confrontation in the hall as well. But he had seen it somewhere else too.

Was it ... the brothel? Yeah, it was hanging on the rack on the ... the left side.

As Jimmy's words came crashing down on him, his heart skipped a beat.

"It's love, Henry. Love and vengeance ..."

Love ... for who?

Another memory came to him.

It was of Leonard wearing that very hat. He remembered it atop his former boss's head—and wondered how he hadn't recognized it before. The distinctive cardinal feather that adorned it was a cherished relic from Leonard's childhood. And now Forrest wore it, apparently everywhere he went.

How fucking cute.

So Forrest was a homosexual, one who had been in love with Leonard.

"It was Judith, wasn't it?"

Love and vengeance. William killed Leonard, so Forrest, grieving his love, killed William's love—Henry's daughter—in return.

But what about Leonard?

Without any sudden moves, he came behind Jimmy's shoulder to whisper in his ear. "Did Leonard know, Jimmy? Was it about love for Leonard too?"

Jimmy's head craned back to him. "He didn't know. And no, it wasn't. The *obsession*—what Forrest had for my brother was an obsession—was forever unrequited."

"Forrest's *interests* would have been one thing," Henry said as the picture painted itself, "but if Leonard had known the feelings were for him—"

"At a minimum, Leonard would have exiled him," Jimmy finished for him. They looked at their rival at the same time. "So Forrest kept him to himself as much as he could. The ruin of all of Leonard's sabotaged relationships—from the boys' mother to each romance after—was orchestrated by him. Over time, it ruined Leonard."

"And you found out, didn't you?" Henry asked. "It's why you're here. You stuck your nose where it didn't belong."

Without looking at him, Jimmy nodded. "Now you know."

"Now I know."

And it changes nothing. No less than all of it, no less than the entire operation.

"No guns?" Jimmy asked as Forrest grew closer, his now-projected voice echoing in the streets.

With a frustrated look, Forrest grabbed the arm of the man next to him and lifted it, revealing nothing underneath. "No guns, no tricks. We just came to take what's ours and get back to business."

His agitation was something Henry very much wanted to capitalize on. "All the same," Henry said, stepping forward, "considering what y'all have proven yourselves capable of, we'd be fools not to have a couple of ours head over there and give y'all a quick pat-down."

"He does have a point, Forrest," Jimmy agreed. "We'll send your boys your way. But before we do, I need to know I'm not gonna get a helping of bullets in return. I had a big breakfast this morning, and I'm stuffed as it is."

Forrest shrugged and waved two of his own forward. In response, Henry nodded at the Hawley brothers. They marched on without qualm. The four men met in the middle to pat each other down. Each was a picture of ire and attempted intimidation. After the first checks were clean, each pair crossed over to the enemy's side and frisked the men one by one.

"Boss," Terrance said at the heel of one of the last of Forrest's men to be searched.

"Wh—?"

"Yeah? What is it?" Henry asked out over Jimmy. They exchanged a look, and Jimmy rolled his eyes.

Rising to his feet, Terrance held a small pistol in the air. "Gun. Ankle."

"Toss it aside," Jimmy said.

As Terrance followed the order, Henry died a little inside. How much he would have loved to take the shot at Forrest if it were him doing the frisking. At the same time, though, he reminded himself that a gunshot death alone would have been too easy.

Nathan turned once he finished the last in the group. "Otherwise clean."

"Same over here, sir." Forrest's men finished and headed back, crossing paths and brushing shoulders with the Hawleys along the way. "You better learn to watch your fucking steps on our side of the line, boys."

In response, the brothers backpedaled with taunting stares the rest of the way. Nathan, who was smiling ear to ear, pointed two fingers at his eyes, turned them to his new rival's, then back into his neck, making a startled face as if he'd been stabbed. The grit he showed was encouraging.

"So this is your game?" Henry asked as he ushered the Hawleys back to their side with a pat on their shoulders. "You play dirty and expect us to just give you what you want?"

"No—no, I do not expect it. I fucking demand it. I don't know who you think you are, but you're in over your goddamn head. Now, Jimmy, you got ten seconds to hand over my boys … ten."

"Enough of this, Emory." Jimmy approached the two men who had escorted the captives to their holding place. Henry followed him.

"Nine … eight … "

Henry was unwilling to give up the bargaining chip—he needed to make this hurt. Under his breath, he pleaded with Jimmy, "No, stop, you're gonna fuck this up. He's desperate. We can use that."

"Seven … six …"

"I'm gonna fuck what up? They threatened us, and we held them in contempt for it. You might not realize it, but we've never been so bold before. I appreciate your enthusiasm, but I've worked too hard to lose it all now to your ego." Jimmy physically pushed the two men toward the building holding the captives. "Fellas, go and bring them back, and let's get home."

"Five … four …"

"They're going now, Forrest," Jimmy said.

"No, they aren't." Henry jumped in front of them when he realized what he needed to do.

"Three … two …"

"We got guns on them right now," Henry said.

Forrest paused and looked at him sideways. "Bullshit. Jimmy wouldn't—"

"I want your hat." Pointing at his temple, Henry couldn't help but smile.

"What?"

"You heard me. You give me the hat off your head, and I give you your boys breathing right now. You refuse, they'll get a bullet, and you'll get them in a bag. Simple as that."

With a curious squint, Forrest moved his hands to his hips. "Who are you?"

"I thought you knew all about me."

"No, I mean beyond your taste for whores. Who in the hell *are* you? And why would you want a silly hat anyway?"

So, Forrest knew where he'd been. The knowledge of that, the threat of it, made him hesitate for a moment. But he steeled his resolve. "Let's say I like the look of it. Why wouldn't you give up a *silly* hat?"

Forrest, who Henry could see was distraught, dropped his eyes to the ground and shook his head. The dejection of his rival was like a drug. When it hit him, vivid images of Judith when she was living and surrounded by love filled his mind. With this first taste, he knew he needed more of Forrest's suffering and in greater degrees.

"I need to see them first," Forrest said, glaring at him now.

The high Henry felt faded.

Still facing Forrest, he waved a hand at those behind him. Footsteps darted off before Jimmy approached him and whispered into his ear. "You're digging yourself a hole I won't be able to pull you out of."

"You're right," he whispered back. "I'm digging straight to hell. And no matter the cost, I'm taking him with me."

Without another word, Jimmy receded. After a few minutes, the two guards emerged with the captives. Two additional men of Jimmy's broke ranks to help usher them to Jimmy's side.

Once they arrived, Henry walked to a point halfway between the two sides and held out his hand. "The hat."

One foot at a time, Forrest waded over, removing the hat from his head as he did. The fedora rested in his hands with the gentle touch of a child. Again, Henry sucked in the sorrow. The gap soon closed between them, and with a few feet of space remaining, Forrest stopped. His finger ran along the outline of the feather, closing around the tip at the end. Without lifting his head, his menacing eyes turned up. Though he'd never let it show, Henry's heart was beating a mile a minute. Before anything could be said, Forrest extended the hand that grasped the brim of the hat. Taking a giddy step forward as if it were a gift being presented to him, Henry grabbed at it. It didn't budge. He gave it another tug, but Forrest still wouldn't let go.

"Perhaps you forget how close we are to the district," he said with an irritated grunt. "This could get ugly fast."

The resistance on the hat ceased, and Henry pulled it toward him with joy. Caressing it in his arms, he observed Forrest for signs of defeat. There were none, though. In a way, Forrest appeared relaxed as he rejoined his men. "I hope you're happy. You can go ahead and send them over now."

Feeling as if he'd been cheated, Henry grew furious.

Is it not Leonard's hat?

Scrutinizing every stitch of the hat, he saw what was missing.

"I need the whole package, Forrest," he said, thickening his accent in his glee. "Feather and all."

Forrest froze in his retreat. Though he was looking at the man's back, Henry could tell Forrest was gazing at the real prize he thought he'd swiped—the true piece of his deceased love. Now he would have to let go. Whether or not there was more to remember Leonard by didn't matter; Henry knew every little thing mattered to Forrest. Leonard's number two had always been the most careful, meticulous person he knew.

After another deep breath, Forrest whipped around, approached him again, and held out the feather. Henry plucked it right out of Forrest's hand. Without hesitation, Forrest turned his back on Henry the second it left his fingers.

Admiring the soft, red feather, Henry raised a hand. "Send them over."

"Thank God," he heard Jimmy say.

Everyone involved seemed relieved—except Forrest.

"You should know you aren't safe here, Wallace. Not in the district, not in my city, not anywhere." Ignoring the threat, Henry reached into his pocket for a match. "You wouldn't even be safe in the Murrieta."

Henry's stomach flipped at the reference—at something knowing in Forrest's tone—just as Forrest whipped around and their eyes met.

Forrest exploded, shouting, "I fucking knew it! You're—" Henry sparked the match. "No! No!"

"Emory, don't!" Jimmy's plea bounced off the buildings.

He touched the match to the feather hat before he tossed both to the floor between them. Forrest rushed after it in a mad dash to put it out. Unwilling to let him, Henry tackled him to the ground. Around him he heard Forrest's gang members and those of the Forgotten yelling and charging at each other for an all-out brawl.

Recalling that a member of the Forgotten had stabbed Forrest in the arm, Henry leveled a swift punch at the spot. Forrest wailed in pain. His subsequent effort to restrain Forrest was successful too; he pinned him by wrapping one arm around his neck and yanking up his head by the hair with his other hand to force him to observe the smoking fedora.

"Look at it, you piece of shit," he hollered in a guttural roar.

"Fuck you!"

"Watch it burn. This is only just—"

A sharp impact on his cheek forced him to relinquish his grip. His view of the scene blurred, but he could tell he'd been punched by a gangster who was now helping Forrest to his feet. Forrest sent a kick or two to his gut, and he gasped involuntarily. The gangster hurried his boss away, preventing additional blows.

All around him, fists and elbows flew. The Hawleys in particular appeared scrappy and excited to be in the action. As Henry writhed in pain at the hits he'd absorbed, he saw them tag-teaming the friskers from before. Their punches were surgical, and they took the return blows in stride. Terrance sent one down to their knee with a kick to the back of the leg, and Nathan came in with a swift uppercut. Forrest's second frisker reared back to strike during the follow-through of Nathan's swing, but Terrance lifted an arm in front of the man and dropped him to the ground with the other.

Together the brothers traded kicks at their downed enemies.

However, the rest of the fight wasn't going so well. Faces were bloodied and bodies bruised, and the large majority of those suffering wore Forgotten gray. After their initial knockouts, even the Hawleys appeared outnumbered and struggling. Rolling over onto his back in pain, Henry saw reinforcements from the district charging onto the scene. A cry rang out among Forrest's men, prompting them to retreat.

Then a battered Jimmy stormed into view and stood over him. "You son of a bitch!"

"Hey, what are you—?" Henry said, resisting with what strength he had as Jimmy grabbed him by the front of his shirt. "Cut it out."

Jimmy pulled him up by the collar and threw him back down to the ground. His upper back absorbed the brunt of the blow, but his head slammed back, dizzying him. The Hawleys ran over, and Nathan pulled Jimmy off of him.

"Let go of me, damn it. He could've gotten us all killed." Jimmy cast him a furious look. "You still will, yet. And for what?"

But Henry wasn't really listening to Jimmy. He still reveled in the suffering Forrest had endured at the sight of the hat, which was still burning on the ground. A laugh escaped him as he thought of the hat and the man burning together.

A few scattered clouds dotted the sky, but it was clear for the most part. Taking a moment to soak in the course of events, Henry was pleased with the outcome, though he knew the others might not share the sentiment. Lifting himself up on his elbow, he winced and clenched at his bruised rib, which was the only thing that could distract him from his heady rush. There was also a pain in his lip, and the finger he put to it came away bloody.

Now finished resisting the younger, stronger Nathan, Jimmy paced back and forth in a rage. "Do you have nothing to say? When will this end? When will you be satisfied?"

As Henry struggled to stand, a guard came to help him. To save face, he refused politely. All eyes were on him now. "Satisfied? What the hell does that word mean anyway? You show me a single soul who claims to be satisfied, and I'll tell you to give them an hour. Hell, give them a second to take a breath, and their mind will be onto the next conquest."

"Speak for yourself, Emory," Jimmy said with a sarcastic laugh. "I mean, is that your only explanation for this madness?"

When he gave no reply, Jimmy spun on his heel and marched off into the district in a huff. Once he was gone, Henry smiled at the crowd. Many of them smiled back. "Look, folks, after this little scuffle here, I just have to say this: now it's us with the gun, not Forrest. We have the power. And there is a time for mercy. Because a guy who pulls a gun on a good person, a person like each of you, he only loses a piece of himself when he pulls the trigger—whether he knows it or not."

The others murmured among themselves, nodding in agreement.

"But on the other side of the same coin," he continued, "there are those who know nothing of mercy. In fact, some people, some violent people who live on a diet of instilling fear in others, they wouldn't give your life a second thought, even if they had every bit of your potential for good on vivid display before them."

The group nodded. Their murmurs lifted into confident chattering.

"So a guy who pulls a gun on a person of fear—a person like Forrest Hayes—he liberates himself and all those around him. His action brings good to the world. And that's what unfolded here before you today. Yes, it was violent, but y'all fought for what you *know* is right. You fought against oppression, fought against fear. And in doing so, you took the first step in liberating our city."

Henry paused, making sure he had their attention. "Now I ask y'all this: will you swear to finish the fight? To me and all our brothers and sisters in the Fraternal Forgotten, will you make this oath?"

Stomping their boots, Nathan and Terrance stood at attention. A thunderous stomp followed as all others around them did the same.

CHAPTER 8

BEAUTY IN BALANCE

A shuffling sound snapped William out of the darkness of sleep. He welcomed the interruption because it ended his repetitive nightmare in which a pregnant Judith's grasp falls out of his. His dreams always seemed to be worse when he felt too hot or too cold, and this evening's air was crisp. Once his eyes adjusted to the darkness, he noticed the noise came from Elan leaving his tent and then the grounds altogether.

He noted it without a care. It didn't much matter to him anymore where Elan went. The young Tokali was the only one who would even hear him out about Cerebism, but the futility of his task was beginning to set in. With heavy eyes, he couldn't shake the feeling that maybe he came to believe the priest too easily.

How could such a promise be kept? How does Kubler know she can return if he hasn't already brought anyone back himself? If he lied, how can I go on without her? Why would I?

Doubt mixed with bitterness until he half-heartedly convinced himself to hold onto his belief. Eventually, he dozed off again. And there she was. This time dancing in the yard.

"William," a female voice whispered from behind him.

"Uh-wha?" he said, disoriented for a moment. It was still dark out. It'd been a dream—a good one this time. "Goddammit."

"Shhh—"

"Oh, don't shush me, Nova." Despite snapping at her, he obliged and lowered his voice. "For once I was having a good dream. I could feel her."

"The others are back and asleep now, so I have come only to be brief. I am certain this is the last time you will see me, William."

"How many times have you told me that now, huh? No false promises, my ass."

Her hand came to his shoulder. "I tend to misspeak at times, and for this I am sorry."

"Don't touch me." He shook his shoulders to shrug her off as best he could. "Thanks to y'all, the Tokali ain't got no more time for me, even though my message is a righteous one. Why is it so hard for y'all to believe there's more to life than this small world you live in?"

"Because the words are preached from a hollow heart. And trust me when I say I have learned there is much more to this life than we can fathom. But you must understand: your love, Judith, is gone."

He couldn't formulate any words in response, so he only shook his head.

"She is. It pains me to say so, but you must accept it now."

Still, he continued to shake his head in denial and began to dig his fingers into the tree at his back.

"What can live on is her spirit, though, William—and the spirit of your child—if you choose to honor them."

The splintered tree rind scraped under his nails as he pressed harder. "And how do I do that?"

"By living up to her memory. By acting how she would want you to rather than in the selfish manner your priest would have you act."

William relinquished his grip on the tree. Physical pain didn't distract him from the pain inside him as much as he would like it to. But what Nova suggested ... it wasn't good enough for him. Whether the priest's promise was true or not, the possibility of being with Judith again had been presented to him, and he couldn't let it go. It was all or nothing. Still, honoring her sounded like it couldn't be a bad thing, which brought him to the reason he suspected Nova was really here.

"My debt to you ain't really forgiven, is it?"

"I said it was and I meant it. Do you not feel it has been paid?"

"We both know it hasn't. But ... what can I do now?"

Nova came around from the back of the tree and sat beside him. The lack of personal space was somewhat uncomfortable to him, but she seemed to have no problem with it, sitting close as if they had long been friends. He supposed they didn't feel too far from it as she stared out at the natives' campsite.

"When I informed you that Judith was pregnant, there was a glow on you, William. In my lifetime I have been a mother and a nurse, so I know where it came from. In your moment of discovery, you became transparent to me. I saw you for what you are."

Thoughts of his lost child who had his own face ran through the garden of his mind again, and he took a deep, shaky breath. "And what is that?"

"A good man."

William choked and shook his head. A good man wouldn't have

put his selfish ambitions ahead of his wife and unborn child.

"You are."

"But why does it matter to you anyway? Why do you care if I'm a good man?"

Nova sighed. "You know it is my daughter who leads you south, yes?"

"I do."

"Well, I know you do not believe in my religion, but as the vessel for the Maiden who watches over this territory, I was given a Calling. You can think of it as a mission that She required of me. Through Walking Widows like me, She seeks to keep the peace here. So my duty was to observe Eastern intruders like yourself and learn from you. However, now that my Walk has ended, I do not know what She has determined must be done next—what She determined about your people from my observations. But as the power of the gangs has continued to get out of hand, I have feared my daughter might be called upon to face the consequences—to balance out their power."

An itch shot up his spine, and he rubbed his back on the tree to rectify it. "And you think I can stop it so that she won't have to."

"Because I have seen your determination, I know you can. And when I saw your reaction to the confirmed conception of your own child, I believed you would."

Finally, he looked her straight in the eye. "Maybe I can try, but—"

Nova embraced him. "That is all I can ask of you. Thank you, William."

Again he was surprised, but this time there was no discomfort.

Simultaneously, he felt both warmth and a sense that he was being used. However, in this brief moment of emotion, at least he wasn't alone, so he held as tight as he could to the feeling before it, too, went away.

With his mouth buried in her shoulder, William realized that deep down, though he'd never admit as much aloud, he didn't want this familiar person to leave. But accepting the inevitable, he found himself letting out an anguished cry.

When she squeezed him tighter in response, he inaudibly croaked, "Goodbye, Nova."

And this time, he knew it would be true.

*

Upon releasing the Highlander's daughter, Gregory received a predictable verbal lambasting from Clovis and a gentle talking-to from Father Kubler. Their good-cop, bad-cop routine was already well cemented. If he weren't so pleased with himself, he might have been more concerned.

In fact, it had felt so right to let the little girl go, to get an innocent out of harm's way, that he had barely heard their respective rants and lectures. On top of that, his action got their foot in the door with the free folk, which was his doing and his alone. Only once they had finished throwing his error in his face did he reveal the good news of the Highlander's promise, and it brought him great joy to see them eat their words.

As they prepared to depart, Gregory returned the father's bandana and hat. The man tied the bandana back around his face with a smile, which disappeared as he pulled it up over his nose.

Hat in hand, he threw himself up onto his horse, then placed it on his head. At a quick tip of the man's cap, Gregory nodded and fetched his own ride. Beside the tree, Kubler was kneeling and reached out to him for one last prayer before they went. While he hoped it wouldn't go on too long, he figured it otherwise couldn't hurt.

"Oh Lord, we thank You for guiding those souls that are lost toward the path of faith and reason."

Glory be to the Enigma for guiding those lost souls ... but none for the man who put in the work, though, eh, Kubler?

"It is not without gratitude that we accept this kindness as we work tirelessly, with our hearts whole, to spread Your good word. We also thank You for sending Clovis Keagan to us."

What?

Gregory's eyes shot open. Standing behind the priest with a bowed head and a hand on Kubler's shoulder was Clovis.

"Clovis is proof of Your will—proof there are signs You provide us in these worlds we are blessed with. May the beacon You shine on us through Clovis continue to light our way."

Clovis, Clovis, Clovis. This is getting out of hand.

"In His name, we pray."

Though he was supposed to repeat the line, Gregory couldn't manage more than a mumble; he hurried to rise and prepare his things.

"Great sermon, Father," Clovis said. The twisted piety sent a shiver up Gregory's spine as he headed toward his horse.

Once they had all mounted, Clovis drew his horse up alongside the Highlander's, and he peeked his head down under the brim of the man's large hat with an endless smirk. "Lead the way ... pal."

The Highlander's path took them northeast through Prayer's Passage. Along the way, they passed by the occasional abandoned house but nothing else. Every turn taken was calculated and seemed to be inspected with precise care by their guide. While it was quiet in the vast, dry fields they crossed, Gregory knew the serenity was a mirage that this place was known for. Attacks could come from any direction at any time since there were no settled lands or specific groups with a desire to claim them.

As the hills started to slope, a ridge formed before them. The swath of land on the northern side of it splintered off and down into what appeared to be an arid valley. Upon reaching a trail that descended into it, the Highlander paused and looked behind them. For a good five minutes he stalled, squinting out into the mirage of heat waves lining the horizon from whence they came.

Gregory's companions exchanged a look that converged on him, as if he were responsible for the man's behavior. Unwilling to accept the burden, he shrugged them off.

"Expecting someone?" Clovis asked.

"No ... no, I'm not," the Highlander replied.

"Well, th—"

"But you can never be too sure."

Clovis's lip curled at the interruption, and Gregory was amused by the way he spit his impatience onto the ground. The eye rolling and head shaking that ensued for the next few minutes were much less amusing. He wondered how a person so many followed to the point of worship could be so child-like. One answer came to him: fear.

"All right, go down the path—be quick about it," the Highlander said, waving them on. In the time it took the fellow to spit out the phrase alone, Gregory was sure they could've all been down beneath the ridge. First went Clovis, followed by Kubler, Gregory, and the Highlander, who rode much faster than he spoke.

Once out of sight beneath the ridge, their guide stormed to the front of the group, jumped off his horse, and indicated they should do the same. It seemed like they would be walking from here. One by one, they followed his lead.

The way down was steep and rocky. Beside the path, about twenty paces to his left, was the cliff-edge drop—a view Gregory had no desire to look down. Despite the uneven terrain, though, the trek was no challenge for Gregory. At a young age, he had attained a fondness for horses and found it easy to connect with the ones he'd been around. Others used to poke fun at him by saying it was because of his size, but he took no offense to it. In fact, he agreed.

What he did worry about, as the path looped left, was what had the Highlander on edge before. The dangers of Prayer's Passage were clear, but as far as he was aware, the free people were known to be mostly tolerant of those who lived like them. Their raids and thieving weren't for those who shared in their cause. This common ground was seen as a deterrence to outsiders and was part of what made traveling through Prayer's Passage into the Murrieta so dangerous.

The farther down the spiral they went, the more the landscape at the foot of the path was revealed. Above them, Gregory could see the cliff hung over what appeared to be a cove. Far off at the bottom were thick trees leading to a small mass of water nestled into the corner. No one said a word as they beheld the mini oasis, which steadily disappeared behind the height of the trees as they descended.

When the slope ended and the path curved into the woods, Gregory tensed. For the first time he wondered if his pride at securing this trip had blinded him into trusting this man he didn't know. The closer they got to the cove, the more difficult it would be to turn back and run. An ambush would mean certain death.

The atmosphere in the woods was heavy and ominous. Every sound was accompanied by a faint echo.

"If you don't mind my asking, are we close to your settlement, friend?" Father Kubler asked, his eyes darting in all directions.

The Highlander didn't turn around to answer or stop his march.

Clovis reined in his horse ahead of Gregory and glared at him as he grasped the handle of the pistol in his right holster. "All right, what the fuck is going on here?"

Still no answer.

Riding past Clovis and Kubler, who had also stopped, Gregory thought of William. "Remember why we're here."

Clovis removed his weapon and carried on again.

Although Gregory had urged them on, the hair on his neck was beginning to stand as well. Their guide had gotten several paces in front of them in the dark, shaded woods, and he had to pick up his speed to keep up. Among the trees, he noted scattered huts and strewn shelters, which were well blended into the environment. He urged his horse forward faster.

"Something doesn't feel right, Gregory," Father Kubler said, his tone hoarse.

It wasn't clear whether anyone was inside the huts until—a rustling.

"What the fuck was that?" Clovis clicked back his pistol's hammer and pointed it toward the sound.

Nothing was there, but when Gregory looked ahead on the trail, their guide had disappeared. "Put your gun down," he said, raising a hand to it. "If this is a trap, it won't do us much good anyway." The order was followed with no lack of resentment; they circled up with their backs to one another. The air was warm, but the quiet was cold. "Hello? Is anyone there?"

"Should we go back?" Kubler asked in a whisper.

A whistle rang out, causing a tremor in Gregory's shoulder.

"Hello? Is anyone there?" he called again.

In the trees, he saw a pair of eyes over a black bandana emerge from behind a shelter without a sound. Another taller figure stood behind the first. Gregory's heart sank, and time stood still. More and more bandanas materialized, and the Highlanders approached them at a snail's crawl. Frozen in place, Gregory noted a trend of frailty and slim builds among them. His partners and he were surrounded by this mass of weapon-wielding thieves who looked ready to feast upon them.

A hand came to Gregory's shoulder from behind, and he jumped. It was Clovis, who grunted, "Guess they heard you."

*

Two more days of southern travel passed, and the pace of Latera's group was slowing. The fault of their lag was as much hers as anyone else's, though. While fatigue was kicking in for them and their horses, she also didn't want to go faster than Nova and Kai could keep up with. Wherever they were, her mother was always on her mind, and she longed to catch up more on their years spent apart. Every night she'd stayed out as late as possible, hoping the crow would return. It hadn't since Nova's guidance to connect with the Mother though, and now, as she sat in the dark, there was only an hour of travel between them and the Hold. In the morning they'd arrive, and she'd finally have her chance to release her people, the V'ahani of Riverlands, from the captivity of the Keagan gang.

"What are you doing awake, Chieftess?"

"Oh, hey, Winnie. I was just about to go to sleep."

Her friend came to take a seat beside her in front of the red, fading embers of their campfire. The weight of Winona's head fell on her shoulder. "We are so close now, you know?"

"I do."

"Well, you should also know it is thanks to you."

While this moment had been such a long, impossible time coming, the knowledge that she would have to one day leave them made it so bittersweet. A smile tugged at her lips, but she felt guilty for it.

"Look, I understand you do not feel like you can talk to us about whatever has been bringing you down. But you can if you need to, okay? If not with me, then Mika would happily hear you out."

Latera chuckled. "And if I speak to Mika, it would not be the same as speaking to both of you?"

Winona's head came up, and her hands came to her chest as if she were taken aback. "Do you think I am so nosy I would not respect your privacy?"

"Winnie …"

"Well—I … obviously I would need to inquire about the topic at least. How could I not while being aware there was something he knew that I did not?"

"Inquire?"

"Okay, okay. I would tie him down and interrogate him until he told me every detail." They laughed. "Why, though? Do you need to talk to him? What do you need to tell him that you could not tell me? Is it about the boys? Do I need to kill one of them? Two of them? All of them?"

"Yes. I need them all gone." Still laughing as the fire's sparks flew into the air with an easy breeze, she gave her friend a serious look and nodded. "What gave it away?"

"I thought they had been acting strange—especially Elan."

What Winona said was true. It pained Latera to think how her sudden hesitation to show Hammond affection as of late might have made him feel. Since the incident between the boys and her, Elan's subsequent odd behavior also troubled her. There were bags under Elan's eyes every morning, and he tended to sit alone, whispering to himself in what appeared to be deep, manic thought. The other Tokali boys discussed the strange questions he had asked them. Warrick in particular was worried when Elan asked what had possessed them to leave the Hold in the first place, as if he had no recollection of the events.

While her inner chieftess worried about his loyalty, Latera was much more troubled to think that his apparent insanity was a result of her controlling him. Elan was a child of the Mother no matter how petty she thought him to be, and as the Walking

Widow, she needed to be better.

"Girl, what did they do?" Winona asked, breaking through her thoughts. "Just say the word, and I will do them in, however you ask. Strangled in their sleep? Spear to the gut? Picked apart by the birds? Name it."

She laughed again. "You are too much. No, any issues I have with them are my own doing at this point."

Winona's head came back to her shoulder. "Well, that is no fun. They will be behind us soon, so I guess I will spare them for now. And do not worry, we will find you a nice V'ahani boy when we get home."

The thought of being with anyone but Hammond made Latera sick, but the lighthearted talk with Winona continued to bolster her spirits. After giving Winona a kiss on the head, she rose to her feet. "On that note, I am ready for bed. Thank you for this, my little assassin. I will see you in the morning."

Winona also stood and bowed in dramatic fashion. "At your beck and call, Chieftess. Good night."

Before crawling inside her tent, Latera went to find cover to relieve herself. A tree trunk she spotted looked thick enough, so she went to squat behind it but stopped when she spotted a figure behind another—it was Nova.

"I feared I would not see you again before we arrived at the Hold. Did you see Winona and me talking?" Latera asked.

"I did. And I thought about showing myself. Believe me, I have struggled with the desire for longer than you can know. But the truth is I am afraid. Perhaps one day I will get over that fear. But for now, I must go north."

The air seemed to thicken around Latera. "What? No. Why?"

"Just as there are two objectives every Widow must follow during her Walk, there are two responsibilities she must complete once her Walk ends. The first is to inform the next Widow of their duties, and the second is to expand upon the Maiden's Canvas. I have completed the former. And with you closing in on the Hold and the northern V'ahani centered in the Riverlands, the timing could not be better to make my way to the Canvas undetected."

"Right," she said, folding her arms, unable to look at her mother. "I am informed, so I guess you can leave me … again."

"Please do not get me wrong. This is not goodbye, Latera. I will find you and return to you."

"How can you know that? There is so much danger in this territory. How can I be sure I will see you again?"

"Against all odds we were fortunate enough to be reunited. That is more than most who suffer a loss can say. It is certainly more than William Keagan can say. At the same time, you are right: I cannot make such a promise. But on my word, you can be certain I will try with every fiber of my being."

The empty look in Elan's eye following her indiscretion came back to her. "I controlled one of the Tokali again."

"Did you?"

"Yes. And it was like I learned nothing from what you said. I failed the Mother, and he seems to have lost his wits because of it. If you go, I do not—"

"If I go, you will keep failing," Nova said, prompting Latera to shake her head, though she couldn't get a word in before her mother continued. "If I stay, you will keep failing. Because it is Her will for you to fail. This is the only way you will learn and grow, as you have to a startling degree from your past failures, no?"

Latera sighed as reality set in and she realized it was the Mother's will for her to go it alone again. She could certainly admit she had learned a great deal both before and after being told she was the Walking Widow. While uncertainty would always remain in this big new world, she believed her light was ready to shine upon the Hold. "Uncle Orrin took me to see the Canvas once. He had told me the images are carved into the trees from time to time by the Mother Herself."

"And in a way they are, aren't they? They are carved by the Mother's vessels, by Her Widows."

"Why does the legend not say it is the Widow, then?"

Her mother smiled at her. "Why do you suppose it doesn't?"

It was clear she was being tested. "The first objective: a Widow must use her secret to spread faith in the Mother."

"Very good. We see the past in our dreams so that we may add to the Canvas when our Walk ends. From one Widow to the next, we fill in the blanks and record the story of Her domain. This way Her children may learn from its past."

"Well … perhaps I can meet you up there once I have brought our people home."

"The Canvas is a work of art. Any such endeavor that bears the soul of its creator takes years of time and dedication. So, yes, I will be there creating and waiting for you, Latera. It would mean everything to have you with me while I leave my mark."

With a nod, Latera came and hugged her mother. "I will see you there, Mama. Until then."

"Until then, my love."

Her night's rest was full and peaceful. Dreams passed by, as they had the previous two nights, of her peoples' plight in the Hold. From what she saw, they continued to be mistreated. However, the gains she had made in her time there to earn them shelter had lifted their spirits. They were no longer a shell of the people who had once roamed free in the Riverlands.

At night they would gather in tight spaces for moments of prayer to the Mother and to console each other. One touching moment Latera held on to was a V'ahani mother she recognized telling her daughter they would be freed—more specifically, she assured the girl that Latera would return. The light in the young one's eyes stuck with her until the moment she woke.

When she exited her tent at the crack of dawn, she was surprised to see the others were already up and organizing their things. In fact, it appeared they were almost finished.

"Gannon, would you please?" Mika asked, tilting his head at Latera's tent to indicate that he break it down, then approaching her. "We are ready to go, Chieftess. Your horse awaits you."

Latera's heart felt full for the first time in a long time. She placed a hand on Mika's shoulder and pulled him in for a hug before turning to the nearby Winona and doing the same.

"Thank you," she said in a whisper.

The couple backed away and bowed, to which Latera returned the favor. Her horse's hooves clacked as Shelton led it to her side, signaling it was time to go. Climbing up to the top of her horse, she placed her hand on its head and whispered to it in the Mother's tongue. "You honor Her will, my dear. Almost there now. One last push."

The horse whinnied, and with her comrades atop their steeds behind her, it charged onward. Over open fields they tore until they reached the familiar sight of the wooded area before the Hold. Weaving in and out of trees, flying like the wind, they finally reached the edge of the tree line. They had made it.

Today was the day she would deliver her people from darkness. *Ready or not, Walter Keagan, here I come.*

*

Two nights had passed since the brawl that shook the Viridian District. Though Henry had been riding high since the incident, the Hawley brothers convinced him it would be best to stay in for a few days to recover from his injuries. Since Forrest knew more than he realized, too—including his identity, it seemed—a temporarily low profile would be ideal, however unfavorable.

During his downtime, he kept in close contact with Nathan and Terrance, whom he'd promoted to the new title of his First Lieutenants. The brothers made various arrangements for him and continued to prove their worth. While Jimmy sulked about without a word or productive action, Henry ordered the brothers to garner support within the Forgotten for Henry's plan and candidacy as their new leader.

The brothers also completed smaller tasks such as cutting a deal with the owner of the All Appetites brothel to send over two girls, disguised, under the cover of darkness. With the forthcoming election, Henry knew he couldn't be caught in such places again— or make too blatant his activities. Precautions were necessary now. Though it might be safest to abstain, he was too hyped from the fight to have *no* fun. While his all-out assault on Forrest was paused, his energy levels never could be—he was all in until the end now.

Before he even opened his eyes, he could feel the weight of naked bodies sprawled atop him. He felt disgusted by it. Last night had been filled with temptation and desire. But in the morning, he felt as if the nature of the act revealed itself to him and to the world. A part of him resented the women for tempting a married man, while a different part resented his own hypocrisy. Both parts wanted them gone. Groaning, he rolled over, out from under them, and opened his eyes to tell them to leave.

"What happened to you?"

"Fuck!" He nearly jumped out of his skin in shock and fright. Searching for the source of the question, he could make out Jimmy reclining in a chair on the other side of the room.

Momentarily stunned, he took a second to cover himself with the sheets. "What the fuck, Jimmy?"

"What's wit awl the noise?" one of the girls asked with a whine and a yawn.

Wondering how long Jimmy had been there, he realized he didn't want to be seen this way—even if he already had been. "Hey, hey, you, wake up," he said to the other, tapping her on the cheek.

Swatting his hand away, she opened her eyes and buried her face in a pillow. "What the hell? Cut it out."

"Time to go, both of you. Get decent, get your things, and get out. Ask the lobby boy downstairs for Emory's guys, and they'll see to your pay."

The groans from the girls filled the room as they followed his orders. While they did, Jimmy and Henry sat quiet.

When the door closed behind the girls, Henry expected Jimmy to say something. But Jimmy only shook his head at him.

"Don't you fucking look at me like that."

Jimmy shrugged but still said nothing.

Averting his gaze, Henry couldn't take the judgement. "So did you just come here to stare, or what? If that's your thing, you know where Forrest lives."

"I asked what happened to you."

"I got a sucker punch to the face and a kick or two in the ribs. It happens. So what?" Henry said, attempting to avoid answering Jimmy's true question.

This time Jimmy's tongue clicked three times to accompany a more evident head shake. "If you were to succeed in killing Forrest, would you still stay here?"

"Of course I would. I ain't built for the West, and it ain't built for me."

Despite Jimmy's effort toward frank discussion, Henry didn't have enough faith in Jimmy to give him the real answers. Besides, any further vulnerability or connection between them would only serve to make his ongoing coup of the Forgotten more difficult.

For a moment Jimmy appeared to contemplate pressing the issue, but he merely sighed. "What about Maria, Henry?"

"I don't gotta answer your questions," Henry said, fidgeting. The mention of his wife made him irate, partly at Jimmy for prying and partly at himself because he didn't know the answer. He pulled open a dresser drawer beside him and hastily threw on a pair of pants under cover of the sheets. "What the hell do you want from me, anyway? I'm turning your fantasy into reality as far as I'm concerned." He stood and grabbed a shirt off the floor, which he threw over his shoulders. "I mean, seeing that hat burn crushed him. Didn't you feel it, Jimmy? After all he's done to you, how could you not have felt the rush?"

Rolling his head in disbelief, Jimmy shot back, "For God's sake, it was my brother's hat, Henry! Did you even consider that for a second? And you can't just ... just come into a situation you don't understand and wreak havoc without consequences."

"Yeah, well, someone should've told that to *him* a long time ago."

Jimmy pushed off the arms of his chair to stand, causing the legs to make a sharp, uncomfortable high-pitched skid on the wood floor, and pointed a finger at him. "That's it—right there. There you go again."

"What are you on about?"

"You think you're hiding the truth from me, but you're not. There's something you're burying. And you know what?" Jimmy's finger wagged at the door. "I might not know *what* it is, but I know it starts with those prostitutes."

"Fuck you," Henry said, his accent dropping in his fury.

"Yeah, whatever, *Emory*. I promise you one thing, though: you won't find what you're after if you ignore the things holding you back from it."

"*He's* holding me back from it, goddammit." The accent returned as he tried in defense to convince both of them of his righteousness. "Once he's been burned at the stake, I'll be able to give the people what they need. And maybe *that's* what I'm after. Truth is, you had the right idea here, and you don't even realize it. But me? I'm gonna tear down

191

the foundation Leonard and him built their empire on and construct a new world where the welfare of the people is guaranteed."

"And who'll be the one to guarantee it? You? Look at the damage you've already done. Now you want to completely tear down structures that built New Berkeley tenfold? That wasn't my goal at all. You've just distorted my vision for the one thing this city and everyone in it needs most, including yourself."

"And what's that?"

"Balance—balance, Henry—balance! In all things, in all the world, it's the presence of the scale alone that gives us justice. When we fight and we bicker and the powerful abuse us, it's not because of the side they picked. It's because they picked one side and weighed it down with the vilification of all who stood against them. And if we follow your path? If we follow your path, we too will become the abusers—"

"Oh, come on."

"—and I can't stand for that."

"Ours will be a better system, and you know it."

"*Your* system! Yours." Running his hands through his hair, Jimmy appeared to be near losing it as he collapsed into a squat. He took a deep breath and rubbed his eyes with his fingers, appearing to cool down. "If you go forward with this, I'll have no part in it. But, please ... you'll only become them if you do. And it won't bring you the closure you think it will. Please, just tell me you'll look inside yourself and try to see the beauty that can only come from balance—for all our sakes."

Staring at his toes, Henry shook his head. "I had beauty and balance. But he took them away."

For the first time, he saw the heart in his counterpart, and he spoke with honesty because of it. He was sorry—to Jimmy, to his family, to himself—but there was no going back now.

"I'm sorry, Jimmy. Forrest started this, and I need to finish it."

"I'm sorry too—truly." And without another word, Jimmy left.

CHAPTER 9

BROTHERS IN ARMS

A knock came at the door. Jimmy had left twenty minutes ago, and Henry had remained on the corner of his bed, his head in his hands, the entire time. Rubbing his eyelids, he dragged his cheeks downward to wake himself and stretched his back as he yawned drowsily.

"Come in," he called.

"Sir?" He heard Nathan reply on the other side.

"I said come in."

The Hawleys entered. "As one of your First Lieutenants, I gotta say, you really should keep your door locked, sir."

"Let's take a walk, boys."

The brothers exchanged a furrowed glance.

"Well, yeah, we can do that," Nathan said. "But we were really hoping to provide you an update on the gray coats. We've been talking with some people and discussing it ourselves, and we have a few ideas."

"Perfect." With a pep in his step, he approached them and ushered them to the door. "We'll talk about it on the way."

Terrance resisted.

"Are you sure you don't want to hear it from us in private first?" Nathan asked.

"I'm sure. Follow me."

He led them out of the hotel and down the streets of the Viridian District. Henry greeted each person who passed by on the way, Nathan and Terrance trailing behind him without a word. It was clear to him that they weren't comfortable talking out here, but he didn't care. He led them on until they came to the dividing line of the district.

"All right, what's y'all's update?" he asked. He walked with his arms behind his back, his feet stepping along the line as if he were on a balance beam.

He heard the brothers whisper to each other.

"I really don't think this is the place to discuss it," Nathan said.

"No? Why not?"

"Because, sir ... the wrong person might be listening."

"Ah. Okay, so," Henry hopped off the paint and onto the district side, "what about here?"

Nathan's lips pursed.

People *were* watching, so the Hawleys weren't wrong. But still, he jumped to the other side. "Or here?"

"The force has room to grow," Terrance said as if he'd been holding his breath.

"Now we're getting somewhere!"

"To elaborate on Terrance's point, there are still able-bodied men within the Forgotten who aren't serving at present. We believe there's an opportunity to recruit further and bring them in."

Glancing down at the line and back up at them, Henry raised his brows. "So there's room to grow?"

"Yes, sir," Nathan answered.

"But only to here?" This time he jumped back onto the line.

Neither responded.

"Y'all get the point I'm trying to make? No? Well, here it is: I want y'all to think outside the lines." He pointed at the border. "If we're gonna win this, we need the support of an entire city. Because as I've said, this is the start of a movement—a movement and way of life enforced by law. What we have here now—this, this district—is only an illusion of independence and influence. That just ain't gonna cut it. Not anymore."

"So you want us to recruit outside the district?" Nathan asked.

With his hand in an OK gesture, he replied, "Boy, now you're speaking the language of the new order."

As a passerby shot them a dirty look, Nathan shook his head. "Fair enough, but what if there are risks?"

"What's the mission you were sent here to complete, Nathan?"

"The primary objective was to help you deal with Forrest Hayes, sir."

Henry nodded and placed a hand on both brothers' shoulders. "This is how you help me deal with Forrest Hayes. Any more questions?"

The Hawleys shook their heads and stood at attention, and together they returned to the district.

*

Latera stood before the Hold with William, Hammond, and Elan. It was silent there on this early morning. They'd decided on a position closer to the trees rather than the Tokali Hold so that they could escape if necessary.

Activity from Keagan and Tokali guards had stirred once their march had begun. At his own request, Hammond had led the charge with a blade in one hand and William in the other, while Elan and Latera followed, their weapons at the ready. A string of rifles atop the Hold had been aimed their way and remained trained on them. Latera had instructed Gannon, who stayed back in the trees, to keep his rifle at the ready and aim true once Walter Keagan appeared atop the walls of the Hold. The other Tokali were asked to stay back as well to keep their flank well monitored.

"Who's there?" one of the guards finally shouted.

"Do you not recognize your own leader?" Latera asked with as much projection as she could muster through the field. "Tell Walter Keagan his cousin William has come for a visit."

No reply came but the sound of scurrying. Ten minutes of stress and frustration passed. Latera wished she could see Walter's reaction when he was told of William's capture but realized the moment would have long since passed: the men who had plotted to attack them earlier in their journey would've relayed the news.

Perhaps this evening she would witness it in her dreams.

Walter Keagan slowly came into view. Even from this distance, she could see that the situation bothered him. Behind him, she recognized Malik and Adila, Elan's parents. The sight of Walter and Adila together wasn't one she cared for.

"What do you want?" Walter asked.

"Now, Walter, what kind of a welcome was that?" Latera asked with a grin. He had treated her imprisonment at the Hold like a game. It was only fair she return the favor. "Did you not miss me?"

"I'll have the V'ahani ready in an hour's time. But if any harm comes to my cousin, I'll have them all hanged. We good?"

Better not to waste time anyway.

"My comrades in orange would like the Tokali released as well," she said, repaying them for their support by making the request. "Or at least to be provided freedom in their own home."

"Our people chose this path and do not wish to divert from it," Adila replied with more venom than even Walter had. "Elan— friends of Elan—it is time to come home now. I know this princess has made you promises that sounded nice at the time. But she will not deliver. She is just a girl."

"They will—"

"My mother is ... she is right," Elan struggled to say, turning back to the Tokali in the trees, as he interrupted Latera. "She is only here for h—her own people. She has no plan to unite us the way William and the Keagans do." Dropping his weapon, Elan backed away a few steps. "I will see William back to the Hold, but I plan on staying with my people once I do. And, brothers, I ... I hope you will follow me."

Latera wasn't surprised in the slightest, and she wasn't angry either. At this point she still pitied Elan and felt bad about his current state. Deep down she knew being with his family would be the best thing for him, and she hoped the Mother would agree for the sake of his recovery.

"Latera!" Winona yelled from the trees. Turning toward the sound, Latera could see a man emerging from the tree line to the west, with a pistol pointed her way. Without Elan beside her, she was exposed.

"Let him go, or I'll kill the bitch."

"No, stop!" Hammond cried.

"Devin?" William asked, rotating to face him.

"Latera, I have the shot!" Gannon said.

"Well, you'd better be quick on that trigger, boy," Devin replied.

She wished she could give Gannon the order to shoot without saying it. Doing so might cause Devin to shoot her in reaction. The thought of controlling Gannon occurred to her, but she wasn't sure if his ability to shoot at that distance would carry over. And she didn't know if she could control Easterners the same way, so controlling Devin wasn't an option.

Hammond let out a sudden yelp, and Latera saw that William had elbowed him in the gut. Terrified for her friends and her people if he were to get away, Latera gasped, and her chest tightened. Rather than making a break for it, though, William ran to her and stood between her and Devin.

"Put the gun down, Devin."

"What are you doing, sir?" Devin asked, lowering his weapon as soon as William had gotten in the way.

"Latera, are you okay?" Hammond asked as he rushed to her side and wrapped her in his arms to shield her further.

Panting in the wake of her near heart attack, she nodded and tried to collect herself. "I am now, yes," she replied.

The sight of William Keagan covering them, protecting them, astonished her. She wondered what it could mean. Did he have some selfish incentive to do so? Was he simply attempting to appear noble to further his agenda of converting the natives to his people's religion? Could that be the case with such a risky action? Or was this genuine? Had something changed in him?

For the sake of so many lives, she needed to find out.

"What the fuck's going on down there?" Walter echoed. "Y'all can consider the deal off until this shit's sorted."

One of William's hands had been raised at Devin, and he pointed a finger on the other hand toward Walter. "One hour, Walter. We'll talk again in one hour. You," he said, addressing Devin, "meet us back in the trees."

One careful step at a time, they all retreated to the trees until they were safe from the fighters at the Hold. Upon their arrival, the Tokali got right to arguing, especially with Elan, who didn't seem capable of returning the favor in a coherent fashion. Mika and Winona discussed what could be said to ensure they'd see the V'ahani of the Riverlands at the end of an hour. All alone, on a tree stump with his face in his hands, was William.

Latera stepped toward him with caution. She saw his suffering in his body language and worried he would shatter at any moment.

"You saved me," she said.

At first there was no response besides a long exhale. Then he shrugged.

"You did. Why did you do that?"

"Why did I stand against my own gang?" he asked, shaking his head as if dumbfounded. "I honestly don't know. I just ... did. Maybe because I owed a debt."

Looking around to see who he could be referring to, she couldn't imagine he had owed anything to herself or anyone involved. She remained wary of his past attempts to convert her. "A debt?"

"She believed I would," he said to the ground. "And I did. To do right by them. But it isn't right. None of this is right. It can't be."

It was evident he was conflicted. This didn't seem like an act. And with all she knew he'd been through, she wasn't surprised. She probed further to keep him reflecting. "Who believed you would, William?" she asked.

Now he met her eyes. "Nova. Your mother."

"What do you—?"

"My brothers," he continued. "My Judith. No one else ever believed I would. But I did. They did. And now in one way or another ... they've all left me."

Her heart broke for him in a way she never thought it would. As she struggled to find the words, his forehead fell back down to his folded arms. Though she wanted to know more about his familiarity with her mother, she recognized his need for time alone. Before departing, she said, "Thank you, William. For what it is worth, you have made me a believer. Now I believe in you too."

The snapping of twigs signaled Devin's approach, though he had another in tow with him. Gannon lifted his weapon again. Latera recognized Devin's prisoner was none other than Charles Langston. Putting two and two together, she feared what it might do to William to see Charles. The others did too: Mika led a charge to restrain William. This time, though, William didn't react. Instead, he just sat and stared at the man.

"Why is he here?" William asked.

"Clovis wanted me to bring him to you, William. As a gift," Devin said.

Charles resisted. "Fuck you and your gang."

Devin raised his gun as if to pistol-whip Charles, who flinched. "What did I tell you about speaking?"

"Okay, okay," Charles pleaded. "I get it. Not again."

"A gift for what?" William asked.

"A pick-me-up. For the bad news I'm to bring you of Daniel sabotaging our operation in the Riverlands."

Recalling William's comment about how few people he had left, Latera snapped her gaze to him at the news of his brother's alleged betrayal. He slid off the angled stump and landed on the ground, leaning his neck back against his previous seat. "What are you talking about?"

"He turned on us and sided with the people of Harran—"

The news dumbfounded Latera. *And now Daniel has turned? Maybe there could be hope for these brothers, yet.*

"Bullshit."

"No, sir. I was there. No lie to speak of."

William's fingers ran through his hair before he shook his head. "No. No, no, no, that can't be."

"Unfortunately, it is," Devin replied.

"No," William said again, rocking back and forth.

"They brainwashed him, surely," Devin followed, forcing Charles forward. "Don't let it get to you. For now, take this man. Have your justice or vengeance or whatever you want to call it. I will go to the Hold and ensure things move along over the next hour, as you've ordered."

"And why would we let you leave?" Latera asked, unsure of the intent of this man who just pulled a gun on her.

"Well, first of all, Walter said the deal's off. Clearly his confidence in the situation is shaken. And second, it's like I said: my orders from Clovis are first and foremost to serve William right now. And

I follow Clovis's orders. So if William asks for your people to be freed, then your people get freed. Besides, what other inside man might you have in this case?" Latera squinted and scanned him top to bottom as she considered the valid points he'd made. "Of course, if you want me to stay with you, I'd love to keep you company, gorgeous. I could help you pass an hour like it was nothing, trust me."

Rolling her eyes, Latera waved him on. "Go."

And so Devin left for the Hold. Once he was gone, everyone reverted to the same conversations they'd been having before, only now they had to keep an eye on another prisoner.

Latera took a seat by William, who was still shaking his head. "If you want your piece of Charles, I will make sure no one does anything to stop you."

"I have no use for him," William replied. "He's nothing—a cog in a machine. A meaningless, hollow machine."

"All the same," she said, placing a dagger beside him and standing up. As she was about to go talk to Winona and Mika, she stopped herself. When she turned, he was playing with the weapon in his hands. "You know, William ... you are not alone."

In return, she received a nod and the closest thing to a smile she'd seen from him in some time.

*

With desperate-looking Highlanders on all sides, Gregory and his group had their hands raised for mercy.

"Gregory and friends of the Keagan gang." A gap opened before them as the Highlanders on the trail moved aside for the outsiders' former captive. A swell of relief came over Gregory as he saw the man approaching from among them with his daughter. "As promised, in return for your kindness, you have the ear of the Highlanders."

Rubbing the sweat off his forehead, Gregory replied, "Thank—"

"Now it's on you to explain why it is you think we should merge with your gang. And please … do so as if your lives depended on it."

Gregory scratched like mad at his head, the stress of the threat making him break out in hives. What could they say? The three of them each had distinct motives, and the possibility of speaking in coherent unity seemed nonexistent. The heat of hundreds of eyes burned into him. Since the faces of the Highlanders were covered, those intimidating stares were all he had to speak to. He inhaled; he exhaled. No words came.

"What if it's y'all's lives that depend on it?" Clovis suddenly asked in a defensive grunt.

"Come again?" Though he couldn't be sure who the question had come from, he knew it was a female, and it was followed by the readying of countless weapons.

I can do this.

"You heard him right," Gregory said, looking to the Highlander father. "We mean you no harm, as we've proven. But if you weren't under threat, why would you bring us here in the first place?"

"You've done plenty of harm." This time a different woman spoke. He followed the direction her voice had emanated from and saw a head of dark black hair and a scarred cheek around fierce blue-green eyes.

"We have all done wrong by those we encounter, in one way or another," Kubler said, with his hands clasped together before him. "It is the nature of drawing breath and making choices. But under the word of God, we may yet be united. This is what Clovis Keagan has been sent to the Murrieta Territory to offer."

Murmurs rippled through the Highlanders. Some sounded hesitant, others curious. But none lowered their weapons.

"Whether it be natives, the beasts of this territory, or stray Easterners, we have faced existential threats on all sides and seen too many of our own suffer for it," the Highlander father said. "We would like to maintain our free lifestyle. What we need is protection."

Clovis smiled at Gregory as if a joke had been told. "So I take it what you're hoping for is a merger."

"Yes, that's right. It's something we have been contemplating for some time."

"A merger with a gang?"

"Well ... yes."

"What does that make y'all, then?"

The Highlander shook his head. "I'm not sure I follow."

"Ah, I get it. You don't want to say it. Well, you know what? I'll tell you. Because I've seen this before. I've been in this position too many times to count. And each one I've come out the other side with people at my back who'd give their life for me. So here it is: y'all are a gang too. A weak, hungry gang."

Gregory didn't like that Clovis was talking down to them, but it didn't seem to scare off the Highlanders like he thought it would. Instead, Clovis's words, uttered as he paced around the circle, seemingly speaking to each of them individually, appeared to strike a chord of truth—at least in terms of acknowledging their condition. So Gregory refrained from interrupting, as much as Clovis's behavior horrified him.

"We've had no choice," a man said from behind them.

"Live free and die, or stand together and survive," the black-haired woman said with her head hung.

Clovis tilted his own head like a curious dog as he stepped toward her. She trembled in place until the moment he was at arm's length. Still Gregory suffered through his patience at his violent associate's prowling. He cringed as Clovis reached out toward the woman's face; his hand froze when she pulled away.

"May I?" Clovis asked with more softness than Gregory had ever heard from him.

Kubler flanked Clovis and whispered, "His is a blessed hand, child."

The woman nodded, and Clovis placed his worn, dirty palm on her cheek. Refraining from pushing down the bandana on her face, he grazed his thumb over the scar by her eye. "This is new, isn't it?"

The woman's shoulders were tense. "Fresh enough to remember the feeling."

With a loud, bothered breath, his hand still settled, Clovis nodded.

"Good. Wear it proud."

Their eyes locked as Clovis froze for what was, to Gregory, an awkward minute or two. When the hand came down, Clovis wound through the Highlander ranks again.

"You should all wear this moment proud. And take it from

the horse's mouth, because it's just like the preacher said: Clovis Keagan's followers aren't only provided safety. Survival ain't worth shit if you don't have a reason for it. I can give y'all that reason. And I'll tell you what: if you let me—mmm-mmm-mmm—I'll give it to you like no one else can."

With a snappy raise of his brow, some hushed laughter followed from a crowd sure to have long been lacking it. The word *genius* passed through Gregory's mind, but he fended it off. He watched in astonishment as one by one, the Highlanders lowered their weapons.

"In all seriousness, though," Clovis continued, "if y'all want to feel free, there is no other option. True freedom is something only the Murrieta Territory and my Keagan brothers have ever been able to give me. Now all I want is to give it back to each one of y'all. But I'll tell you this: Clovis Keagan doesn't merge. Nuh-uh. He takes and he brings order, but the people who try to threaten that peace—your peace—will suffer his hand. So what do y'all say?"

Some whispers were shared. "May we have a moment to discuss?"

Seeing Clovis begin to shake his head, Gregory decided to jump in. "Yes. We will await your decision."

"If y'all need it, then fine," Clovis said, climbing onto his horse above them all. "But know this: I ain't got room for any one of y'all with a second thought. Like all good things, the cost is commitment. And if you ain't ready to pay it, you ain't got nothing good coming your way."

Silence. Each one of them seemed to be waiting for another to speak up. There was no leader among them. This, Gregory realized, was their greatest flaw. It was what put them in Clovis's pocket even before he spoke a word. They had no alternative.

But what about Gregory's own tribe? Could he commit Maria and her children to this world of gangs that he felt alienated from? Could he promise them to the endless threats this life presented? Now, as he reflected on the feeling of setting the Highlander's daughter free, he understood why the woman he had professed his love to was still willing to leave him: he wasn't being the leader she knew she needed.

Without hesitation, he dug into his bag for a sheet of paper and something to write with.

He wrote the entire time the Highlanders took to deliberate, which, as expected, was brief. After their discussion, they agreed to join the ranks of the Keagan gang. At their submission, Gregory felt a sense of relief and pride. Though Clovis had sealed the deal, he knew this meeting wouldn't have occurred without him. The Keagan gang also needed the Highlanders as much as the Highlanders needed the gang. So, however he felt about Clovis, Gregory knew Clovis wouldn't let these people starve under his command. And he hoped these reinforcements would make William happy.

Clovis and a giddy Father Kubler broke apart after a brief chat following the Highlanders' decision.

"Before we leave for the safety of the Tokali Hold, my children, I would ask you all to please meet me at the cove. Together, we will make official your affirmation of commitment to Clovis and the Keagan gang, through your undying faith in the almighty Enigma."

A rush of hopeful Highlanders made their way to the cove. At a much slower pace, Gregory followed behind, Kubler beside him.

"Somehow I knew this day would come," Kubler said. "You've done well, Gregory."

"Thanks ... I guess."

"I'll be sure to tell Billy you contributed when we see him. I know his condition's been troubling you." Kubler gave him a look, which Gregory interpreted as a reference to talks they'd had in the confessional following Judith's death.

Reaching into his sack, he pulled out the quill and ink he'd used, as well as his letter. Holding it against his thigh, he signed his name at the bottom. With one last look at it, he sighed and rerolled it before handing it to Kubler. "When *you* see him, please do. And also give him this." Taking the letter, Kubler unrolled it and gave it a quick glance before stowing it away in his robe. "Please, Father. Please make sure Billy gets it."

"Of course, Gregory. He will have it. But if he asks, where should I tell him you're going?"

Clovis dashed over to them after celebrating with the Highlanders. "Going? What's this about you going?"

"I'm going to Fayette to take Maria and the kids farther west."

"Hmm. Well, may the Enigma be with you on your journey. I must go tend to the flock now." After a handshake, Kubler left for the water, where the Highlanders were waiting. The priest would soon dip Highlander after Highlander into the clear blue water. The look of ecstasy on Kubler's face made Gregory uneasy. But, just as with the scene of an explosion, Gregory couldn't take his eyes off the spectacle. It was a sight that only further solidified his decision.

"Not Blanton and Donna," Clovis said with a tilted, sidelong glance. "I know the boy and you are close. But if you even think about taking them, I swear I'll find you—"

"No, not Blanton and Donna." It was difficult to spit out, and it would be even harder to say goodbye considering how close he'd gotten with Blanton in particular, but he heard the threat in Clovis's voice. "They're Keagans, and I know it isn't my place. I'll be sure they're watched after too."

"Good. Blanton's fast approaching the age, you know? Gonna take his rightful place as one of the heads of this gang. The boy's initiation will be a proud day for Walter, too, let me tell you. One he's been talking about for some time now."

Gregory shuddered at the thought of Blanton becoming like Walter, while Clovis took a moment to revel in the idea.

"You know we're only gonna keep pushing further toward where you're running, though, right? I mean, once we clean up our current mess, we'll be continuing right along toward whatever's out there."

Gregory nodded. The madman had put into words a point he had considered. "We're all just pushing westward. Endlessly, it seems. A time will come, though, when we'll have no choice but to look back and see what we've left in our wake." For the first time, Gregory stared straight into Clovis's eyes without hesitation. "This war you're looking to fight is a terrible storm. And if all I can do to protect the people I love is outrun it, well, then it'll have to chase me to the ends of the earth."

Gregory departed before the last of the Highlanders completed their cleanse, starting back up the hill and leaving the madness behind. Thinking of Maria the whole way, he had no intention of looking back.

The southern hills went by in a blur as Dominic's horse paced up the inclines and trotted down the slopes. Hardened dirt and rocky paths made the clacking hooves a constant, rhythmic companion. He and Daniel spoke little, saving their energy for the breakneck speed. They raced to reach William before Clovis and Devin could, and they were determined not to lose.

On they went like this for days, closing as many miles between them and their goal as they could. Nearing the end, they pulled up to a stop just before a wooded area, where they spotted some water for their horses.

"Just want to be clear: when we find them, Clovis is mine," Daniel said, looking down into the water beside his ride. "You got that?"

"Whatever I have to do to get this over with and back home, I'm gonna do. So I won't discriminate when shit hits the fan, Daniel."

"But if he's alive when the dust settles?"

"If it plays out that way, then sure, he's all yours."

Daniel would experience a ton of emotion once the moment came—Dominic knew this. Whatever the plan of attack, it needed to be Dominic's, whether Daniel agreed or not, because no matter how determined Daniel felt now, he'd likely falter, overwhelmed, when the moment came. It was to be expected. Daniel wasn't a natural killer, and Clovis, however much Daniel agreed he needed to die, was his brother. This was why Dominic had come along—to ensure the trigger was pulled, one way or another.

During their brief pause, Dominic readied some of his smoke

bombs. He knew they were nearly there. Perhaps he'd have another type of performance sooner than he thought. The prospect excited him, even if it would once again accompany a fight.

When the horses were satiated, they resumed their straight shot through the trees and onward south. While Clovis needed to die, hunting him was second to finding William. Dominic hadn't started this journey with this mentality, but he had come around to it. Daniel had a point: If Clovis got to William first and corrupted his mind enough, they'd have even less chance of taking down the monster than they already did.

Their horses pushed and pushed until they saw figures at the end of the wood ahead—Charles Langston among them.

"Ready?" Dominic asked as he grabbed for a smoke bomb. "When you see him, you shoot to kill."

The click of Daniel's weapon answered his question.

A commotion brewed as they got closer—some cried, "Ambush!"—but Dominic didn't pause. He hurled the smoke bomb forward, and its cloud expanded between them and their targets until there was nothing but gray to be seen. A rush came over him as he entered the haze. Under its cover, he changed his direction a slight bit so he'd exit at an unexpected trajectory—the look on their faces would be priceless.

"Dominic Turner?" a female voice shrieked in joy.

Surprised, he burst out of the cloud at full speed. He was right on top of what he realized was a group of natives.

"Stand down!" he called to Daniel.

A spear whipped through the air just over his head and sliced into a tree, startling both him and his horse. The beast reared, causing him to lose his grip and fall off its backside. Its hooves landed, and he cowered to try and avoid being trampled by it. Soon enough, one of the natives stood over him, speaking to it in their language. She was a woman who looked a lot like the V'ahani of the North, and she wore their characteristic white.

"Y'all the ones with my brother?" Daniel asked the others as he circled around them. "Wait a second ... Elan? You're in on this? Where is he?"

Still dazed, Dominic rolled about on his back, trying to regain his senses. Recalling the moment he emerged from the smoke, he felt ashamed. In his longing to get back to the stage, he had rushed into a dangerous tactic. If they had only conducted minimal reconnaissance, they could have avoided this dangerous mishap altogether. His actions had put lives in danger—his own life included. This wasn't the stage. One truth remained: until this task was complete, there couldn't be another show, and if he didn't give it the focus it demanded, there might never be one again.

Rotating onto his side, he looked up at the young woman. "How did you know my name?"

"My brother, Hanzah, told me all about you and your tricks," she said, reaching a hand down to him to help him to his feet. "He told me what you have done."

"Oh—?"

Before he could say anything more, she wrapped him in her embrace. "I cannot thank you enough, Dominic."

Relieved, he hugged her back. "It's nice to finally meet you, Latera."

"Where's Billy?" Daniel asked from the campsite. "And ... why is *he* here?" Again, Daniel readied his gun as he pointed at Charles Langston. "Clovis and Devin—where are they?"

Dominic had all the same questions Daniel did. Once Latera let him go, he looked to her for answers. She lifted a hand, indicating that he give her a moment, and walked toward the site, searching in all directions.

"Clovis did not come. Only Devin. He left Charles with us for William, and he is at the Hold now. Winnie, Mika, did you see where William went?"

No one around the camp seemed to know.

"I told him he could have his time with Charles if he wanted it," Latera said. "I know what Charles did to him."

"You didn't," Daniel replied with a groan. "Billy!"

Remounting his horse, Daniel stormed off into the woods. Fearing the worst, Dominic did the same.

"Dominic," Latera said as he settled atop his horse. "I am sorry. I did not think he would run off. He has been in good spirits—better ones. Please, find him."

With a nod, Dominic was off. Not only was William missing, he realized, but so was Clovis.

*

The handle of the blade in William's grasp was sticky with pine tar. His mind stalled as he traced the grooves with his finger. Only the most basic observations occurred to him. The ground he sat on was messy and uncomfortable; the air was getting hotter; his skin was smooth and thin. In the midst of the smoke covering the camp, of people scrambling to protect themselves, the truth had flooded his mind: he had no reason to keep fighting, to try. Sitting there, under attack, he'd felt his deeply buried denial, his intense grief, and his damning failure all come rushing to the forefront of his mind. And with the flood came the judgment: all he had done, all his effort, was futile. So, he'd wandered off into the woods, with no particular motivation, the knife an afterthought. How a world so simple at its core could lead a man to such suffering was beyond him.

"Billy!" The shout sounded like—

Daniel?

But it couldn't be. Daniel had turned on their gang for the people of the Riverlands. He couldn't have come this far south. The thought of his allegedly traitorous brother, the person he'd most trusted his entire life, disturbed him. And though the tiniest voice inside him fought against it, his dark thoughts drowned out any lingering hope. He glanced at the knife in his hand.

"William!" This was a new voice. One he didn't recognize. But it persisted, sometimes drawing nearer and sometimes farther away.

It occurred to him that maybe he was hearing things. Lifting the blade before him to observe its jagged edges for a moment, he placed it onto his folded thigh, pointing it in the direction of his gut. Perhaps it'd be simpler this way.

"Billy!"

Warmer.

"Billy!"

Warmer.

"Billy!"

Clovis lied. What if the priest lied? What if Devin lied?

"Daniel!" He roared the instant he sensed a feeling of hope he wasn't just hearing things.

"Billy!"

He began to weep. "Daniel!"

If Daniel had turned against their gang, he would at least have his confirmation that there was no one left. If he hadn't, then William could simply see him one last time. Either way, though, there was no one else he'd rather have by his side.

"Daniel! Daniel! Daniel!"

A horse darted his way. And sure enough, there his brother was. Daniel dismounted and rushed over to him. His brother's first move was to grab for the dagger; he parried Daniel's wrist.

"I'm here, Billy. I'm here. Just give me the weapon, please. There's no need for it."

"You turned," he said, spit escaping him as he bellowed. "Devin told me."

"No—no, Clovis is the one who turned. Long ago."

"That's not … he said—" The struggle for the knife interrupted him: Daniel repeatedly tried to sneak in and take it, and William resisted less and less each time.

"Please," Daniel said, retreating with his hands raised. "You have to trust me."

"You want me to trust you? Tell me you didn't fight against the Keagan gang in Harran."

Daniel lowered his eyes and shook his head.

He did rebel. Then it's all over. Dad was right—I am nothing.

William was unable to process the confirmation of his closest brother's betrayal; his eyes watered. "You tell me!"

"We thought we could control him, but we can't, William!"

It was rare for Daniel to address him by his formal name, and this struck him to his core. No longer did he see his adventure-hardened, aged brother before him. With one word, he flashed back to their childhood, when the only person in the world who seemed to understand him was Daniel. The destiny they had envisioned for themselves was just a dream then. Like a talisman, his brother speaking his given name brought him back from the place his mind had gone, and he suddenly could hear Daniel's words crystal clear.

"Clovis burned down Adonis Morrell's home against our orders. He's murdered, and he's taken more than we ever knew. But our past ignorance is irrelevant because we let it all happen. We knew what he was capable of, and we unleashed him on this territory, thinking we held the reins. We didn't. And we, in our carelessness, did more damage than we can even imagine. So, yes, I fought against our own gang in Harran—the same gang I helped build. Because, like it or not, it's on us to stop him."

Now here it was, the destiny they'd dreamed about as children, but it had manifested in a way they never could've imagined. And somehow, after all their mistakes, after all his mistakes, Daniel still seemed to believe they could fix it.

"I don't know if I can."

"I know it's been hard. But you have to, Billy. I can't do it without you."

"You don't know, Daniel. In New Berkeley, I …"

A gentle hand came to William's head, and it weakened him again. "I know, buddy. I do. It's okay."

As Daniel pulled him into his shoulder, William's hand with

the blade shook. Daniel's other hand reached for it, and William loosened his grip until Daniel was able to snatch it and throw it away. Once it was gone, they hugged each other as if they'd only just been reunited.

The touch broke William down further, and he struggled to speak through labored breaths. "Judith … she …"

"Yeah. I know. And I'm so sorry I wasn't there to stop it."

"My child."

"What's that?" Daniel asked, releasing him as William hung his head and sobbed.

A shiver ran up his spine as if to shake the memory away. But it didn't work. "They took my child from me."

"Billy," Daniel said, shaking his head. "Are you saying Judith was pregnant?"

William breathed heavily. Daniel seemed to recognize that his sorrow was building and pulled him close again. On impact, a cry erupted from him, each salvo of which made him feel lighter. "I was finally gonna have my chance. After all the dreams I've had of it. My whole life. I was gonna give them the love we were never given. It's all I've ever wanted."

"I know it is." Daniel patted him on the back. "They know it too—wherever they are, I know they do."

The walls had closed in on the last part of his hope for Judith's return. The priest wouldn't be able to resurrect her; he could see that now. Nothing would.

"She's … she's gone. Isn't she?" For the first time, William said the words. "She's gone, and she isn't coming back."

Daniel's lips pursed, and he shook his head. "No. She isn't."

She isn't coming back.

Though he and Daniel had said it aloud, William was surprised to learn that the image of Judith didn't fade in his mind. In fact, it became more vivid. He could think of no words for her clear, emanating beauty, so he let her words ring in his head.

Everything's going to be all right, William.

"Doesn't mean you shouldn't have faith she's watching you, though," Daniel said as William saw her smile. "You can still do right by her memory. That's what she'd want, man. She'd only want for you to do what you know is right."

Brought back to the present for the first time in what seemed like ages, William was steadied by Daniel's presence. It made things simple again. The principles they had learned along the way became clear as it dawned on him that Daniel was right. Judith wouldn't have wanted him to suffer or wallow. She had shared in his vision from the moment they had met, and this wasn't it. When she had been alive, he'd promised her it'd come to fruition. He felt as if a curtain had been lifted: it was clear that he needed to see this purpose he'd set for himself through. He'd seen the truth in New Berkley, but only now, having heard that Daniel had come to the same conclusion on his own, did William fully accept it. Their future, the world he'd promised Judith, everything—it all started with stopping Clovis.

So he looked his brother in the eye, cleared his throat, and swore, "I will."

CHAPTER 10

SUNRISE AND SUNSET

The Hawleys had spread the word for the Forgotten to assemble in the roundabout of the Viridian District for an announcement. No longer would their talks be hidden away in the main hall. There was no maximum capacity on these torchlit streets, and unionists of all ages gathered around in excited tension.

As Henry watched their numbers grow from the windowed door leading to the hall's balcony, he saw a body of people starving for liberation. Their hunger was his too. Knowing he was among his own emboldened him like never before. After a week of recovery, he was feeling ready for the moment, despite some butterflies. While the bruises he had received remained and would for some time, his spirit was healthy and fierce.

Terrance stood on the balcony like a true sentinel, scanning and observing the crowd from where Henry would address them. If he had learned anything about the brothers, it was that they were opposite in more ways than not. In particular, Terrance was no talker, while Nathan, who stood inside with him, tended to speak for both of them.

"Are you ready, sir?" Nathan asked.

He stretched his limbs and took a deep breath to get in his

right frame of mind. "What happened before was a skirmish. This campaign will be a war. And tonight I'll be telling our troops that they'll be on the front lines. It's been a long time coming for me. So my question is, are *you* ready, Lieutenant?"

"My Lord above," Nathan said, shaking himself straight as if he had a chill and straightening his tie in a suave motion. "If I wasn't before, I sure am now."

"Well, good. Now how do I look?" Henry asked, presenting himself and the long-tailed coat he wore. "Leaderly?"

"Oh, well, yes, you look prepared. But, uh, sir—and not to be a pest, but—that's not a word."

"What isn't? *Leaderly*?"

At the second mention, Nathan's faced scrunched up. "Yes. That. It's just, our mom was a teacher, and when we were younger, she'd be all over us when we spoke incorrectly like that."

Though he was the opposite, Henry would forgive Nathan for correcting him.

"Well, she sounds, uh, sweet. But wait a second—you're telling me Terrance can actually string a whole sentence together?" Henry asked jokingly.

"There's more to my brother than meets the eye. And I wouldn't try to impart wisdom on an elder like yourself, but you might want to mind your vocabulary during your speeches."

Looking through the window at the crowd, Henry was ready to go. "I can respect that. Now let me leave you with a little something: the truth is, it doesn't matter what I say out there. Deep down they don't want promises of prosperity or change or even happiness. People only *think* they give a shit about those things. What they really want is a flag to rally behind. Because they need something to be a part of—a cause to join that'll make them bigger than they could otherwise be alone. And they need to be bigger so that they can fight what's holding them back from their potential. See, Nathan, the worst kind of chains are the ones we put on ourselves. But it ain't in our nature to admit fault, so we thirst for distraction and projection. By giving them those two things, we make them feel free."

"But … then they aren't really free? Right?"

"Are any of us?"

"Hm. I guess that's a good question," Nathan said with his hands behind his back. Almost on cue, Terrance glanced at them over his shoulder. "Before we go out there, I wanted to ask: have you truly given up on William and the Murrieta?"

He gazed at Nathan as Terrance approached and opened the doors for them. Then, looking straight ahead, he walked out onto the balcony without answering. That said it all.

Handling Forrest and rebuilding New Berkeley were his priorities. Only then would he think of the Murrieta—and even then for no reason other than to bring his family home.

A roar of cheers erupted as he appeared on the balcony with a wave. He raised his hands to settle the crowd.

"Thank y'all, brothers and sisters. Thank y'all for accepting me as one of your own."

"The Forgotten heed the call!" a voice shouted, followed by riotous howling.

Henry gave a warm smile and a tip of his hat in the direction it came from. "Y'all most certainly do. But I come to you tonight because it is time someone returned the favor. As y'all heard me say in the hall, the time has come for the Fraternal Forgotten to rise to new heights. Together, and only together, we can bring New Berkeley the change it deserves." He provided a moment for the applause. "So, for the first rung on our ladder toward prosperity and freedom ..." Again he stopped and allowed them a moment of painful anticipation—not too much, but just the right amount to make them sweat. "It is my pleasure to announce, first to you and soon to the rest of our city, my candidacy in New Berkeley's first mayoral election"—hysteria ensued—"to be held in six months' time. It'll be announced outside the district for the first time, during a new rally at the very same factory where they threatened to silence us with their guns."

The Forgotten chanted in unison. "Em-o-ry! Em-o-ry! Em-o-ry!"

A spark at the center of the roundabout lit into a flame. A shadowy figure held up the source of the ignition. From his balcony, Henry couldn't see who stood there. In response, the people scattered but soon settled and quieted.

In the silence, the figure spoke. "I, too, would like to announce my candidacy for the mayoral race. And unlike my challenger, I'd like to do so from the place I'm most comfortable: among you all."

Recognizing Jimmy's voice, Henry tightened his grip around the railing as if it were Forrest's throat. "That's not—"

"Forgive him, though. Despite all he's told us, he's still getting used to being on this side of the Viridian line, the same way I've told you all I had to," Jimmy said, staring straight up at Henry. "Oh wait … did he not tell *y'all* yet? Gee, I'm sorry, Henry. I thought you'd come clean by now."

This wasn't supposed to be happening. Forrest's resistance to the cause would have been difficult enough to overcome.

"Don't listen to this nonsense, brothers and sisters," Henry said. "He's only bitter because a new day has come, and he isn't prepared to climb with us."

A portion of the Forgotten gave a dull call of support, but he could feel how uncertain the crowd had become.

"And how can we trust a man who's lied about his entire background?"

A separate group echoed Jimmy's question.

He couldn't lose them. The accent needed to end now for better or worse. "I didn't lie. I had to hide my identity when I came back to New Berkeley because Forrest—"

Half the crowd jeered, half still voiced support for him.

"Oh, here we go. It's always Forrest, isn't it? The source of all your ills." Though Jimmy's words referenced him, they were delivered for those around them.

"Don't let him misguide you, comrades," Henry responded. "When I returned, Forrest would have had me killed because of how dangerous he considers me to be. And of course he's our enemy, you fool. I would question your intentions to suggest otherwise."

The retort was a good one, and he mentally patted himself on the back for it.

"The point is that you don't know a thing about the systems in Alvenika that you keep bragging about. So how could you ever hope to implement them here?"

Henry narrowed his eyes at Jimmy. "I have six months to prove my abilities, and I swear to each of you on my life I'll do so. I will earn your trust and show you that together we can rise like a phoenix against the likes of Forrest and all his cronies. We'll build a new, better New Berkeley in the wake of the one you all know he's drowned in a pool of lifeless cement. If that's the future you want, you simply can't afford to take a different path than the one Emory Wallace will pave for you."

The crowd seemed somewhat receptive again, and there was much less pleasure on Jimmy's sour face than when he'd first revealed Henry's identity. If there was one thing Henry felt good about, it was the advantage his charisma gave him.

"Six months, Henry," Jimmy said. "You've got yourself a race."

*

When Gregory returned to the mansion, he jumped off his horse and stormed up the stairs of the porch with a smile on his face. The inside was quiet, with no one to be found.

"Maria!" he called.

No response.

The place was big; he started his search in the bedrooms. "Maria!"

Nothing.

Back downstairs, he passed through several other rooms until reaching the kitchen. "Maria!"

There, through an open window, he could hear the Abigale children laughing in the backyard. He ran for the door.

It was a bright day, and sure enough, there she was. Like an angel, she watched over her children as they played. For him, too, they were precious cargo—far more important than the rush of conquest and exploration. "Maria!"

"Gregory, h—"

He pulled her into his arms and kissed her before she could finish. "Let's get out of here."

"What?" she asked with a smile.

"I love you, and I want to take you and the kids to start a new life."

"Are you serious?"

"Of course I am. We can go west. We can make roots and live together as a family, and I'll take care of you all every day, just like we dreamed about in our talks. I thought we could have all that here, but this is no place for it."

Looking out at her three children, she paused for a moment.

Had he overwhelmed her? "I understand if it's too much, and—"

"Okay."

"Okay?"

"Okay. Yes. I love you, too, Gregory. We'll go with you." She jumped into his arms, and he kissed her until she pulled back. "But when?"

"Now."

"Now? Like, right now?"

"Yes, right now."

"But aren't you going to say goodbye to Blanton and Donna?" The wind was ripped from Gregory's sails. William's young cousins had been on his mind since Clovis had mentioned them, but he didn't know how he'd leave them behind.

"I will. We all will."

Over the next hour, they rushed to gather their things, and Gregory had a carriage prepared. Once they were all ready, Maria loaded Henrietta, Florence, and Francis into the wagon, and Gregory started them off toward Fayette's town. The last stop would be the circus, where Blanton was training with the strongman, while Donna, ever dependent on her brother's presence, watched.

Maria turned to him and placed a hand on his arm when they arrived. "Do you want me to go with you?"

The threat Clovis made came back to him. "Let me break it to them first, and then I'll bring them out to say goodbye."

By now he knew the location of the strongman's tent, and he marched straight toward it.

The promises Gregory had made to William to protect his loved ones in his stead came back to him. The times Blanton had confided in him came back to him. The memories of his son, Leroy, came back to him.

At the entrance of the tent, he lifted the yellow drape over his head and saw them.

In the middle of a curl, Blanton froze and perked up. "Gregory!"

Donna sat up. "Why are you all dressed up?"

With desperation, he shoved the words out of his mouth. "Hey, guys. I just came by to, uh—to tell you the Abigales and I are gonna be leaving Fayette. We'll be seeking somewhere quiet to settle. Somewhere far from this dangerous place."

The barbell fell to the floor, and Blanton walked toward the exit of the tent as if the lesson had ended. "When are we going?" he asked.

"We?" Gregory shook his head and steeled himself. "No. I'm sorry, but you can't come with us."

"But why not?" Donna asked.

"Because you're Keagans." His voice cracked as he said it.

"Well, what if we don't want to be Keagans?" Donna asked again.

"I—" He stopped as he realized Blanton hadn't spoken first. "Donna, did you just … ?"

The brother and sister gave each other a surprised look before each smiled at him. Then, as if it were the most casual moment in the world, Donna shrugged. "We're coming with you, Gregory, whether it's permitted or not."

"I …" Donna's steadfastness stunned him. He would have expected this from Blanton, but he hadn't perceived the impact he'd had on them collectively. It seemed Donna felt the same affection for him as he felt for her, perhaps thanks to how much he'd helped her brother. These two felt like his family. *Right. Family.* "I can't ask you to leave your family."

"You aren't," Blanton said. "This is our choice."

"So?" Donna asked, as she pulled up the tent curtain to leave. "Where to?"

To hell with Clovis.

"West," Gregory said, his heart full, warm, and prepared for this responsibility. "We're going west."

And they would. Gregory didn't know what the future held for them, but he knew he would do everything he could to build them a life in which they could live free and in peace, away from the struggle to come. Most of all, though, he knew they'd be together. And in the end, he felt that's all any of them wanted.

The hour came and went. With William accounted for, it was time for Latera and her followers to return to talks to free their people. Again, the same four entered the field: William and Hammond ahead of her and Elan beside her. Elan would only be a further bargaining chip now that he had established his allegiances. Their new comrades, Dominic Turner and Daniel Keagan, remained behind in the trees with the others. Daniel had made it clear that his Keagan ties were all but severed and that he'd have no leverage, especially with Devin at the Hold whispering in Walter's ear.

Within minutes of their emergence from the wood, a bevy of faces appeared on the wall of the stronghold. Malik and Adila returned to their place beside Walter and now Devin. Alongside them were a string of armed guards—more than before, it seemed.

"Well? Here we are again," Latera said, menacingly grasping her spear behind William. "And you have had your time to reflect. What value have you decided to place on the life of your leader?"

"I told y'all, the deal's off," Walter said to cheers from his men.

William resisted Hammond's grip, which Latera was sure was for show.

"Walter! What the fuck are you doing?" William shouted.

Latera's fists balled as she stared at Walter.

"You've been through a lot, Billy," Devin called from behind Walter. "And we're gonna bring you back from it. Clovis is sure of it. But we're just not going to surrender to this so-called chieftess."

"She just does not have the control she thinks she does," Adila said next.

No control?

As William replied again, Latera's fiery gaze shifted to Elan's mother, one of the leading voices of the Tokali. With instantaneous focus, she ripped into Adila's mind. Before her now were Walter and Devin—both unsuspecting and vulnerable to the pistol in Adila's grasp. The hand around the grip was sweaty. She was breathing heavily, and her fingers were dancing on the handle.

Do it. Finish it. Kill them both.

A pain slipped into her head. With her free hand, she rubbed her eyelids.

"Adila?" Her stomach dropped as beside her, Malik placed a hand on her arm. "Are you all right?"

The greatest of care in our choices. Remember Elan.

Without a moment's hesitation, Latera released Adila and retreated into her own body. Back in the field, she continued to contemplate her mother's words and the impact her power had made on Elan; she brought a hand to her knee. A heat flash darkened her vision of the scene for an instant. The Keagans continued spitting back and forth, tensions flaring as she regained her senses.

"We're going to come down there and rescue you, Billy," Walter said, waving a hand. The gates to the Hold started to open.

"No, goddammit. You heard them. They're going to kill me!"

Devin came forward. "They wouldn't dare, sir. Don't you worry."

Hammond tensed, with William in his grasp, as a mass of armed Tokali and Keagans emerged from across the field. "What do we do, Latera?"

"Let him go," Elan said. "It is our only option now. She is finished."

If Adila pointed a gun at Walter, she'd question her own sanity the moment I released her. The same way Elan did when I made him say what he didn't believe. It can't be her. But Malik? He is more empathic to Elan and his friends—I have seen it during my time in the Hold.

"Wait," Latera said aloud, turning her attention to Malik, who was still consoling his wife. Latera called on him, snapping out of her mind.

Observing his hand on Adila's shoulder, she noted she was atop the Hold again.

"Yes," Adila said, grasping her forehead. From the corner of Malik's eye, Latera noticed Adila's pistol was holstered again. "I think I am fine. I just—the heat got to me."

"It is going to be okay," Malik said.

"I know, I said I will be—"

"No, Adila." Latera flashed to the motivation she had decided Malik would be able to accept. "The boys … I cannot see them punished for this."

"Elan will be fine. He admitted his mistake."

"You know that is not enough."

"What are you saying?" Adila asked.

"It is going to be okay."

Malik grabbed the gun from Adila's waist.

"Malik!" she cried.

Now with a pistol in each hand, he approached Walter and Devin and touched one barrel to each head. The click of the hammer caused both men to jump and turn with tense hesitation.

"What in the hell do you think you're doing?" Walter asked, a frustrated calm in his tone.

Adila shook, eyes bulging, but Latera knew she would at least comprehend Malik's decision. "Malik, stop this!"

Since other Keagan guards were positioned along the wall, Latera knew she needed to keep Malik covered. Grabbing Walter by the throat, she backed up to a wall with the other gun still on Devin, who sported a snide glare.

"Keep your hands where I can see them," Malik said. Devin raised them. "This ends now, Walter. Give the order: release the V'ahani and let the Tokali below go as they please."

"The fucking balls on you," Walter said. Latera could laugh at the irony. "Do you know what Clovis is gonna do to you and yours when he finds out about this?"

"If he cares at all about his cousin or his brother, he will do nothing," Malik replied, his grip tightening. "Give the order."

As Latera turned Malik's attention down to the field, she could see the gang members and warriors were halfway to her and her comrades. By now, the other Tokali in hiding had joined them, including Gannon, who had his rifle raised. All of them were shouting in desperation at her body, trying to shake her out of her trance. She'd have to find a way to explain that, but now, she had other things to take care of.

The veins in Walter's reddened head bulged as she tightened Malik's grip. "Do it now!" Malik said.

"This is war," Walter replied with a laugh, causing her stomach to turn. "Tell them to stand down, Devin."

"Sir?"

In a swell of relief, Latera loosened Malik's grip so Walter could speak up. "Stand down! All of y'all! Gather the northern savages and let them free. We'll slaughter them later."

The Tokali guards and Keagan gang froze at first, but after a moment, they dutifully commenced their retreat back to the Hold. Inside its walls, the V'ahani—already celebrating their freedom— were rounded up in no time. At long last, the cries of joy Latera had prayed for filled the air.

His guns still raised, Malik smiled at his wife. "Come now, Adila. It is time for us to leave."

"Leave? I cannot leave—I will not," Adila said, to Latera's dismay. She worried about the impact this would have on Malik. "This is my home."

"But we have no choice."

"He's right," Walter said, rubbing and stretching his neck. "If y'all two want to live, you'd better run with the rest of them."

She is a child of the Mother—just like the rest of us. I am responsible now.

"You would let the boys go north alone?" Malik asked his wife. Despite her disdain for Adila, Latera hoped she would make the better choice rather than stay.

Adila folded her arms. "I will not bow to the will of the V'ahani, Malik. After all we have suffered to broker this unity, all the sacrifices our people have made … I will not let them be in vain."

"Don't you worry," Devin said as he sauntered toward Adila. "We'll keep her safe while you're gone."

Malik's grip tightened again. "You will not touch her."

Waving his fingers, Devin chirped, "But my hands, they are so difficult to control at times."

Enough. No more running from them. It is time they answered for their crimes.

"Well, she will not be within their reach," Malik said.

"Didn't she just—?"

"I am staying. She is staying," Malik interrupted Devin. "But the same cannot be said for *either* of you. No, you will go back with the V'ahani, and you will answer for your crimes. William Keagan will stay, and he will lead our people as we intended."

To Latera's relief, Adila's expression lightened as Walter and Devin went pale. "You fucking coward," Walter raged. "I swear to God I'll be back, and when I am, every single one of you will be—"

With a crack, the butt of Malik's pistol knocked Walter out cold.

"Any of your own objections?" Malik asked Devin.

Without a word, Devin raised his hands into the air.

While the Tokali warriors followed Malik's order to take Walter and Devin to Latera, William told his own men to stand down. Latera had to bear an authentic hug and kiss—uncomfortable, at least for her—with Adila before she was sure the exchange was complete. Looking beyond the walls, she marveled at the enthralled masses of the V'ahani of the Riverlands, sprinting toward her group and her.

It was done. And she needed to be present for this moment.

Releasing Malik, she returned to her body and fought off the initial dizziness.

Though Hammond and Gannon tried to question what had happened to her the moment she came to, Winona and Mika took one look into her eyes and together simply said, "Go."

With that, she charged toward her people, leaving the Tokali behind. She knew Winnie and Mika would quickly make an excuse to cover up what they thought were her "seer" abilities before they, too, would run to join their people.

Like a lone soldier rejoining her army on a battlefield, Latera was mobbed with hugs and tears and laughter and smiles from faces she recognized even though they were thinner than they had been back home. A small figure grappled her legs from behind, nearly causing her to trip. She knelt and hugged the young girl back.

"Latera!" the girl cheered. "We have waited and prayed, and you have come!"

"Every day I dreamed of seeing you all again, my love. I am so proud of you."

A shadow cast over them. When she looked up, she recognized the girl's mother from her dream.

"What did we say we would tell Latera when we saw her?" the mother asked the girl, with the crowd listening.

"By the grace of the Mother, thank you, my Chieftess." The young girl kneeled before her—the daughter of Chieftain Arkouda and once a simple nurse—and all other V'ahani in the field followed. It would be her greatest honor to lead her people back north to their rightful home, even if it was the last thing she did as their leader.

*

With the V'ahani of the Riverlands accounted for and in preparations to leave the Hold, Latera had two things left to address before their journey back home. First was the state of the Hold and what it would mean for both the Tokali and the future of the Keagan gang. It was her duty to ensure balance would remain, and if the wishes of all the Mother's children were respected, she would feel secure in her departure.

Scanning the masses of the Tokali, the V'ahani, and Keagan gang members, she soon spotted William, Daniel, and Dominic standing and talking in front of the gates of the Hold.

"A word?" she asked as she approached them.

"Of course," William said, his face filled with a warmth it hadn't been since she'd captured him.

As surprised as she was to admit it, she was glad to see him in good spirits. "First, I wanted to thank you for assisting me in freeing my people. For you to do so after all the effort you took to capture them in the first place—"

"I ain't usually one to say it, but I can't tell you how sorry I am for all that, and—"

"No," she interrupted, "please. Let us not dwell on what is behind. What I have come to discuss is what is ahead of us."

"Peace," Daniel said. "Pure, lasting peace."

"Peace with your men still residing at the Hold?" Latera asked. While pleased with the answer, she was still concerned about the best interest of the Tokali.

"Only if the Tokali will have us." William shook his head. "And our stay won't go a day past Clovis's return."

"With his defeat in Harran, he'll have no choice but to head here, considering all his remaining men are here," Daniel added. "We'll be able to keep them under control, though, and capture him as soon as he arrives."

"I want to believe you, but how can I be sure?"

"Because I won't leave until it's over, Latera," Dominic said. Reflecting on all he'd done for her brother in the past, Latera recognized that it was exactly what she needed to hear. "And you better believe I'm itching to get back home to Harran."

"Thank you. I am sure Hanzah will be awaiting your return."

After a nod from Dominic, William stepped toward her. The look in his eyes was the opposite of the one she'd seen at the mansion. It was softer and more careful, but, at the same time, stronger.

"You gotta know, even after we deal with Clovis, all I ever want—all I've ever wanted—is peace and trade. When I saw what Adonis Morrell had with y'all natives in the Riverlands, I just ... I thought it'd be easier. I was raised to be jealous and greedy and resentful, and that's the truth. And I've paid dearly for it, for my decisions. But now that I have, I can see those things only blinded me to what I wanted most—the thing everyone here deserves— and that's freedom. Freedom is what this place, this territory, has come to represent to all us Easterners."

Latera reached out her hand, and his met hers to shake it. "And we will have it. We will all have it."

As she shook hands with Daniel and Dominic as well, she felt confident that the Hold would be in good hands for now. "Along with Dominic's presence, I am sure you know I will have eyes in the sky as you await Clovis's arrival. I trust you will keep these people safe in the meantime."

"For trade and protection, look no further than the Keagan Company," Daniel said.

"What's that?" William asked.

"Rebranding." Daniel gave a wink.

Hearing what she needed to hear, Latera felt ready to address her second concern. "I will see you all again soon," she said before leaving them.

Returning to her people, she saw that the V'ahani were all set to go. Knowing she was running out of time, she went to find the Tokali boys, who were assisting her people in preparing for their journey. She gave her greatest thanks and gratitude to Warrick, Gannon, and Shelton, all of whom decided it was best to stay at the Hold, since William and Daniel Keagan would oversee it.

Hammond, who was also standing among them, was the last to hug her. "Goodbye, Latera."

"Hammond, I—"

"It is okay," he said, holding her close in an embrace as she tried but failed to pull back to look at him. "You do not need to say it. I understand. Our people are just different. I have accepted that."

"But I—"

"You have a responsibility to your people as chieftess." He softened his grip, and she found herself looking up into his big hazel eyes. They made her smile now, just like they had the first time she saw them. "I would not expect you to bear the added burden of having a Tokali lover to explain to them. Not after what we have done. As much as I want to be with you, I could never ask—"

Beaming like she had never beamed before, she shut him up the only way she could think to: by smashing her lips against his. In his surprise, he was slow to react, but soon enough he was pulling her close as their tongues danced to an elegant tune all their own.

A cough from one of the other boys ripped them out of their daze. They all stood in a line with obnoxious grins on their faces. Hammond blushed.

"Are you not going to say goodbye to your friends, Hammond?" Gannon asked.

Hammond gave her an excited, questioning look, to which she held his hand and nodded. "I do not know what is to come, Hammond. In fact, my road might never be a steady one. But I can tell you there is not anyone else I would rather have by my side to walk it."

"Well, Latera, for as long as you will have me, you will never have to face it alone," he said, planting another, gentler kiss upon her lips. When he released her, he turned back to his friends. "Now just let me get my things and say my goodbyes to these crybabies. The Mother knows how miserable their lives will be without me!"

Once Hammond was ready to go, it seemed all Latera's affairs were as in order as they could be. The Keagan *Company* would await the weakened, murderous criminal Clovis Keagan to bring him to justice; her people were finally safe; and the boy she loved was by her side. She'd have to wait and see wherever her Widow's Walk would take her. But for now, it was time for her long-awaited, mad dash home.

CHAPTER 11

WHEN YOU SOUND THE CALL

The march back to the Riverlands was more of a charge. It seemed neither as long nor as arduous as the journey south had, because they all knew that at the end of it they'd find the home, family, and friends they'd all been waiting for so long to see again. Latera guided them over hills and plains, through stormy nights and calm ones, and ensured they were fed and hydrated the entire way. The first signs of the dense forests of the Riverlands were met with feverish enthusiasm. Running along the paths as they drew closer, Latera came to a halt at the head of the group when she spotted two massive grizzlies standing on either side of the trail. A smile extended across her face. The beasts remained still and on all fours, their eyes glowing as she approached. When she stood within five feet of them, they rose to their hind legs and let out powerful roars.

Looking back at her people, Latera howled out in chorus with the bears, her fist balled above her head. Not a single V'ahani failed to join in on the exuberant cheer. With their support, she sprinted forward again through the sentinel grizzlies—her people were close. The trail continued until she saw the first shelters of her home. "V'ahani!" she cried.

The first white-clad warriors from the northern V'ahani camps of the Mountainlands and the Great Fortress emerged from their tents to meet the rush of their lost brothers and sisters. Latera ran into the camp, unable to process her emotions, and hugged the first person she saw. A shy, hesitant Hammond stayed close behind her, and she introduced him as an ally.

"Grand Chieftain," the warrior called in her embrace. "The V'ahani of the Riverlands have returned!"

With so much joy to absorb, she let the man go and sat down to bask in the earth of her home.

"Latera!" She rose up on her knees when she recognized Hanzah's voice.

"Hanzah—oh!" Just as she saw him, he tackled her to the ground in a hug. In her arms, her brother sobbed. "Oh, Hanzah," she gave a warm laugh, "do not cry, brother."

"I am not crying. I just thought …" he paused with a sniffle. "I thought I would never see you again."

"Well, I am here now, and—"

"There she is!" Uncle Orrin hustled over merrily.

Rising to her feet, she met another hug—and she was certain there would be too many more to count. "Uncle Orrin!"

"There are no words, my dear. Although, at the same time, there are too many words. And I could not possibly say them all—though I wish I could—because you deserve each one for what you have been able to accomplish. And to think about how proud your father would be is just … it is just …" Orrin took a moment to catch his breath. "It is just amazing, my dear. Amazing. And beyond me, to be frank. I cannot even fathom it. That is how much it blows my mind. I cannot begin to comprehend how you managed it, but you saved them. You saved them all. And you would not give up, and … oh my … I do not know … but you know what I am trying to say. Well done, I suppose."

As Latera laughed, Hanzah wiped away his tears and smiled. "Oh, how I have missed you, Uncle," she said. Now, like never before, she noted the chieftain regalia Orrin and the rest of their leaders wore. Despite her exaltation for the return of her people, a part of her couldn't help but wonder if she'd be given the same formal recognition. Whether Grand Chieftain Varek would go against tradition in doing so would be a question answered another time.

Stroking his beard, Orrin gave a little bow before rising and jumping at the sight of Hammond. "And who is this orange-clad fellow, my dear?" he asked.

"Hello, Chieftain Orrin. My name is Hammond," Hammond said, coming forward and giving a bow.

"Hammond is my friend. He also opposes the Keagan-Tokali alliance, so he has come back with us to stay." Latera knew the clarification would be necessary, especially for her brother, who would resent the Tokali after Elan's betrayal of the V'ahani of the Riverlands.

"Your *friend*, you say?" Orrin asked, curling his whiskers with a coy grin that made Latera blush. "Well, it is a pleasure to meet you, *friend* of Latera. Please know that if at any time you have a hankering to hurt my niece or try to convince any of our people to go south with you, I will have one of our grizzlies turn you into a four-course meal. Otherwise, welcome to the Riverlands!"

Hanzah laughed.

"No hankering to speak of, Chieftain," Hammond said with certainty Latera found cute.

"Please, forgive me, Latera. I should allow your brother and you some more time to catch up while I welcome the others back. I will return to you with a mouth full of questions and ears eager for answers once this all settles down. Hammond, how about you come with me, and I will introduce you around?"

"I would very much appreciate that, Chieftain," Hammond said, exchanging a nervous glance with Latera, who chuckled.

As Orrin and Hammond left, Latera faced her brother with a thumb pointed at her departing uncle. "So, how much have your listening skills had to improve since you reached the Mountainlands?"

Her brother's lips pursed in exaggerated consideration. "Not enough."

"I can imagine. He is a piece of work. Did you learn anything from him, though?"

"Hmm." As Hanzah scratched at his messy hair, she noticed it had grown a bit longer. "Oh, yeah—he taught me the difference between a frog and a toad."

Her brows furrowed, which made Hanzah chuckle. "Um ... what?"

"I can explain."

"Well, I would hope so. After all this time, for *that* to be your first answer ... I mean, it is not surprising coming from a student of Uncle Orrin. But still."

"So," he said, sighing, "do you want to know?"

"The difference between a frog and a toad? Are you kidding? I need to know!"

From overhead, a small shadow zipped by. Despite the hysteria of the crowd running around her, Latera noticed it. The crow landed on the shelter beside her and looked right at her.

"I see you," she heard the crow say.

"Who are you?" Hanzah asked, which surprised her since she hadn't realized her brother had noticed it.

The bird craned its neck. "The River White," it hissed.

Mama.

Grabbing Hanzah by the wrist, Latera started off through the camp and to the trees to head toward the river. The crow flew overhead at the same time.

"What is going on?" Hanzah asked.

Without an answer, she raced on until they burst out of the trees and onto the riverbank. Scanning to her left, to her right, across the running water, and back from whence they came, she did not see what she was hoping to see. "This is where it happened," she said.

"Yes, this is where they killed him."

"No, I—"

"Hello again, my Hanzah," Nova said. "My little chieftain."

The little chieftain—as he was born to be.

Despite being stung by the reference, Latera was glad to see Nova emerge from the trees behind them.

"Mama?" Hanzah asked, just as she had.

As they raced into each other's arms, Latera turned and spotted Kai hiding behind the tree from where Nova had appeared. With a grin, she waved, and he did the same. After reuniting with Hanzah, Nova was light on details in her explanation to him for why she had disappeared and why she'd have to leave so soon, without returning to the rest of their V'ahani family. Proud of her mother for revealing herself to Hanzah, Latera assisted in reassuring him in whatever way she could. Nova had just overcome not only her own fear but one of Latera's as well: it gave her hope for her newfound destiny. Despite whatever Calling she might one day receive, maybe she would be able to find a way to live the life she had come to desire. For Hammond's sake, at least, she would be sure to try.

*

"Take me to them," Latera said to Winona, whom she had found once she had finished reuniting with all the V'ahani she'd missed.

"To who?" Hanzah asked. Her brother had been flanking her at her request.

Before the trees to the south of the camp, Winona stood and scanned the grounds. "You do not think we should tell the grand chieftain we have them?"

Though she told herself this was about seeking justice, she couldn't deny a feeling of resentment for her leaders' lack of formal recognition for all she'd done. She'd earned it, she thought. "They are not his to judge."

I do not need their formalities. I am the Walking Widow.

Back through the woods they went, until they came upon a growling grizzly, who was stalking Walter Keagan, Devin Turpin, and Charles Langston, each tied to a tree. Squatting off to the left beside a boulder was Mika, whose eyes were rolled back as he controlled the beast. At their approach, it turned to spot them. Once it did, it stood on its hind legs over the men and let out a saliva-showering roar in their faces. They each cowered at the display—much to Latera's content.

Under the watchful eye of Mika's furry escort, and with the help of Hanzah and Winona, she had the captives' feet untied and marched them through the woods and toward Harran. The sleepy town appeared empty when they entered, until their presence caught the attention of a couple swinging on a pair of rocking chairs. One by one, others noticed and congregated in the streets, forming a small mass before her bunch. The collective scorn in their gaze as they glared at the men who had wronged them hung like a dark smog.

"I have a gift for the Morrells," Latera said to them. "Three gifts."

From within the crowd, she could see people ushering Jeannie and Harrison Morrell to the front.

"Hanzah, Latera, welcome to Harran," Harrison greeted them with a warm salute. Latera was glad to see him again; she knew him because he had frequently carried out his father's trade routes with her people.

"Charles," Jeannie acknowledged him with a blank expression. "Walter, Devin, welcome to Harran."

Circling behind a trembling Charles Langston, Latera kicked him in the back of his leg, and he shrieked as he fell to his knees. "We have come to let you know the hand of justice is yours now."

"Just put a bullet in our heads, and let's get this over with," Walter said to the Morrells.

Hanzah shoved him from behind. "You will join Charles on your knees and beg for such mercy."

The grizzly grunted as Latera turned to Devin. "You too."

He smiled at her and came to his knees, puckering his lips on the way down. "You don't have to tell me twice."

Disgusted, she wanted this to be done as soon as possible. "If it is the grizzlies they have earned, just say the word," she said to the Morrells.

Jeannie and Harrison took a brief moment to confer with each other before facing the men again. "We've been through so much here in the Riverlands—us Easterners and our allied V'ahani alike," Harrison said, addressing all in attendance. "I know I speak for Jeannie as much as myself when I say we've dreamed of this moment since our family's senseless murder. These men have taken from us what we loved most in this world. And yet, knowing what we know now, we're certain seeking vengeance upon them will only make us lose more of what makes us better than them. With all we've been able to rebuild, we're not willing to give them the satisfaction."

While Latera understood their choice, she knew she could not let these men go free. "Very well. So we will take them, then?"

"Yes," Jeannie said. "To the coldest, darkest cell your people have constructed at the Great Fortress. So they may feel the bite of our northern winters for the rest of their days."

Unable to think of a better solution, and happy that this one would give her allies their closure, Latera pulled Walter to his feet. When he had risen, he shook her hand off of him. "You can do what you want with me, girly, but you won't win, you hear me?" His eyes were bloodshot, and he became frantic. "None of y'all will! Clovis will be back—I promise y'all he will. For any of y'all who want to be shown mercy, this is your only chance to stop this. Set us free now, before it's too late."

Not a peep was made.

"Enough," Hanzah said, yanking Walter's wrists by the rope that bound them.

Walter kicked Hanzah to the ground. "Fuck you."

Off Walter ran, kicking up dirt as Latera hurried to help Hanzah up. Everyone else stared at Walter—everyone except the grizzly, which raced after him. The man didn't make it ten yards before the bear leveled him to the ground. Again he cowered as Mika's beast let out its merciless cry. This time, though, he whimpered and begged for his life.

The crowd was entertained, as was Latera. To see her tormentor, the one who had laughed at her in her imprisonment, in this position was fantastic, but at the same time it was almost too pathetic to enjoy. Spinning a finger at her comrades to signal them to leave, she said, "Let us gather these sad men and give them what sad men deserve."

"No, please," Charles said, stopping everyone in their tracks. "They'll kill me if I'm locked up with them. Jeannie, Harrison, please."

Throughout Walter's pitiful spectacle, Devin had remained silent, wearing his strange little grin. "He's right. We will."

Tugging on Harrison's sleeve, Jeannie pointed to a pile of rubble. "The jail. He can stay in the jail."

At first Harrison looked confused, but then he nodded. "Good idea. Charles, you will serve your time in our prison once it's been rebuilt—by you, under our oversight."

As Charles stared dejectedly at the remains of the jail, Harrison and Jeannie sent two women standing by them in the crowd to collect him.

"And thank you for this, Latera," Harrison said. "Our appreciation here in Harran for the V'ahani is limitless, and like I've said, we look forward to rebuilding where our fathers left off. I hope you all know that."

"We do know it," Latera said, putting an arm around Hanzah's shoulder. "The Morrells will always be the V'ahani connection to our Eastern allies. We will be in touch soon, my friends."

Gesturing for Winona, Hanzah, and the grizzly to usher Walter and Devin back to their camp, Latera felt clear for having dealt this justice. Though Grand Chieftain Varek wouldn't be happy to find out she'd withheld them, any reaction he had would pale in comparison to the way he'd treat their prisoners, anyway. If he even allowed Walter and Devin to reach the Great Fortress alive, they'd be made to wish they hadn't for the rest of their days. And she wouldn't lose any sleep over it.

*

The summer was winding down, and the V'ahani had been gone for a few weeks. The Hold was quiet now—especially at this hour. Every morning at the break of dawn, William would come to sit atop the wall of its entry gate with Daniel. For hours they'd stay there observing the new day's rise. The Hold was a more peaceful place with them helming it, and his mind was the same. For the first time in a long time, he no longer felt alone. He and Daniel finally had achieved the vision they'd had when they had first left New Berkeley all those years ago. Even Dominic Turner seemed to be enjoying his time here; he performed for the Tokali in the afternoons.

This particular day was going to be a nice one—William could see it in the cloudless, dark, navy-blue sky. As he sat, he thought of Judith, like he did every morning. But he did so in a healthy state of mind, reflecting on his fondest memories. He vowed that with every step he would take, he would do what he could to honor Judith and build the world the way the two of them had envisioned it. In the meantime, he would try to forgive himself for living while she did not.

The trees sang as a gust whistled through the large field before the Hold, and the air was cool on his skin. Noticing a bed of goose bumps lining his arm, William ran a fingertip over it. A faint sound snapped him out of his distraction.

"You hear that?" he asked Daniel.

Sitting up wordlessly and squinting ahead, Daniel pointed forward. The noise was coming from the forest, and he could make out a silhouette emerging from behind a tree—then another, then ten more, then hundreds more.

In bewilderment, he turned to Daniel. "Hey, am I dreaming, or are you seeing this?"

"I'm seeing it," Daniel replied.

When he honed in, he could make out the hats and bandanas on the faces of the stumbling walkers.

The Highlanders … Gregory. He did it.

While this secondary objective had faded from his mind, he supposed it couldn't hurt to have the extra support on his side. These new followers would help them build, and he would give them safety and community in return. As far as he saw it, the more people he took in, the easier it would be to show his intent was pure.

Hundreds of people swarmed the field, and about a quarter of them were on horseback. As he scanned the riders for Gregory, he spotted Father Kubler in his robes atop a black mare. Though William still wore his Cereb pendant, he kept it beneath his shirt now by his heart. The priest would notice soon enough, but it wouldn't matter.

Walking along the wall from left to right, William kept scanning the crowd, but Gregory was nowhere to be found. One last rider burst out of the trees. As William ran over to see who it was, the Highlanders parted ways to allow him through. This person, too, wore a bandana and hat. Once he reached the front a few paces ahead of the rest, he slowed his horse to the speed of the others. William's stomach dropped as he glared right down into the newcomer's eyes. Beside him, Daniel launched out of his seat and charged down the stairs. Before the rider removed the bandana and lifted the hat, William knew: Clovis.

"Brother!"

The mood took an immediate turn. With Clovis and Kubler guiding the Highlanders, he had no idea what their sentiments and motivations could be. He only knew that he would somehow have to take control. It was like Daniel had said: they let it happen, and they had no choice but to stop Clovis.

Racing after Daniel, he called to him. "Where'll you go?"

"Not far, but he's protected now, and it won't be safe here," Daniel said as he ran through the streets. "As much as we've calmed these men down here at the Hold, they'll still react to him. With these new recruits he's managed to bring in too … I don't know. But I'll stay close, okay? And I'll have Dominic."

Outside the shelter Dominic resided in, Daniel stopped.

"We're still gonna stop him, right?" William asked.

"Or die trying." Daniel pulled him in for a hug. "I love you, Billy. I'll be in contact soon, okay?"

"Love you, too, Daniel."

"Now go on and distract him so I can get out of here in one piece, yeah?"

With a solemn nod, William ran off to do as Daniel said. Clovis soon entered the Hold with the Highlanders, to a false welcome from William. The Highlanders filed in gleefully, to the confusion of the Tokali and Keagan gang members. There was work to be done in many ways.

After some time of forced assimilation, William decided he needed a moment alone to think, but Father Kubler intercepted him. "William, it is so fantastic to see you. How was your journey?"

"Yeah, it was fine."

"We will talk more in the days to come. For now, I wanted to give you this." Kubler reached into his robe and pulled out a rolled up paper. "It is from Gregory—"

"Where is he? Is he all right?"

Kubler gave a smile and a nod but no words.

"Well?"

"He is. And he was a help in securing the allegiance of the Highlanders. He ached over how we would do it and wanted to ensure it was done for you, William. But I am sorry to say he has left and taken the Abigales with him."

"Left? Left where?"

"He said he was going west—to find a place to settle down away from all this. Please do not worry, though. I gave him a blessing and ensured he goes with faith in his heart before we parted ways."

Despite the priest's self-important remark, William's heart warmed. He was happy his friend hadn't come; Gregory had earned a break from all this. After parting ways with Kubler, William wasted no time in returning to his place atop the walls of the Hold. In the most secluded spot he could find, he read Gregory's letter with a smile on his face as the sun began to rise.

Billy,

Before I left New Berkeley and met you, my son, Leroy, was my best friend. As often as possible, I'd take Leroy to the park because it was his favorite place. I didn't quite understand why he liked it so much back then (parks had never been something I much cared for). To me they were just a patch of land, and since there are plenty of those, I didn't see the appeal. Nonetheless, one of the memories I most cherish about my boy happened the very first time we went to one. After a day of running around and playing, Leroy approached me and said, "Dad, I was born to be at the park." Again, I didn't understand what it meant at the time, but it was cute and made me laugh.

You know the story between those days and these. When no one else would or could, you gave me a moment of your time. And without you, I don't think I'd have made it through the dark valley I found myself wandering in. Which is why I might have been even happier than you were when Judith came along. It brought me so much joy to see you so whole.

Another story played out between those days and these. It's one that, like mine before it, I can't bear to tell. And now you know the reason we reach out to moments like the one I had at the park with my son. We reach out as if we could grab them and bring ourselves back to a better time—but we can't. I know you wouldn't want me to apologize, but I'm sorry, buddy. We just can't.

All the denial, the anger, the broken promises, and the outright sorrow do is distract us though. They make us feel we have to change course in some dramatic way. The truth is, we don't. In fact, we shouldn't. Yes, we should learn from our mistakes. But we need to accept that even though it's a new path we walk, we must stick to the values we had on the old one that are worth upholding. For me, that means remembering that the happiest moments of my life came in the simplest of places, with a son I loved who just wanted to run around on a silly patch of land, as well as with a best friend who just wanted to go west on a wild adventure.

I realize that now. And I'll be praying every day that the Enigma guides you to realizing it too. Because, oh, what a miracle it is, to simply see the world again for the miracle it is.

With all a brother's love and gratitude,

Gregory Calloway

With a joyous, salty tear falling down his cheek, William rejoiced at Gregory's escape. How he wished he could have had the same with Judith. From beyond the Hold, a tiny glare caught his eye. As he searched for the source of it, he could just make out Dominic and Daniel in the distance, looking up at him from within the trees. With a brief wave, he watched as they turned and darted off.

The simplest of places.

William thought of the mornings he and Daniel had been

sharing atop these very walls. At the same time, he knew he couldn't have those back, or anything like them, without first bringing an end to one of their lives' greatest dilemmas.

Quick as a switch, he darted back down the stairs. The streets were empty now, to his surprise, so he marched through the Hold, searching left and right until he came upon the massive square, which was packed with Highlanders, Tokali, and Keagan gang members.

An icy terror seized his limbs as he noticed all their heads were bowed and their hands clasped as if in prayer. He turned and saw, atop the main balcony, looking out over them all, Clovis and Father Kubler, whose arms were outstretched as Clovis yelled out to the faithful.

This part of the world he found himself in was no miracle. There was only darkness and tyranny here.

"No," William said quietly to himself, determination straightening his spine. "No, this isn't how it ends."

*

It had been a nice few weeks in the Riverlands since the V'ahani had returned. Although Grand Chieftain Varek had been upset with Latera over the initiative she had taken regarding the judgment of Walter Keagan and Devin Turpin, the tension had seemed to fade a bit by the time the men had been sent off to their doom. The days that followed had been filled with helping her people resettle, a task she supremely enjoyed.

One quiet evening, after a long day of hiking with Winona, she lay in her tent. The summer was coming to a close, and the air was tinged with the first signs of the forthcoming winter. To pass the time until she fell asleep, she carried on knitting a blanket—a hobby she had enjoyed with her mother at a young age and had long refrained from when Nova was believed to be dead. About a half hour or so into her activity, the flap of her shelter opened. In came Hammond, who had been out hunting with Hanzah.

Looking up from the task at hand, she felt her daily elation at his presence. "Hello, my love. How was it?"

"Your brother is quite the shot for his age," Hammond said as he took off the coat he had been wearing—a V'ahani-white coat, heavier than his own, which Orrin had given him. It had been his prized possession ever since.

"He certainly is … the little chieftain." While it wasn't her brother's fault in the slightest, the lingering question of whether she or her brother would come to assume their deceased father's position in leading the V'ahani of the Riverlands still remained—and still bothered her. The chieftains would be "meditating" on and "debating" it in the coming days. It would be a while before they came to a conclusion.

"Hey." Now settled, Hammond sat beside her, wrapping her in his arms. "No matter what happens, no one can take what you have earned away from you. The people know their chieftess, and they will never forget."

With her rock by her side to stay, she felt warm even in the chill of night—she felt invincible. And he was right: it wasn't the time to fret. There was no reason to. Because she knew what she'd accomplished, and she was proud of what she'd become.

As she fell asleep in his arms that night, she did so with this pride at the front of her mind.

Her dreams held darkness—not the flurry of visions that Latera had grown accustomed to. And in this darkness she stood, clear as day, looking around her into emptiness. "Hello?" she called, her voice reverberating in the void.

Silhouettes began to materialize on all sides of her. Ten or more figures, at her estimate. She soon made them out to be women, all marching toward her. Their garb was a mix of white and orange.

"Behold," one of them said.

"The new Widow walks." A second spoke this time as Latera turned to try and keep up.

"And like those who came before her ..." Their movement dizzied her as they came from different directions into her line of sight.

"So, too, shall she answer the Mother's Call." This fourth sounded from behind, and she knew this one.

"Mama?" Sure enough, Nova stood before her when she turned; her mother stilled beside the others, who she could see all around her. They looked similar despite their varying clothes, and as she observed them she could tell: these were Widows of the past. The circle of her ancestors looked upon her, and their hands came together. When they did, the darkness grew into a glowing light, until they all disappeared.

"It is time, my child." The ubiquitous voice from her dreams was all that remained, and its words were spoken with greater clarity than ever before.

In this glorious, shining kingdom, Latera came to her knees.

"Oh, Mother—Oh, Maiden—when you sound the Call, I will answer. What is your will?"

A pause elongated into silence, though the sense of euphoria Latera felt remained.

"War," the powerful voice hissed.

Everything started to shake. The sound of breaking glass echoed all around her as she was whisked along to a dark scene. There, standing atop the main balcony in the square of the Tokali Hold, were Clovis Keagan and a Cereb priest. From front to back and all along the surrounding balconies, the square was packed with Tokali and Keagans. However, there was a new crowd as well—a people she had never seen before. Where these numbers came from, she could not imagine, but they made it seem as if the flow of Easterners would be endless.

Everyone in attendance—natives and Easterners alike—wore both a Keagan pin and the Cereb pendant necklace. And they were all on their knees, repeating the words of the priest in between Clovis's manic ranting. Off to the side, in the cover of shadows, she could see William Keagan, who did not wear the pin. She hoped and believed this meant he remained her ally.

"Clovis Keagan and Priest Ross Kubler," the Mother said. When She uttered Clovis's name, Clovis seemed to stare straight at Latera as if he could see her. Her breathing grew heavier. "Rid my domain of them." The Mother's Call overpowered the chaos unfolding before her, and it was the only thing that softened the grip of Clovis's gaze. "At all costs."

The Mother's words repeated in her mind at a greater pace and volume as if to combat the manic sermon in the Hold.

The curtain of Clovis's mouth drew back, revealing his crooked, yellow teeth. He laughed as if taunting her. Then fire started to overtake the Hold and spread up to the balcony behind them. Neither reacted, though. Kubler's words only grew more impassioned, while Clovis's laughing became hysterical.

The onlookers, however, felt the flame.

They all cried. They all suffered. And a desperate Latera tried her hardest to reach out to help the victims.

"No!" she cried as she was pulled away from the scene. "No!"

Her eyes burst open, and she gasped for air, now awake in her shelter in the Riverlands.

"Latera—are you okay? What is it?" Hammond asked.

Still panting and looking down at the ground, she whispered, "War."

~

CURIOUS ABOUT WHAT HAPPENS NEXT?

Continue to Amazon to buy the next book in the series now:

https://www.amazon.com/author/nbaustin

Need more than that?
Check out Nicholas Austin's website!

www.nbaustinbooks.com

ABOUT THE AUTHOR

N.B. Austin is the author, screenwriter, and blogger behind the Civilands Series. His first novel, *Crimson River*, was a finalist for the *2016-2017 BooksGoSocialDaily Book of the Year Award*.

Based in Austin, Texas, but hailing originally from Long Island, New York. University of Texas at Austin educated. His experience as writer and editor for several scholastic newsletter publications combined with a passion for song writing, soon inspired him to divert his attention to storytelling.

Find more about N.B. Austin, including his blog and details on free book giveaways, at:

www.nbaustinbooks.com

www.ingramcontent.com/pod-product-compliance
Lightning Source LLC
Chambersburg PA
CBHW052040240626
47153CB00006B/2163